29

NANCY PENNICK

Allison-Hayes Publishing

ISBN-10: 0996810609
ISBN-13: 978-0-9968106-0-9

To the real Ashley

– the one who wished bookstores had shopping carts

PROLOGUE

I hate my brother. He ruined my life. Now I have to fake it and pretend I like him. I want to scream to the world that Doug may seem courteous and thoughtful, but he's pure evil. No one would believe that underneath those military clothes and good looks lies a psychopath. My parents think he's the protector of our family. He can do no wrong in their eyes. Me? I know better. Because of him, I lost the boy I love.

But I'd do it all over again—the same way. To protect the one I love. Maybe in another life I can be his girl. A life where Doug doesn't exist.

CHAPTER ONE

I walked into AP English daydreaming of anything but school. As I headed for a row of seats, I almost crashed into the back of a guy wearing a black hoodie. He stopped to pull the hood down. My heart went straight to my throat and lodged there. I swallowed hard. It was him.

I glanced around the room and spotted Ashley, my best friend, already slumped in a desk. No available seats near her so I made a quick decision to follow the formerly hooded one and slipped in the last seat behind him. He adjusted the jacket, shook his head and stared straight ahead. He sat close enough that I caught a whiff of fresh outdoors with a hint of spice.

I studied the dark mass of hair in front of me and flashed back to the first time I saw him. Sophomore year. I wanted to call him tall, dark and handsome, but that was so cliché. Still, I couldn't find better words to describe him. On my scale he was a ten—tall, but not too tall, lean and muscular. He had dark hair and chocolate brown eyes that contained hidden secrets.

Last year he became my secret crush. I had a boyfriend, but this guy made my heart stop each time I saw him. The size of the high school kept kids from knowing everyone's name. A person could get lost in the crowd. I discreetly asked around, but no one seemed to know the guy. I decided to name him Loner. When the yearbook came out at the end of the school year, I dove in looking for him. No sign of him, not on a single page.

A tap on my shoulder released me from my fantasy world. The kid next to me pointed to my best friend, two rows over. Ashley pantomimed some message, wildly moving her hands back and forth. I started laughing. I had no idea what she meant. Finally she resorted to pointing. I shot her a look that said, "Cut it out." She spotted the Loner sitting in front of me. We had no secrets between us and supported my good fortune. Junior year *could* turn out better than last. The break up with Josh Reed had been hard. I still liked him, but willed myself to move on from the drama.

"Young lady? Is there a problem?" The English teacher called me out, and I sat straighter in my seat.

"Um, no, Mrs.—"

"I know this *is* the first day of school but you could have learned my name."

"Sorry." I thumbed through my folders hunting for the one marked English. Of course I found it at the bottom of the pile. As I scanned the syllabus, I heard a few snickers spread through the room.

"Mrs. Greene!" I shouted when I found her name. The class burst out laughing.

"If this wasn't the first day, you'd see me tonight after school. Please tell me your name." She didn't appear happy with the start to her school day.

"My name is Allison Sanders, ma'am. And again, I'm sorry."

"I think you've apologized enough. Since this is a shortened period, I'd like to get to the assignment. The first six weeks we'll be reading *Wuthering Heights* by Emily Bronte. It's available at the school or local bookstore. Of course, you can always download your book, but whatever form you choose, make sure it comes with you to class."

After that, I didn't hear anything Mrs. Greene said. I couldn't stop staring at the back of Loner's head, plotting a strategy to meet him. The bell rang, startling me. I jumped and hit my desk against the back of his. "Oh, sorry!"

Loner rotated in his seat and stared at me for about five seconds. He had dark, brooding eyes that I got to see up close for the first time. Dark chocolate brown. I could melt right into them. Just as suddenly, he slid out of his desk and slipped into the crowd to head for the door.

As I left the classroom, Ashley pushed through the other students to join me. "It's him! You were inches away from your dream crush. Did he talk to you? Did you find out his name? Do you want to go shopping after school tonight?"

Some might say Ashley talked too much or didn't really let you answer her question before she went on to the next, but I found it endearing. We met in grade school and have been best friends ever since. She had two qualities I loved—loyalty and humor.

"No, no and yes," I answered as I rushed down the hall to my locker. I forgot my schedule and had no idea what class came next.

"So what do you think his name is? We thought up some pretty great ones last year, but I forget most of them." Ashley stuck out her lower lip. She leaned against the locker next to mine as I struggled with the combination. "Here, let me." She turned the knob a few times, and it magically opened. "Lancelot?" She looked at me. "Romeo? Dante?"

"Dinner. My house. Then bookstore. Have your brother drop you off. I can take you home." I gave her a playful push hoping she'd stop with the names. "I'm going to find out who he is and get him to talk to me."

"Ooh, a girl on a mission. I love it. But don't you

think we'll find out his name in class?"

"Yeah, I guess so. I have a feeling getting to know him will be harder. He looked right through me and didn't say a word."

"He was speechless, that's all. He saw how beautiful you are." Ashley waved and skipped off in a different direction than I was headed.

I stared down the hall wishing she'd change direction. I could really use her support right now. Josh, my ex, and his new flavor of the month, bleach-blonde Chloe, supposedly the most popular girl in the junior class, were walking straight toward me. Chloe was a little over the top—too much make-up, skirts too short, and too much giggling. It seemed Josh had turned into a comedian over the summer. She couldn't stop laughing at everything he said. I hoped she didn't cut off the circulation in that arm she hung on to so tightly.

When they got to my locker, he stopped. Chloe almost ran into him. "Hey, Allie! Good to see you."

I nodded. I had nothing to say to him. I tried to stick my head in the locker. *Too late.* I felt the warmth creep up my neck as he came closer. My stomach clenched in a knot. Inwardly I screamed and yelled all the reasons I didn't like him anymore. *Unpredictable. Cheater. Liar.*

"Maybe we have a class together. Let me see your schedule." His hand almost touched mine. I fought back a gasp. Still handsome as ever, Josh's dark blonde hair and blue eyes reminded me why I fell for him in the first place. I tried not to react to the almost touch.

Chloe's bottom jaw dropped and stayed there. She tugged on Josh's arm as if to say, "Let's go". He didn't budge. I stupidly handed him my schedule.

"See you in American History." He flipped the paper back at me. "Hey, can we talk?" His eyes pleaded with me to say yes. "Chloe, wait here. We'll be right back."

Before I could answer, he ushered me around the corner to a spot less congested. "Josh!" I struggled to break free, but his grip tightened.

His face was inches from mine. I could tell he brushed his teeth this morning by the peppermint scent on his breath. "I just want to ask you something, Al."

Sirens went off in my head. I hated when he called me Al. I asked him not to, but it fell on deaf ears. "Lee." I finished for him. "Al-lie."

"Look. I never got to talk to you. Explain myself. I tried all summer. You never answered my calls, my texts. Can we meet somewhere so I can finally tell you the truth?"

I wiggled under his vice grip. I didn't want to hear anymore lies, stories or what he thought happened. I saw what happened with my own two eyes. He kissed another girl right in front of me. I broke up with him on the spot. What more can he say? "You need to let go," I said through clenched teeth.

Out of nowhere a boy in a black hoodie had his hand on Josh's arm. "You heard the girl. Let go." The two stood in a stare-down of epic proportions that I feared would never end.

"Let go," Loner said again, and Josh dropped his hand. His eyes grew wide. He started to open his mouth to say something, but the hooded one continued down the hall as if we had been a pit stop. He took such long strides I could barely catch up.

"Hey! Wait up! I just want to say thank you." I jogged along side of him until we hit a mass of people.

"It wasn't a big deal." He shrugged as he faded into the crowd.

"Thanks," I croaked. I wanted to ask how he had heard me, but it was too late. "Ooh!" I stamped my foot and headed back to my locker.

Thankfully, Chloe no longer waited there like an obedient dog. Josh was nowhere in sight. I let out a sigh of relief. "That was strange," I muttered as I walked down the hall to my next class.

I floated through the rest of the periods, thinking of how Loner rescued me, seething over Josh's arrogance and longing for the school day to be over.

* * * *

When I got off the bus that afternoon and walked up the drive, an oversized, intimidating black SUV greeted me. It signaled that my oldest brother, Doug, had come for a visit. Sixteen years older, he felt more like an uncle, one you see on holidays, your birthday and occasionally in-between.

As I stepped into the kitchen from the garage, I smelled pulled pork. Ashley would be happy. "Hi, Mom, I'm home," I called out.

"We're in here, sweetie." Her voice came from the formal living room, a room we hardly used. "Doug's here."

I put a smile on my face and headed for the front of the house. Mom had a tea set on the coffee table. I settled in next to her as she poured tea into a beautiful china cup. She held it up. "Tea?"

I couldn't believe she served my brother, the commando, tea but he balanced a saucer on his knee. Always the good boy, he did whatever my parents said or wanted. If Mom wanted him to drink tea, he drank tea.

"Thanks." I took the cup with two hands.

"Aren't you going to say hello to your brother?" Mom smiled brightly, almost too brightly.

"Hey, Doug." I stared at him. He wore a dress uniform loaded with medals. His close cropped brown hair, army issued, looked good on him. He left home when I turned two and joined the Army. He worked his way up the ladder over the years and became part of some special military unit headquartered in the Pentagon. The family couldn't ask questions about his work because it was top secret. I could care less. I found it boring and didn't really want to know what he did all day.

"First day of school, huh?" His cold blue-gray eyes sent a jolt through me. Doug tried to be friendly, but we rarely had long chats. I always felt self-conscious when he first arrived.

"Yeah." I nodded.

"That's it? Nothing exciting happened?" Mom set her cup in its saucer.

"Ashley's coming for dinner, and we're going to the bookstore." No way would I share the news about Loner.

"Do you ever bother to ask Mom if it's okay? You just tell her?"

"Doug, it's fine. Ashley's always here. I'm sure Allie has to buy something for school." She looked at me for an answer.

"Right." I wished Mom didn't always feel the need to protect me. I put my cup on the table, not in the saucer. "How long are you staying, Doug?"

"I leave in the morning. Want to see how Pops is doing. I'll see you at breakfast."

"I don't do breakfast."

"Everyone needs to eat breakfast, Allison. It's a good start to your day." Doug pulled his brows together and studied me.

"It makes me sick." I twisted my hair around one finger. He made me feel like I was under interrogation with a lone light bulb dangling over my head.

"She takes water and a breakfast bar for later, Doug." Mom jumped up from the sofa. "I'll check on dinner. Your father should be home soon. You two stay and catch up." She disappeared before I got a chance to leave.

"So." I tried to go through the files in my mind and find the one marked *Doug*. "Still at the Pentagon?" *Oops, off limits.*

"Yes. Yes I am." Doug's eyes narrowed to slits and he sneered at me. "Brat."

What? Mom left the room and his real personality came out, just like always. Ignoring the comment, I tried again. "Great! Still doing spy work and mission impossible stuff?"

Doug threw his head back and laughed, exposing perfect, straight white teeth. "Yeah, something like that. Hey, I heard you're not seeing that Reed kid anymore. He might have a breakout season this year. What was his position? Tight end?"

"Wide receiver."

We went from name calling to talking football in a matter of seconds. I remembered giving him the name Jekyll and Hyde a few years ago. Old emotions churned up inside. My stomach rolled, and my head pounded. I couldn't think clearly. Doug had a knack for making me uneasy and feeling unsure of myself. *It's the age difference. That's all.*

"That's right. He's a wide receiver. I bet you can't

wait to watch him in action."

"Not planning on going to the games this year, sorry." I'd been saying "sorry" a lot and really wasn't. I didn't like talking about Josh. Last year I had it all or thought I did. I had the popular, athletic boyfriend and the golden life. We became the chosen couple of the sophomore class. I admit the popularity never felt right, but it really helped pass the time in this small town. Kids invited us everywhere.

My phone buzzed. I pulled it from my jean's pocket, thankful for the distraction. "Ashley's here." I held up my phone. "Got to run." I popped up and sped to the front door to let her in. We headed straight for the stairs.

"Hi, Doug!" Ashley called from the staircase after she spotted him in the living room.

I closed the bedroom door behind her and made a face. "It's getting harder and harder to talk to him."

"Well, he's an old man. What is he, thirty-two?" We both giggled.

"Something like that." I needed to change the subject. "Guess who I saw right after you left my locker?"

"Josh."

"How'd you know?'

"Who else can make you turn bright red?" Ashley flipped her long, silky dark brown hair over her shoulder. "You still like him, don't you? Was he with Chloe? Did you check out her make-up? Her eyes reminded me of Halloween. Just saying."

This time I chose not to answer so quickly. Did I still like Josh? I wanted to say "yes" but something didn't feel right. "No, yes, and yes."

"Allie." Ashley crossed her arms and stared at me

with hazel eyes on fire. "I decided it's time for you to stop with these yes and no answers. It was funny for awhile, like grade school, but now we need to share more. I know you like Josh and still hurt over the break-up."

"It really wasn't a break-up, Ash. It was more like 'I see you're kissing another girl right in front of me' moment. What was I supposed to do? Congratulate the happy couple?"

"Painful."

"So let's not go there."

"Girls, supper!" Mom's voice stopped the conversation. We headed down and joined the family for dinner.

"Hi, Mr. and Mrs. Sanders. Thanks for having me for dinner. My, don't you look handsome in your uniform, Doug."

I rolled my eyes, and she wrinkled her nose at me. I longed to call her Miss Manners as a joke, but not with Doug around.

"Jim, could you help me?" Mom lifted a huge pot from the stove.

"I will." Doug sprang into action before my dad had a chance. He glanced back at me and smirked.

Really, Doug? Are we playing a game?

"It's so nice to have our boy home, isn't it, Clair?" Dad beamed; probably glad he didn't have to do the heavy lifting.

Routine conversation filled the air as we ate. We discussed school and the weather. It helped having Ashley at the table. The talk couldn't get too serious. After dinner I grabbed the keys to my Jeep, and Ashley and I headed out.

As we stepped inside the building, I took a deep

breath. I loved the smell of a bookstore. Some might say it was all those books in one place, but I disagree.

We rushed over to a huge round table stacked with books for the high school English classes. Ashley and I circled the display until we found the book. We each grabbed a copy and thumbed through the pages. I read the back cover, searching for clues about the book.

"So did you see Loner anywhere after first period?" Ashley whispered as she snapped her book shut.

"Nope, not after he rescued me from Josh. I have no idea what to say to him. He doesn't seem very friendly." I closed my book, too, ready to explore other sections of the store.

"I'd like a good mystery, maybe a romance, but no vampires. Dystopian is okay." Ashley gazed at titles as we walked down an aisle.

I browsed the shelves but felt distracted. "Ash, I'm going to get a coffee and look over the book." I held up *Wuthering Heights*.

"Okay, meet you in a few."

Something caught my eye—a guy in a dark hoodie at the end of the aisle. *He's here.* My heart raced as I slipped down the row pretending to search through the books. My fingertips grazed the binders as I walked along. When I glanced up, he disappeared. I skirted around the corner and stared down the next aisle. *Crap! Empty.*

I headed for the café and ordered my caramel latte, hoping it wouldn't keep me up all night. A little corner table called to me. I slipped into the chair against the wall and placed my book on the table. I mindlessly play with the whipped cream on top of the coffee and reviewed my day—the good, the bad and the ugly.

Well, not ugly in the literal sense. Doug could be

considered quite handsome in a military sort of way. We had an ugly vibe between us. After all these years, I couldn't figure out why we did. He only lived at home with me for two years. What could I have done in that time? I shrugged and moved on to the next part of my day.

The good? That award went to the Loner. He sat in front of me first period. I finally had a chance to meet him.

The bad? I made a pact not to let Josh get to me anymore. To think I almost, and I say it very adamantly, *almost* slept with him made me shudder. He would've been my first.

Ashley found me in my private corner and slipped into the seat across from me. We sipped coffee as we looked at our books. She had her mocha. I had my caramel. I had a pile of one book. She had four. She consumed a book a night and was the reason I went to the bookstore so often. She'd read those books in less than a week and want to come back for more. I'd need a few months to read her pile in my spare time. Ash wished bookstores had shopping carts to make her life easier.

"Hey, Ash, I just found a name for you know who." I set *Wuthering Heights* in the middle of the table. "From the little I read, Heathcliff seems like a tragic figure. Who knows what the Loner has gone through, so let's name him—"

"Heathcliff! What a great idea. We can talk about him all we want, and no one will know. They'll think we're discussing the book."

"Ashley, you read my mind." I held my coffee cup in the air and saluted her. "I think I'm done here. I'm going to check out and will meet you up front." I gave the bookstore one more sweep before I headed toward the cashier.

"Are you looking for someone?" Ashley closed one eye and gazed up at me. "Does he wear a hood? Did we just name him Heathcliff?"

"No, yeah … maybe. It's just so frustrating, Ash. I thought I saw him."

"Makes sense. He has to buy the book, too."

"Why hide? He could say hi."

"Maybe he's shy." She smiled sweetly. "Go buy your book and quit obsessing."

I gathered my things and walked to the counter. A strange feeling came over me. *I'm being watched.* I spun around to see Ashley at our table and people milling about, nothing suspicious. After I paid, I sat in one of the large, overstuffed leather chairs by the entrance. Glancing around, I kept thinking eyes were upon me. Finally, I decided having Doug home put my imagination into overdrive. After all, his work involved highly secretive military operations. He could be the one spying on me and reporting back to my parents.

"Okay, ready." Ashley appeared in front of me as if she materialized from a puff of smoke. I grabbed my bag from the floor. As I looked up I saw a hooded figure in the back corner of the store. *Heathcliff!*

I grasped Ashley by the arm and spun her around. The mystery man disappeared again. I scanned the aisles and coffee shop. No Heathcliff.

"What are you doing?" Ashley checked out the store then looked at me.

"Nothing. Never mind." I pushed the door open and walked out into the cool night air. I gazed up at the twinkling stars in the black velvet sky, and wondered why I was so infatuated with this boy. I knew nothing about him. If I was truly Doug's sister, I should want to run a background check, fingerprint him and get to know everything I could before I talked to him.

A warm humid night greeted us. I stopped and pointed my remote at the Jeep to unlock it. Suddenly a gust of wind kicked in, blowing my hair across my face. A piece of notebook paper, caught up in the blast of air, swirled toward me. It smacked into the side of my leg. *Just what I need.*

I laughed as I reached down to pull the sheet off, tossing it on top of my book bag in the backseat. The lights from the car bounced off it, making me give the paper a second look. *Strange.* I looked again to be sure. Only four letters were written in black marker on the paper—XXIX.

CHAPTER TWO

After dropping Ash off, I decided to take a detour and stop next door to see my friend, Nathan Kalas. I parked in my driveway, but instead of heading inside, I ran around to the backyard.

Since we were kids, Nate and I hung out together. We wore out a path between our two houses over the years. Our parents finally gave up trying to seed it over and turned it into a gravel walk, making it the best shortcut to his house. Nate left the backdoor open, alone or not. Although at this hour, he probably wasn't.

"Hello? Anyone home?" No answer. *His parents must be out.* I maneuvered through the sprawling ranch until I reached his bedroom in the back corner of the house. "Nate?" I didn't see him.

His head popped up from behind his computer desk. Golden brown eyes stared back at me, showing surprise. "Yes?"

The reddish-blonde hair on his head stuck out in every direction. He continued to crawl around on the floor connecting some wires to the back of his hard drive. "Present and accounted for, little one," he said from under the desk.

Nate's nickname for me came from a time when I was much shorter than him. I finally caught up in middle school, but he surpassed me again. He stood over six feet tall.

"Hey, give me a break. I didn't see you." I sat in his computer chair and spun around, taking in the familiar posters. Motorcycles and dirt bikes hung on every wall. People who knew him would expect to see music and movie posters. "Got time to talk?"

"For you? Always." He crawled out from under the desk. His eyes traveled from the top of my head to my toes and back up. "You have an agenda. I can tell."

"You know me too well." I shoved the paper in his hand. "What do you make of this?"

"Twenty-nine?"

"No, I mean those lines and x's."

"Allie." He gave me his grumpiest face. "Have you been paying attention in math class? Those are Roman numerals."

"They are?" I grabbed the paper back.

"X equals 10. The I in front of the X means minus one. X-X-I-X. Twenty-nine. Someone dropped their homework."

"But why is it the only writing on the paper?"

"You're up past your bedtime, kiddo. You're tired and over-thinking. Someone was just doodling."

"Come on, Nate! Use your director skills. How would you map out the scene? Girl in parking lot finds mysterious note with secret code."

"You got me there." He bounced on his bed, placing his hand under his chin. "Hitchcock would play the scene for all it's worth, like in *The Birds*. Close ups of the number would appear throughout the movie with more and more clues until —"

"Until what?" I believed he had an answer.

"Until some kid searches the parking lot looking for his lost homework." Nate let out a loud guffaw. "I know you want out of this Podunk little town, Allie, but don't go looking for drama when there isn't any." He stuck out his bottom lip as if to pout for me.

He could be right. I wanted out. Nothing exciting ever happened in our hometown. It was the typical small town. Dull. Uninteresting. It had the customary white gazebo, with accompanying red, white and blue fan flags hanging from the railings, in the middle of the square. Football was king, and the town rocked the high school colors every Friday night in the fall. My five year plan included graduating, attending a big name college, get a fancy art history degree and never returning except for Homecoming. Big city here I come.

"How about if we go riding tomorrow?" Nate asked as his face lit up.

Nate loved dirt bikes. The kid had eclectic tastes, not what a person would expect from someone so into computers and film. Our houses stood on wooded lots with tons of acreage. Nate had built trails with ramps and speed bumps throughout his backyard for his bike.

We worked endlessly in the summers improving the course and adding to it. My parents wouldn't allow me to ride until I turned sixteen. When the time finally came, I had to admit the thrill and freedom were hard to explain. "Sure, after school would be great."

"Not directly after school, give me an hour."

"Okay, Mr. Audio/Visual president. I know you have important work to do." I kissed his forehead. "See ya." I paused and turned in the doorway. "Oh, I forgot to tell you. Doug's here." I made a face.

Nate pretended to choke himself, placing his hands around his neck and fell back on the bed. I left with that image in my head, giggling. I stepped in the backdoor of my house, still chuckling.

"What's so funny?" Doug's voice burned through me. He stood in front of the refrigerator, digging around the cartons of milk and juice. He finally picked juice and drank from the container.

"Ew! Now I'm really glad I don't do breakfast."

He wiped his arm across his mouth and smiled.

"Dean and I did this all the time before you were born. If you grew up with us, you'd be used to it." The smile turned to a sneer.

"Dean told me you guys had chugging contests," I said smugly. I was fully informed, thanks to my other sibling. "One time you threw up a whole carton of milk in the sink."

My favorite brother, Dean, was a few years younger than Doug. The two were total opposites. Dean lived on the Atlantic coast in a great house by the ocean. He made a living through his photography and art. Neither was married but Dean had an awesome live-in girlfriend, Autumn, who I adored. I visited every summer for a month. They doted on me the whole time, making sure it was a magical, memorable time. Doug took me to a local amusement park once that I could remember.

"Oh, Dean always liked to embellish the truth." Doug walked over to the sink and poured the rest of the juice down the drain. He tossed the container in the wastebasket. "There. Happy now?"

"Goodnight, Doug." I really wanted to say that he wasted a whole container of juice. Instead I spun on my heels and headed for the nearest exit. I couldn't stand to be in the same room with him. Why didn't he like me? Mom said it wasn't true, but I could feel the bad vibe oozing off him.

"I'll see you in the morning, sister dear." His voice trailed after me, the tone condescending.

"Like hell you will," I whispered as I reached the top of the stairs.

* * * *

I didn't get much sleep after drinking that giant coffee the night before. Now I had to face Doug, and give him a sisterly send-off despite swearing otherwise. I debated staying in bed to the last possible second and rush out of the house with a quick goodbye. I couldn't do that to my parents. They felt bad I grew up alone, like an only child. Not my fault they had me when they were in their forties. They shouldn't worry about me so much. They had a good example next door. Nate was an only child and pretty darn self-sufficient.

My brother, Dean, turned twelve after I was born and was around for some of my growing up years. I could do no wrong in his eyes. We never fought. He and Doug had their share of fights, but I only heard second-hand stories from Dean. He always started with "you weren't born yet" and went on to tell about their adventures. They were fairly close for two boys who turned out so differently.

I padded into the kitchen, hoping my socks muffled any sound. I needed a bottle of water and wanted to retreat to my room before anyone showed up.

"Allison, I'm glad I got to see you before I left." I jumped from the sound of his voice. Doug made his grand entrance into the kitchen, dress uniform and all.

I gave him the appropriate hug. "Have a safe trip."

"You know something? I realized I neglected you all the years you were growing up. We need to correct that, get to know each other better."

I searched for the right words but came up empty. I finally said, "That's okay, Doug." Whatever that meant. Was it okay we didn't know each other very well or that he neglected me? I was too tired to explain.

"I'm going to try to come home more often. Make an effort." Doug put his arm around me causing a cold shiver to shoot down my spine. Something in the back of my mind warned me to pull away. "Would you like that?"

"Sure." *Whatever, Doug. Not really. I'm sixteen and a junior in high school. I don't really want to hang out with my thirty-something brother.*

"Before you leave, I have a question." He retrieved an index card from his pocket. "Ever see this?"

Doug held the card in front of my face. The Roman numeral XXIX stared back at me. I swallowed hard and opened the bottle of water, taking a long drink.

"Allison?"

"Doug?" I had to give him a hard time. He never teased me like Nate or Dean. He could be *way* too serious.

"Well?"

"They're Roman numerals. I think you learn about them in fourth grade. You want me to tell you what they stand for? I think a big, smart, Army guy like you should know." I gave him a quick smile, trying to give the impression of a bratty teenager. If he knew the reason I stalled, I'd be given a truth serum and tied to a chair.

He grabbed my arm, squeezing to the point of pain. My brain sounded the alert to back away. Memories of other encounters just like this one flooded into my mind. "Why are you so difficult to talk to?" He hissed. A drop of spit landed on my cheek. "I just asked a simple question. Have you ever seen anyone write this or maybe wear it like a tattoo?"

"Oww, Doug! Damn it!" I pulled away and took a step back. His nostrils flared and a scowl crossed his face. If I thought I could trust Doug, I would have told him what I found. But an inner voice told me to play dumb. "No! I've never seen it. I gotta go. I'm late. See you next time."

I made a quick exit and took the stairs two at a time. I rushed into the bathroom and examined the red fingerprints on my arm. A bluish color formed around the throbbing marks. "All because of twenty-nine," I said to the mirror. "What's the big deal?" I turned on the shower hoping to stay there until he left. Let him have Mom and Dad all to himself.

I stepped into the steamy water, letting the pounding force hit my body until all my thoughts washed away. I stood hypnotized, staring at one bathroom tile in a trance. I drew an X, then another, followed by I and X on the tile. If Doug had reason to believe those Roman numerals stood for something dangerous, he should have told me. No way would I help him, let alone turn in a fellow student. A knock on the door brought me to my senses.

"Save some water for the fish!" Dad called through the door. I laughed as I always did at his favorite saying.

"I'll be out in a minute," I yelled as I grabbed my terry robe.

I rubbed my hair with a towel and reached for the hair dryer to give it a quick blow dry. Luckily, my hair was not too thin or thick and dried into a nice shiny, straight style with just a little curl to the ends. The shortest layers touched just under my chin, the longest swept below my shoulders. I stared in the mirror and wished for blonde or auburn hair, something more eye-catching than medium brown. Mom said we came from a family of brunettes and should be proud of the connection. Just like our eyes, all shades of blue.

I liked to say I had aqua eyes—in between green and blue—to make them sound more exotic. I studied my face in the mirror. Small nose, soft features with large eyes. Dad said I was pretty, but all dads said that about their daughters.

I dashed into my bedroom trying to stay undercover. The hard part began. What to wear? I wanted Heathcliff to notice me but not think I dressed so he'd notice, if that made sense.

Flipping through outfits in my closet, I finally decided to wear a skirt instead of jeans, something I rarely did. A black cotton double ruffle flare skirt stared back at me. I pulled it from its hanger. I tore through my shirts, tops and blouses until most ended up on the floor. Mom wouldn't be too happy if she came in here, but I'd clean it up later. I glanced at my watch. I didn't have much time to make the final decision.

Finally, I chose a pink tee sporting a large imprinted black bow that hugged my body. I slipped on a pair of black plaid ballerina shoes and headed for the stairs. Dad should be gone for work so he couldn't comment on the short skirt, and Mom would just say I looked cute.

When I reached the bottom of the stairs, Mom stood by the door, holding my breakfast bar. I kissed her on the cheek. "Ooh, look how cute!" She put her hand to her cheek.

"Thanks. See you later." I had to grin as I flew out the door. *Predictable mom.*

I patted the Jeep as I went by, wishing I could drive it to school. *Waiting lists!* At least I was on it. I could carpool with Nate, but he went in an hour before school started. President of the Audio/Visual club, he arrived early to set up for the day. Nate immersed himself in that world, loving the creative side of music and movies. He hoped one day to be a director.

Knowing him, he'll definitely be famous one day.

I heard the roar of the bus and knew it must be getting close. Bus fumes filled the air. I coughed a little as it screeched to a halt in front of me. The bus, filled mostly with freshman and sophomores, had a handful of juniors. Seniors wouldn't be caught dead on the bus. They'd walk instead, no matter the distance. I had to ride because our house was on the outskirts of town. Some kids lived even farther in isolated homes along country roads.

I found a seat and sat solo, watching the houses grow closer and closer together on smaller plots of land as the bus made its way along the same route I had ridden for the last two years. The cracked seat kept anyone from sitting next to me. I stared out the window until we squealed to a stop in front of the school.

Ashley stood farther down the sidewalk as we poured out of the big yellow vehicle that hummed and coughed intermittently. I waved as I approached. "Hey, Ash!" I stopped in front of her. "Guess what? Doug's leaving today but wants to come home more often and get to know me better."

"That sounds like fun," Ashley said as she rolled her eyes. "Tell him I'll give up some of my time hanging out with you." She laughed as we parted ways. I walked toward my homeroom.

As I stepped into the classroom, the teacher waved me to her desk. "I have a message for you. Your counselor, Mr. Whitmore, wants to see you. Take this pass. If you miss the rest of homeroom, go straight to first period." She handed me the message and the pass.

"Thanks." Not really sure if I should be thankful or not. I tried to think if I did anything wrong. I searched my brain as I headed for the office, wondering why he wanted to see me. Kids never got called to the counselor for anything good, especially the second day of school. I arrived at the counseling center more quickly than I thought. I handed the note to the student assistant. He motioned for me to sit and disappeared. I paced instead. When he returned he closed one eye and squinted at me with the other. Again he motioned for me to go in without saying a word.

"Allison, please sit down." Mr. Whitmore pointed to the chair in front of his desk. "Let's see." He fumbled through some papers, appearing confused why he had sent for me. "Ah, yes, a parking space has opened up. You're next on the list."

That's the reason I was called to the office? My heart did a little flip of joy. "Thank you." I settled back in the seat.

"You just have to fill out this paperwork, have a parent sign it and bring it back to the office tomorrow. You don't have to see me. Give it to Jacob out there. He'll give you a parking area and sticker."

I couldn't believe my good fortune. Finally I had freedom. I could drive to school and not ride the stinky bus anymore. It felt so great I could almost kiss good, old Jacob right on the lips as I passed by.

The bell rang for first period, and the halls began to fill with people. I headed for English class, searching for Ashley to tell her the good news. My heart pounded with excitement. I almost forgot about Heathcliff until I saw him slip into the room ahead of me. I held myself back and waited for Ashley in the hallway.

"Allie! I thought you'd be in class already discussing *Wuthering Heights* with Heathcliff."

"Very funny. I'm waiting for you because I have great news. I got a parking pass."

Ashley grabbed me and danced around the hallway.

"Do you think I can ride home with you instead of Rob? He always wants to leave so fast to get to work. Plus it's so hot and his air conditioner's broken. Doubt if he'll ever save the money to get it fixed."

"Of course, you can. We better get inside. Second bell's going to ring."

I walked down the aisle to my seat, staring at Heathcliff the whole way. His head stayed bent over a book. As I adjusted my bag, I brushed into his desk. The motion caused him to glance up, but he looked down again. Maybe I finally got his attention by bumping him.

"Sorry," I said, but he didn't answer. I slid into my seat. My folder and books slipped out of my book bag and fell to the floor. *Crap! I thought I zipped that shut.* I reached for the closest one the same time Heathcliff did.

Our hands touched briefly, and a tingle traveled up my arm and back down my spine. He quickly pulled away, handed me the folder and continued to pick up the rest of the mess. I didn't know if I should say sorry or thank you because I couldn't take my eyes off his gorgeous face.

As he placed the pile on my desk he looked directly at me, straight through to my soul. "You're welcome." His dark hair hung over his eyes and those chocolate orbs burned right through me. A slight smile crossed his face. Then it was over, and he turned back in his seat, pouring over that important book.

I brought my hand to my chest, the one he touched. It still tingled. Funny, I never felt that way with Josh. I never experienced anything when we held hands. Josh may have been a teenage crush but this felt like something more—like danger and romance could be right around the corner.

I blinked a few times to bring myself back to reality. My schedule still lay on the floor close to Heathcliff's desk. I debated if I needed it, but didn't want it in someone else's hands. I leaned to the side and tried to extend my leg out into the aisle to pull the paper toward me. It was just beyond my reach. I slipped from my seat into a squatting position, praying no one watched. How embarrassing if anyone saw me. Super powers would be really great right now, and I wished for invisibility. I wiggled a few inches forward to pick up the paper.

As I scooted toward his desk, I admired Loner's sandals. I had the sudden urge to tell him he had good fashion sense. I caught my breath as I spotted something on the arch of his right foot. I couldn't make out the whole thing. Part of the foot was covered by the sandal strap. *Pen marks? Letters? A tattoo?* My blood ran cold. I began to feel dizzy and steadied myself on my desk. I saw something I wished I hadn't. Loner had a tattoo on the arch of his foot. I couldn't make out the whole thing but what I saw was enough to send a chill down my spine—I-X.

CHAPTER THREE

I sent a text to Nate asking how long it would be until he got home. We needed to talk. He shot back a quick message—*the usual*—as if to say I should know by now.

The parking pass application kept me busy while I waited. I rejoiced in the fact that tomorrow would be the last day I rode the bus. After I finished the paperwork, I ran upstairs and changed clothes. I chose beat up jeans and a t-shirt in case Nate still wanted to ride. Finally his message came through. *I'm home, little one. Happy now?*

I rushed across the yards, slipped into the house and burst through his bedroom door. "Are we riding today?"

Nate sat at his desk, leaning back in his chair, hands folded across his chest. His eyes focused on the computer screen. "Sure, it's great weather. That's not why you're here though, is it?"

"I got a parking pass."

"Wow. Great." He sat forward, eyes still on the screen. "What else?"

"Saw Josh. He said he wanted to talk."

"Still like him?"

"Maybe, I have to think about it. Loner's in my English class. I renamed him Heathcliff." I decided to withhold the tattoo sighting.

That seemed to pique his interest. Nate knew all about my secret crush. He tore his eyes away from the screen long enough to look at me. "What's his real name? I'll do a search." He swung back around, hands perched over the keyboard.

When Nate said he'd do a search, he didn't mean the ordinary search that anyone can do. I never asked questions.

"I don't know."

"You don't know. Did the teacher call on him?"

"Not yet, it's only the second day of school."

"She didn't check attendance the first day?"

"I wasn't paying attention."

"Take a picture. I'll do facial recognition."

I placed my hands on my hips and stared in his direction. "How am I going to do that in English class?"

"Well, see what you can find out. What about Ashley? She know anything?"

"If you mean did she meet anyone yet? The answer's no. So you better make your move. She's supposed to be your date for senior prom. I don't want to go as the stand-in."

I promised Nate if he didn't have a date for prom, I'd go with him. It would be fun to dress up, and we'd have a good time, but I didn't want him to have just a good time. It needed to be memorable. He still had the whole school year to ask her out. He didn't answer so I changed the subject. "Doug left this morning."

"Good for Doug." Nate had no use for him. He thought Doug was pompous and bossy and didn't treat me like a sister.

"He wants to get to know me better."

Nate spun in his chair to face me. "Really? I wonder if he has an ulterior motive."

"Thanks!" I had to chuckle. Leave it to Nate to see beyond a simple conversation. "He's going to recruit me or have me go undercover."

"You never know."

"Maybe he just wants to get to know me. Did you ever think of that?" I couldn't believe I defended Doug after the encounter I had with him. Was there a part of me that wanted him to like me?

"Don't get so touchy. You know me. I see evil lurking around every corner. Come on, let's go out."

We headed for the storage barn in his backyard. Two bikes sat inside. Nate kept his old bike for guest riders. We slipped on our helmets, rolled the motorbikes out the door and down the dirt path to the woods. We weren't allowed to start them up close to the house, a lame rule because you could hear the bikes throughout the neighborhood.

As we reached the woods, I started up my bike and coasted onto the course. I revved up the engine, headed for the first speed bump and made a soft landing a few feet away. Nate liked air time and always challenged himself to go higher, stay in the air longer. I just enjoyed a good ride. We ran the course a few times to warm up. The last jump on the track unnerved me. Nate had two paths, one that avoided the ramp and the straight-away path that gave enough speed to take it.

On my final loop, I decided to take the ramp. I needed to find my inner courage and let it come to the surface. My hands shook as I skidded into position. The runway loomed ahead of me. The sloped wooden ramp sat among the trees taunting me to chicken out. I visualized something unknown and exciting on the other side. The only way to get there was to conquer the fear inside and take the plunge. A bead of sweat rolled down the middle of my back. My hands clenched the handlebars tighter. I released the gear and flew through the woods. I felt exhilarated and terrified at the same time. The tire hit the bottom of the wood ramp.

Soon I was airborne, soaring past leaves and trees. Someone laughed and screamed, and I realized it was me. I landed on the dirt path with a bump and a wobble and rode out onto the grassy yard. Nate flew out of the woods a few seconds later and skidded to a stop.

"What the hell was that?" He pulled off his helmet. His grin said it all. He was proud of me.

"Time to take the bull by the horns as my dad always says." I yelled back as I shut down the bike.

We wheeled the bikes back to the shed. The final step of the journey still waited. Without speaking, we made a beeline to the kitchen and chugged a sports drink, racing each other to the finish. Nate always held back and let me win or so I thought. We high-fived and sat at the table.

"Nate, let's make a pact."

"Another one?"

"Stop kidding around."

"Fine, what's it going to be this time?"

"Find someone to love."

"I though you were leaving town as soon as you graduated."

"That's almost two years away. I need something to distract me. I'll help you and you help me."

"Do I have to?"

"You're doing it again, Nate."

"Okay, my part's harder than yours. I have to find out about loner boy, Heathcliff. I barely know what he looks like. You couldn't find him in the yearbook last year. He doesn't hang around school, isn't in any clubs, activities or sports. If he was, I could at least get a picture of him. You have to find out his name. I'll take it from there."

"Deal. And you have to talk to Ashley."

"I always talk to her."

"I mean call her, ask her out, act like you like her."

"I fear rejection." Nate feigned a heart attack holding his hand over his heart. "Plus you promised to ask her—"

"If she likes you?"

"Yes, and you never have."

"It's awkward, Nate, but I will. I promise."

We shook hands to close the deal, and I decided to end his pain. I pulled out my phone and dialed Ashley. "Hey, Ash, do you like Nate?"

Nate pantomimed placing a dagger in his chest.

"She hasn't answered yet." I giggled at his theatrics and planned what I would really say.

"Allie, what's up?"

"Nothing, just got back from Nate's. We were hanging out."

"Dirt bikes?"

"Yeah, you should try it sometime. It's fun." Terrified of any type of motorcycle, Ashley stayed far away from Nate's when we rode. A motorcycle almost hit her when she was a little girl. The man screamed at her for getting in his way. "Nate would be happy to show you how to ride."

"That's nice of him."

"He's nice, don't you think?"

"Yeah, I do."

"And cute?'

"Very."

"So?"

"Allie, where are you going with this?"

"Could you like him in a boyfriend sort of way?" There I said it.

"Maybe. I have to think about it."

"Okay, you do that. I'll talk to you tomorrow." I quickly hung up. I didn't know if I have good news or bad.

"Well, what'd she say?" Nate looked like a panting puppy.

"She thinks she could like you." I couldn't resist. I had to pet the side of his head.

"I guess that's better than no."

"I guess it is." I hoped to have better luck with Heathcliff, if I ever got the chance to talk to him or find out his real name.

* * * *

"Mr. Montgomery." The English teacher called on the hooded boy in front of me. She pointed to her head as if to say "take the hood off". Mrs. Greene believed in the old school way of teaching. She told us that in college, the professors often called students by Ms. or Mr. and she would do the same. *I'll never learn Heathcliff's first name. Couldn't she slip up just one time?*

Class hadn't started so I talked to the back of his head. I gave up trying to talk to the front. "I want to thank you for helping me out the first day of school. I wasn't in trouble or anything, just an ex wanting to talk. I didn't want to talk and that's what you saw ... or heard. How *did* you hear me?" I paused for a response but nothing. Thinking back to that day, I thought it odd that he came out of nowhere and knew I wanted Josh to let go of my arm. We blended in with the crowd. We weren't yelling or fighting. To someone passing by, Josh had his hand on my arm.

The grateful teen girl routine wasn't working so I went with another approach. "And, by the way, how did you know I needed rescuing? Or if I wanted help? Maybe I want to get back with my ex, and you ruined it." I let out a loud huff, hoping he felt my frustration. "Anyway, I'm not going back to him, in case you're wondering. I have big plans to get out of this town as soon as I graduate. A boyfriend would complicate things." I poked him in the back. "Got it?"

I swear his shoulders moved up and down with laughter. "What's your name? First name that is, Mr. Montgomery."

He shook his head slowly back and forth. I couldn't tell if he found me impossible or was answering "no". I poked him once more for good measure then stopped. Mrs. Greene walked to the front of her desk. The signal class would begin.

During her lecture, I obsessed on how to get the guy in front of me to open up. Maybe I should ask him about his tattoo. It'd make a great conversation starter. *So what does XXIX mean? Are you in a cult? A gang?* I chuckled at the thought then frowned. *My brother's out to get you, so watch out.* Why did I feel suddenly protective of Heathcliff?

A better idea hit me. Follow the secretive Mr. Montgomery. *Thank you, Mr. Whitmore, for issuing my parking pass.* I had to wait a few days, but the trusty red Jeep sat right outside, ready to go at a moment's notice.

As soon as the bell rang, I rushed for my locker, forgetting to wait for Ashley. Out of breath, she caught up with me. "What's the hurry? Are you meeting Josh? Did he dump Chloe?"

"I'm going to follow him, Ash." I stared into my friend's hazel eyes and saw confusion.

"Josh?"

"No, Heathcliff," I whispered and exhaled at the same time.

"So I don't get a ride home tonight." Her

shoulders slumped, and she stared at the floor. "That's okay. The Rob-mobile isn't so bad."

"It's just for tonight, Ash. One day." I reached out and placed my hand on her shoulder. "Forgive me?"

"Call me when you get home. I want a full report." She gave me a small smile. "It's kind of exciting. Not much happens in our town."

"You can say that again." We laughed and parted ways. I counted the hours then the minutes to the end of the day. The final bell would be a welcomed release from the suffocating confines of the school walls.

I compared myself to a sly fox, slinking through the woods, stalking its unsuspecting victim. I planned to rush to the front door at the end of the day and wait for my prey to appear. One agonizing minute after another, the bell finally rang, signaling escape time. I jogged to the main exit and stood to the side trying to blend in. I wanted to observe everyone coming out of the building. Kids spilled out the door, heading for bus lines or the parking lots. Some walked and began to cross the street for their trek home.

I almost missed him among the crowd. Heathcliff followed a group of boys crossing the street. He stayed a few feet behind giving the appearance he was with them although I knew better. Hurrying, I made it across the street before the buses pulled out. I kept a safe distance, but also had him in my sights. Doug would be proud of me. Suddenly he darted out into the street and ran across to the other side. *What just happened?*

A large wooded area, fifty acres or more, lay just beyond the school soccer field on that side of the street. He disappeared into the brush. I came to a complete stop, staring with my mouth open. *What the—?*

I had no choice. I dashed across the street and

slipped through some large bushes right at the edge of the forest. No sound came from within, no snapping of branches or rustling of leaves, just silence. I snuck farther into the woods and hoped to be rewarded. A few yards in I saw a cleared path and decided to follow it.

A loud noise startled me. I jumped behind a huge tree, hugging its trunk. *A motorcycle?* Within seconds, one flew by me. I'd recognized the shape of that body anywhere. *Heathcliff.* He hopped onto another trail and disappeared into the shadows.

Odd. The whole sneaking into the woods and riding a bike out in another direction made me all the more curious. I knew he wasn't allowed to ride the bike to school so why go to all that trouble? *Heathcliff. Mr. Montgomery, whoever you are, you're so infuriating!*

I followed the same path I came on to exit the woods, stepping out into the sunny day. No sidewalk ran along the side of the road so I walked through tall grass and weeds, past the soccer field to get back to the high school parking area. As I headed for my car, I noticed Josh in the parking lot. He raised his hand when he spotted me, waving me over.

"How about if we talk now? I've got football practice in ten minutes, but since we're both here—" He shrugged.

"Fine, let's get it over with."

He dropped the cocky attitude and reminded me of the old Josh. He followed me to the Jeep. As I unlocked the doors, he slid into the passenger side. "Nice. Did your dad get you this? What year?" He patted the dashboard.

"It's only a year old. You know Dad. He said I'd get a used car but wanted it to be reliable."

Josh smiled and shook his head. "Daddy's little girl. You always had him wrapped around your finger just like you had me."

I laughed at that comment. "Really, Josh? I thought it was the other way around."

"Does it really matter, Al?"

Al? Already aggravated, the nickname set me off. "Start talking, Josh. Your ten minutes are ticking away."

"Okay!" He held his hands up. "First, when you saw me kissing Savannah last April it was more like she kissed me."

"A kiss is a kiss, Josh." I was now officially perturbed. "Go on."

"It's like she planned it." He threw his hands out. "She knew I was waiting for you and when she saw you coming? Wham! She kissed me. We'd been talking and joking around for a few minutes before you showed up. I didn't see it coming."

I rolled my eyes. "You ended up dating her until the end of the year. How do you explain that?"

"She was easy?" Josh looked down at his hands.

"So what you're saying is that after I broke things off with you, you thought what the hell, I'll just start dating Savannah?" *Oh, my gosh, he slept with her. I know he did.* I wasn't asking any more details. "Thanks for straightening that out. Now get out of my car."

"Wait a minute, let me finish. I didn't want to date her or Chloe or anyone else. I just want you back. Please think about it."

"I will." I sat without speaking for a moment. "No. Now get out of my car."

"I'm serious." Josh opened the car door and got out. "I'll be waiting for your answer." He knocked a few times on the window as he walked away.

I started the car and fumed as I watched him head to practice. Didn't I just tell him no? *Boys! Men! I can't figure them out.*

I had Mysterious Montgomery on one hand and Take Me Back Reed on the other. A push-pull grew inside me. Did I take the easy way out and go back to Josh? Or did I follow my heart and try to reach the boy who wants no one to know him? I mulled over the answer. As I stared out the car window, it came to me. Nothing in life was simple or easy so I chose my heart.

CHAPTER FOUR

I had terrible detective skills. Doug wouldn't want me to be part of his secret Army team. Three weeks of school went by, and I still didn't know Heathcliff's first name. I tried to follow him the next few days, but lost him every time. I got the bright idea to park at the edge of the woods to wait, but he seemed to know. When I did follow him, he never traveled in the same direction.

I waited for Ashley outside class when Heathcliff Montgomery appeared out of nowhere. I gave up trying to impress him with my fashion choices and switched back to t-shirts and jeans. I thought I saw a slight smile cross his face as he slipped past me.

"Hello, Mr. Montgomery." I acted like he was an old friend. He gave a slight nod. Then I went in for the kill. "Don't rush off too fast. I may have some things to discuss with you. Like the number nine." I couldn't say twenty-nine. I only saw the I and X on his foot.

That got him. He flinched and hesitated. For a brief moment, I thought I had his attention. Just as suddenly, he stiffened and continued into the room.

"I'm so sorry I can't ride home with you this week!" Ashley rushed down the hall, skidding to a stop in front of me. "I have to babysit Emma. Mom promised this would be the only week while she looks for a job."

"What if she gets a job, Ash?"

"Ooh, never thought of that. Let's hope she doesn't or I'm stuck babysitting for the year. Do you think we'll get our papers back today?"

"We'll find out soon enough." The dreaded term papers had already started. Our first assignment had been a character analysis of any main character in *Wuthering Heights* using quotes to back up our reasoning. I picked Heathcliff, of course, and tried my best to write a good analysis as the schoolgirl geek came out in me.

We walked into the classroom, and I took a deep breath. I learned how to go down the aisle without bumping anyone, especially Heathcliff. He always stayed hunched over in his seat without so much of a twitch or budge. His stance made me want to poke him all the more.

Mrs. Greene was handing back term papers as I made my way to my seat. She placed mine on the desk. "Good job, Ms. Sanders." *Ninety-two percent. Not bad.*

She paused next to the boy in front of me. "Mr. Montgomery, you wrote a well-thought piece on whether Heathcliff should be considered a tragic hero or not. You gave arguments for both sides. It's insightful and well-written as if someone beyond your years wrote it. You're an old soul in a young man's body, I believe."

Oh, so Mr. Montgomery's a deep thinker, an old soul. I kind of liked that even though my inner competitive self bristled at the one hundred percent I saw on his paper.

"Good job," I whispered and got the usual no response. I decided he was hard of hearing.

After class I got in the habit of visiting my locker. For some reason, I just had to see if Josh and Chloe were still together. Every day, like clockwork, they passed by. I got a polite hello or head nod from him. Chloe looked right through me as if I didn't exist. She probably wished I didn't. As of now I had the record of being Josh's girlfriend for the longest time, and she aimed to break it.

Busy sorting my books, I almost didn't see him at first. Josh stood next to me, alone.

"Hey, Allie, how are you?"

"Good enough to not make small talk with you."

"Ouch! Come on, give me a break. I just want an answer. Have you read the texts I sent you?"

"Nope, deleted them." I rummaged through my locker.

"Can we talk? Alone?" Josh had a cute, pleading look on his face. A piece of his dark blonde hair hung over his sparkling blue eyes making him irresistible.

"Fine, but not today."

"You name the time and place. I'll stop by tomorrow, and you can tell me."

"With or without Chloe?"

"We're just casually dating, Al."

"Oh." *Why am I agreeing to this?* I sighed. *To make him go away.*

"I'll see you in class." Josh strutted away looking a little too happy. I organized my stuff so I could race straight to the main door at the end of the day. I planned on following Mr. Montgomery out the door and right into his life. Just try and stop me.

* * * *

Palms sweating, I gripped the steering wheel of my Jeep. I felt my heart pound through my shirt. Sweat rolled down my back even with the air conditioning running full blast. I sat on the crossroad, pulled off on an embankment, ready to put the car into gear.

I lied to Ashley and told her I couldn't take her home today. I lied to my mom and said I needed to stay after school for a meeting. What kind of girl had I turned into? I was the good girl, with a 3.5 grade average, and did as I was told. Now I sat here waiting for a motorcycle to fly out of the woods and planned to follow it wherever it may lead.

The bike broke out of the woods and headed for the street. It caught me by surprise. My hand shook when I put the jeep in drive and stepped on the gas. "Which way are you taking me today, Mr. Montgomery?"

Excitement took over as the car spilled onto the road, stones shooting everywhere. I turned south on Gilbert, the road out of town, and kept a safe distance. We traveled about fifteen minutes before I noticed the bike turn left at a three-way stop. I hadn't lost him yet, so I followed his lead. I'd driven down Gilbert many times but never turned on that side road. I had no clue where it led.

Without warning, the bike slowed to a crawl and veered into a drive. I let up on the gas to keep my distance. The road had woods on either side. No signs of homes or businesses. I came to a diner sign, and knew that had to be the place to turn in. *Funny. This seems to be in the middle of nowhere.*

I parked in a huge gravel lot and scanned the grounds. Three or four cars sat in the lot but no motorcycle. I slipped out of the Jeep to have a look around. I could have sworn he pulled in here.

"He did it again. He lost me." I stood with my hands on my hips surveying the land then headed for the car. As I opened the door to the Jeep, I heard a voice.

"Looking for someone?"

I swung my head in the direction of the sound. He stood leaning against the diner, my handsome loner. He nodded and strolled toward me.

"Not really, just hungry." I lied.

"Really?" He smiled, genuine and beautiful, all pearly white teeth. As he came closer, I noticed a twinkle in his eyes. They didn't seem so dark and brooding now. "I'll buy you a cup of coffee." He stood inches from me, waiting for my response.

I could barely breathe, let alone talk. I played with my keys, acting as if I needed to lock up the car. I broke eye contact and turned toward the Jeep.

"You got auto-start?"

"Yeah."

"That's good."

I swung back and smiled. "In case I need to make a quick getaway?"

He smiled back. "Hopefully not." He gestured toward the diner. "Shall we?"

We walked toward the diner, and he held the door open. I marched up the few steps to the entrance. The scene appeared so normal, it made me wary. I bit my bottom lip as I glanced around the room. I hoped I hadn't set myself up.

"Booth okay?" He pointed to the one farthest from the door.

"Sure." I wiped my hands on my jeans as I sat down, hoping he didn't notice.

He slipped behind the counter, poured two cups of coffee and grabbed a plate of biscuits. The tray overflowed with an assortment of blueberry, apple and cinnamon that smelled like they just came out of the oven. Unable to eat all day, my appetite suddenly returned.

"Do you work here?" It dawned on me that he helped himself to coffee and grabbed food for us from behind the counter.

"Sometimes." He put a plate and napkin in front of me and offered me first choice.

"They all look so good." I reached for apple.

"Then have all three kinds." Again the smile that made me melt inside. "So what are you doing in my part of the woods?' He gave me a wink. "Oh, that's right, you're hungry."

This time I smiled. "I'm Allie, by the way." I stuck out my hand.

He took my hand. It felt warm and tingled like the first time we touched. I felt myself flush from head to toe.

"Lucas, Lucas Montgomery. Although you already know the Montgomery part."

I laughed. He was easy to talk to, and I felt comfortable. The diner had a pleasant atmosphere. I settled back against the seat. I hadn't pictured our first face-to-face to be so predictable. "Yeah, you're Mrs. Greene's favorite student. What did she call you? An old soul? You'll have to tell me the secret to writing a good paper for her."

Lucas threw his head back and let out a long laugh. "You can't stand that someone wrote a better paper than you."

Stung by the comment, I picked at the biscuit I held. In fake frustration, I threw the small piece and he caught it in his mouth. "Fine, you know me. So what else do you know? Have you been following me?" I regretted saying that as soon as it passed my lips.

"I know you're friends with Ms. Donovan in English, and you drive a red Jeep." He pointed to my car outside. "I believe I saw you at the bookstore the first day of school but was definitely not following you." He looked away, trying to avoid eye contact.

Mmm, I don't think he's telling the truth. "Did you ever see me last year?" I asked.

"Yeah, once or twice."

Oh, he was good at this game, charming yet elusive. "So last year was your first at the high school."

"No, I started freshman year. My parents researched the area before buying the diner. They wanted me to go to a solid, academic school with a good reputation."

Surprised to hear he attended freshman year, I tried to gain my composure. How did I miss seeing him in the halls? "You're not in the yearbook."

"Oh, that?" He rubbed his face. "Who cares? I think I was sick on picture day."

"Both years?"

"I think so. Can't remember."

"For someone so smart, it's strange you can't."

"You know what they say about smart people. Sometimes they can't remember to tie their own shoelaces." He raised and tipped his mug at me to make the point.

I couldn't stop staring into those dark brown eyes and came to the conclusion that he excelled at distraction. I wanted to find out more about him. "Any brothers or sisters?"

"I have a younger brother, Jonas, and a little sister, Hannah."

That sounded normal enough. The family bought the diner and moved here two years ago. They lived pretty far from town so if Lucas didn't drive until this year, he was stuck. "I confess I saw you on your bike. Doesn't look too big. What is it?"

"A Ninja 250."

"Kawasaki?"

"You know your bikes."

"A little. My neighbor, Nate, loves them. We ride dirt bikes in his backyard."

"I'll have to ride with you sometime." Lucas hesitated. "That is, if you want."

"I'd love it." I felt myself blushing so I decided to get back into safer territory. "Have you ridden long?"

"Pretty much my whole life. My Granddad collects all types of bikes, going back to World War Two. Most of his bikes are from the fifties and sixties, the golden age of the motorbike."

"Sounds awesome."

"Maybe you'd like to see them sometime."

"Maybe you'd like to start your shift now." A booming voice came from behind the counter.

"Dad!" Lucas bolted from the booth. "Let me help you with those boxes."

His dad rolled in a two-wheeler from the back of the diner, set it in place and leaned on the top box. Not as tall as Lucas, but I noticed the similarities—dark hair and eyes. Mr. Montgomery's brow furrowed as his eyes swept over me. I got the distinct feeling he wanted an immediate background check. "And this lovely lady is?"

"Allie, Dad. I'd like you to meet a new friend, Allison Sanders. Allie, this is my dad, Sam Montgomery."

"Nice to meet you, Mr. Montgomery." I nodded at him.

"Sorry to tear Lucas away, but there's work to do."

"Not a problem. I was just leaving. See you in class tomorrow?" I gathered my things and dug for money to pay for the coffee and biscuits. His hand went over mine. I wanted to crumble back into the booth.

"Put your money away. It's no good here. I'll walk

you to your car."

When we reached the Jeep, I heard a faraway beep. "Did you hear that?"

"You've got great hearing. It's just my phone." Lucas pulled the device from his back pocket. A sleek design, one I'd never seen before. "Just Grandpa Gene." He shrugged. "I'll get back to him later."

"You live around here?" The street seemed deserted except for the diner.

"Yeah, another couple miles up the road." Lucas cocked his head in the opposite direction from the main street. "Not too many houses out here."

I gazed around and noticed two lampposts by the diner entrance but no other streetlights on this back road. The landscape appeared to be nothing but woods. "Bet it gets dark out here at night."

"Doesn't bother me." Lucas shrugged. He turned and headed back for the diner leaving me alone next to my car.

His sudden departure left me with my mouth hanging open. What did I expect? A kiss goodbye? To be asked out on a date?

I started the car and drove past the diner almost expecting to see Lucas peering out the window, waving to me. The windows remained empty.

I traveled a few miles on the side street, reaching Gilbert in no time. I made a right turn and headed back into town. With each mile, more and more houses appeared then a gas station, a convenience store. Civilization. Funny how driving a few miles away from town can change the lay of the land. When I got to the school I pulled in the parking lot to gain my composure. "I just met Lucas Montgomery!" I shrieked and did a little dance.

I took a breath and grabbed my phone from the visor of the car to send a text to Nate: *Have our bikes ready. We're going on a road trip.*

I headed for his house, passing by my own. I drove right into the open garage. Nate had the loading ramp attached to the back of his pick-up and secured one of the bikes in place.

"You found a place we can ride?" Nate called out as I headed to the shed for the other bike.

"Yep, it's got readymade trails," I answered and felt a twinge of guilt for not telling him the real motive. I wanted to explore the wooded area by the school to find out more about Lucas.

When I returned with the bike, Nate jumped from the truck. "Here I'll take it, little one."

"I can manage."

Nate, the older brother I wished I had, took the handles. "Get in." He nodded toward the cab and rolled the bike into place. I waited in the cab while he pushed the ramp up and in, then locked the door to the truck bed. He climbed into the driver's seat and looked at me with one eye shut. "Where to?"

I swallowed hard, hoping he'd buy it. "The woods next to the school. I discovered some great trails there."

"You just happened to be strolling around the woods next to the school? What are you, stupid? Someone could follow you in there. Who knows what could've happen?" Nate smacked his head.

We drove in silence to the end of the street. I finally broke the icy atmosphere between us. "Wait until you see the trails. If we park at the farthest end of the school by the soccer field, we should be able to ride through the brush and into the woods."

"How about telling me the real reason you

discovered this place? No one walks on that side of the road. No sidewalk. School rule is to cross and walk on the other side. Plus the soccer field between the school and woods is about the size of a football field. I can't figure out how you ended up there."

"Fine! I'll tell you. I followed Heathcliff after school. He ran into the woods and disappeared. I never saw him come out." I lied and also left out the 'meet and greet' at the diner. "That's when I saw the trails. Maybe he made them. He could own a dirt bike, too. Wouldn't that be great if we had something in common?"

Nate pulled into the school parking lot and drove right up to the field, backing the truck into place. "Yeah, great."

I jumped from the truck and gazed at the wooded area. I had said I didn't want any distractions so I could leave town when the time came, but Lucas was the exception. I wanted to find out all I could about him. Slipping on a helmet, I took my bike from Nate as he rolled it down the ramp.

"Stay together. No fancy stuff." He glared at me.

We started up the bikes and cruised through the tall grass along the side of the road. I guided Nate to the opening where I saw Lucas first go in. The path didn't begin right away. He left the front of the woods in its natural state.

A few yards in, the first path stretched out before us. I cruised along slowly, looking around for additional trails. I came to the end of the main one, skidding to a stop in front of a large pile of leaves and brush. Pulling off my helmet, I swept my hair back and waited for Nate.

"What do you make of it?" I asked as he pulled up

along side of me.

"Interesting, seems like he can ride in on any of these paths, ditch his bike there," Nate said as he gestured to the pile, "then walk out on the main path to school. I've got to give him credit. Let's see where these go."

We revved up the bikes, replaced our helmets and continued to explore. I chose the path Lucas took the first day I followed him, curious to see where it led. The trail had an S-shape. I had to lean to the right then left again. Not built for the amateur rider. The sun peeked through the trees as I grew closer to the edge of the woods. The path narrowed to the size of a tire and finally disappeared into tall grass. I drove out into the bright sunlight. I recognized the intersection, the street that led away from town taking people out to the country, Gilbert Road.

"If all these trails just end, it's a pretty lame track." Nate called over the roar of the engines. He backed up and spun around, heading back into the woods.

I followed behind, still interested in the other paths. Surely, they led to other places besides the street. Nate pointed to an almost undetectable one and hung left. We hit a few speed bumps along the way and had to avoid a few obstacles making it quite a find. We circled back to the primary path and came to a stop in front of the familiar pile of leaves.

"The sun's lower in the sky. We've been here longer than I thought." Nate wiped the sweat from his forehead. "We better get these in the truck and start for home."

"Thanks for doing this." I patted his arm. "I owe you."

We walked the bikes out of the woods and loaded

them in the truck. As I slid into the passenger seat, I smiled. One mystery solved. Lucas rode his bike to school, hid it in the brush and walked the rest of the way in. He lived on one of those country roads and used the S-shaped path to come and go.

My phone buzzed as I settled in the truck. "Hey, Ash, how'd your mom's job search go?"

"She got a part-time job, Monday, Wednesday, Friday. So at least we can hang out on the other days. Where are you, by the way? Do I hear country music playing in the background? Are you with Nate?"

"In Nate's truck, yes and yes." I had to stop teasing her, but found it fun to answer her questions in quick succession. Silence came from the other end. "Okay, I'll stop it. We rode dirt bikes, and now we're on our way home. Next time, come with us." I poked Nate in the side.

"I hate those things! Why didn't you ride in Nate's backyard?"

"Trying out something new."

"Why do I think there's more to it?"

"Wow! You're just as bad as Nate."

"Then, I'm right. Let me talk to him."

"He's driving."

"Then put your phone on speaker."

Nate's eye lit up when he realized Ashley wanted to talk to him. "Hey, Ash. What's up?"

"You tell me. What's my girl up to?"

"Chasing dreams."

"Oh, so this has something to do with Heathcliff."

"Yep. We need to get together and discuss what we're going to do with her." A huge smile crossed his face.

"Maybe we should," Ashley said. "Ooh, got to go.

Mom's calling me. See you guys tomorrow. Bookstore? Movies? Do something with me this weekend before babysitting duty kicks in."

"I'll call you." I hung up and leaned back against the seat, satisfied with the progress I'd made with Lucas and now Ashley and Nate.

"Why is she always saying maybe?" Nate shot me a frustrated look.

"I don't know but I think you should hold her to the getting together thing." I looked up my driveway and saw Dad's car. I checked my phone for the time. It was after six.

Nate parked in front of his garage. I jumped out and into the Jeep knowing I pushed my luck. I backed out of the Kalas garage and into the turn-around so I could head down the long drive. For just a moment, I thought I saw a motorcycle at the end of the street, but it disappeared before I got a good look.

It can't be. Is he following me? Maybe he liked me just a little. Or maybe he didn't trust me. I had no clue what twenty-nine stood for and could care less. Now that we met, it would be a good time to come clean about everything with Lucas. Everything, except Doug.

CHAPTER FIVE

My heart fluttered and my stomach flipped as I stepped through the classroom door the following Monday. I couldn't wait to see Lucas and tell him we could ride with Nate whenever he wanted. I negotiated a treaty over the weekend and had to promise Nate I'd get Ashley to come along.

Ashley slipped into her seat and had the "go for it" look as we made eye contact. Lucas' head was bent down as usual, still shutting the world out. Today I knew I wasn't included in that world.

"Hey," I said as I walked by and slid into my seat. No answer. "Lucas?"

I gave him the familiar poke in the back, but he didn't budge. I glanced at Ash and gave her a wide-eyed look. Mrs. Greene started class, and I had fifty minutes of agony to find out what went wrong.

When the bell rang, Lucas darted from his seat and reached the door before I caught up. "Lucas!" I said as loudly and sternly as possible.

I saw his body jerk, and he spun around. A pained look flashed across his face. The dark and brooding eyes were back.

"Wait!" I commanded. "What just happened in there?"

Lucas pulled me over to the side of the hallway. "I can't see you anymore."

"Why?"

"My dad."

"That's it. That's all you got?"

"Nothing against you. He feels we won't be here long. We'll be moving on. The diner's a temporary thing until he gets back on his feet. He doesn't want me to get too attached to anyone at school."

Or anyone in general. "That has to be hard on you. No friends, no girl ..." I wanted to say girlfriend, and I would gladly apply for the position.

"Let me see what I can do. I'd like to see you." Lucas came so close our bodies almost touched. Our lips were inches apart when I lifted my head to meet his eyes. I melted right into them. "Just stay clear until then. They know my every move."

"They? Who are you talking about?" Lucas disappeared into the crowd of people shuffling down the hall, leaving me stunned. Was he in some sort of cult? How could they know his every move? Did he have a tracking chip implanted in his brain like all those science fiction movies I watched with Nate? Nate! He might have some answers.

Ashley caught up to me. "What's with Mr. Personality? I thought you said he was funny and kind. Seems a little stand-offish and rude."

"You don't know him. I think something's wrong."

"My advice is to steer clear of him, Allie. Maybe he and his family are aliens or something."

"You read too much, Ash. He's going through a hard time. His family could have money problems or are running from the law. Maybe they like to keep to themselves."

"Or they are mass murderers, kidnappers, or bank robbers. Whatever they are, be careful. You might have your hands full with that one."

I wanted to change the subject before Ashley came up with any more scenarios for the Montgomery family. "Want to meet me at Nate's tonight after dinner?"

"If Rob will drive me, but I need a ride home."

"I'm sure Nate won't mind."

"What's with all these Nate references lately?"

"Nothing, we've hung out for years. I always talk about him."

"I mean *extra* references, Al."

"Hey, you know I hate that name!"

"I know. Sorry, it just slipped out."

It reminded me of the conversation I had with Josh the other day. I told Ashley all the sordid details.

"He wants you back! I knew it. What are you going to do? Do you think he slept with Savannah? What about Lucas?"

We walked toward my locker. I hoped to avoid Josh today. Arriving later than usual did the trick, he was nowhere in sight.

"If this was the first day of school I might have considered going back to him. I don't even want to think about Savannah and what the two of them did. Right now, Lucas is the only thing on my mind. I finally met him and want to see where this goes."

"You never did tell me exactly how you ended up at that diner."

"The less you know the better." I joked.

I fumbled around in my bag searching for my phone. Phones could be used in school for emergencies and schoolwork. I considered this an emergency. I sent a text to Nate saying Ashley and I would be over after dinner. We needed to brainstorm and figure out what was going on with Lucas.

* * * *

"Lucas, Lucas Montgomery!" I yelled the name at Nate.

"Calm down, little one, I'm typing as fast as I can. Ashley, distract her."

"So what do you think the next book will be for English?" Ashley smiled too brightly at me. "Maybe you can find a new name for Heathcliff ... er, Lucas."

"He doesn't need a name anymore and looking at the syllabus we're reading *Animal Farm,* as if you didn't know."

"Ooh, that's a good one. Four legs good, two legs bad." Nate laughed as he stared at the screen. Ash and I looked at each other and wrinkled our noses. "You'll see what I mean once you start reading. Whoa! I think I got something."

I popped up and looked over his shoulder as he read aloud. "Once a leading member in the racing world, Eugene Montgomery hasn't been seen on the track since the 1970s. An inside source said Gene chose retirement over the opportunity to create a worldwide motorcycle racing circuit. He and his family moved back to their home state of Missouri."

"Eugene has to be Lucas' grandfather." I recalled him mentioning Grandpa Gene. "See if you can find a picture of his family."

Nate worked at his computer for over an hour while Ashley and I gossiped and discussed class assignments. We had a final essay test on *Wuthering Heights* next week. I was sorry to see it end.

"Damn! The trail went cold. That one little piece was from some obscure cycle magazine from the early eighties. Someone scanned the article and posted it on their blog today. That's all I can find. Now I'm intrigued. I can't give up."

That made me happy. I didn't want him to give up either. Being part of the motorbike world might keep his interest. "Nate, isn't it strange for someone to be so prominent in that field to have so little written about him?"

"Yeah, especially since motorcycles became popular in the United States around that time. American Honda Motors was established in 1959. They brought street bikes to America."

"A history lesson?" Ashley threw a pillow at him. He picked it up and tossed it back, accidentally hitting her in the head.

"It's so on, Kalas!" Ashley leaped from her chair, taking the pillow over to the computer desk to give Nate a few playful whacks.

They paused for just a second, and I witnessed something very sweet. Nate got up from the desk seizing Ashley by the wrists to keep her from delivering another blow. They both laughed, looking directly into each other's eyes. The laughs died down, a moment occurred and quickly ended. Maybe they would've kissed if I wasn't sitting in the middle of the bed, watching.

"Well, I guess I better get going." Ashley swept her long hair back and looked around for her cell and book bag.

"Nate has to drive you, Ash."

"Oh, right. Well, would you?" She made eye contact with him, and I swore he dissolved into a puddle of mush.

"Sure."

"Is it alright if I stay here until you get back?" I held up my notes. "This woman assigns too many essay projects. I'm in the middle of organizing my last paper for the book and don't want to lose track."

After they left, my phone rang. Ashley probably forgot her notebook or lost an earring. "What'd you forget?"

"Hey."

It was *him*. I sat up straight on the bed. "How'd you get this number?"

"I have my ways."

"What do you want? I thought you warned me to stay away from you."

His laugh rang through my head.

"Not funny," I whispered.

"Okay, sorry. How would you like to come over tomorrow after school and see the bike collection? Grandpa Gene's dying to meet you."

Oh, I just bet he is. Does he want to size me up, too? "Let me think about it. I'll let you know tomorrow. That's if you plan on speaking to me."

"Of course. I'll wait for your answer."

This time I wouldn't have to lie to Ashley, just my mom. I needed to come up with something really good. I wanted time with Lucas so I texted Ash and asked for her help.

Tell your mom we're shopping and grabbing a bite to eat. I'll cover appeared on my screen. Hugging my phone, I danced around the room celebrating. I might have a chance with Lucas after all.

I got back to my assignment, flopping on Nate's bed, thinking of the book we'd read in English class. Heathcliff's love for Catherine stood out the most. Some might argue he was cruel, and his need for revenge drove him more than love. He had a sad upbringing until Catherine's father brought him to Wuthering Heights to grow up with Catherine and her brother, Hindley.

Heathcliff was treated as an outsider by Hindley. He overheard Catherine say she couldn't marry someone beneath her status which added to his torment. Unrequited love was difficult to overcome, and Heathcliff could never do that. I closed the book, contemplating if Catherine really loved him. Did she say those words because she had no choice? I couldn't do that to my Heathcliff. I shivered as I thought of how I could take the safe route with Josh, like Catherine did, when I really wanted to be with someone else.

Debating those talking points helped me make a decision about my own life. I jumped to my feet and glided around the room dancing to imaginary music. I might not have to zombie walk through the next two years. Things could get interesting in this ordinary small town making it quite extraordinary. My heart raced as I envisioned a life headed down an unknown trail instead of a well-worn path.

Nate slipped into the room and caught me dancing. Surprisingly, no snarky comments. He wore the biggest, silliest grin, and I didn't have to guess why. He kissed her. I wrapped my arms around his neck. He placed his hand on my hips. We whirled around the room. As I spun through the air, I felt Josh cleansed from my mind, clearing the way for a new beginning. I gave Nate a quick peck on the cheek and gathered my things to head home.

As I stepped in the back door, I found Mom pacing in the kitchen. She seemed to be talking to herself as she fidgeted with something in her hand. My mood changed from happy to concerned. When she spotted me she jumped like she saw a ghost.

"Mom! Are you okay?" She fumbled with a black, glossy high-tech phone and tried to hide it behind her back. "Is that what's got you all upset? Let me see it." I stuck out my hand.

"No." She pulled back and slipped it into her

pant's pocket.

"Did you get a new phone? I can help you with it." I spoke softly, hoping to calm her.

"It's fine. I won't use it much." She sank into a kitchen chair and rested her head in her hands. "It's just been a long day, sweetie. Don't mind me."

I joined her at the table and reached out to pat her arm. "Mom, you aren't good at hiding things. Talk to me."

Her face softened, and she tried to smile. "I'm fine really. Now tell me about your day. Make any new friends at school?"

An alarm went off in my head. She was grilling me, not making casual conversation. "Not really."

"Doug said there might be an influx of new kids at your school, and I should keep an eye on you. I don't know why." Her hand shook as she swiped at her hair hanging over her forehead.

Now I knew why she paced. Doug called and filled her head with nonsense. She didn't know whether to believe him or not. "Were you talking to Doug when I came in?"

"No ... I mean ... yes. Oh, my goodness." She brought her hand to her mouth. Her mouth quivered, and her eyes filled with tears. "I don't want anything bad to happen to you, Allie. I couldn't take it. You're my little angel."

Her statement made me tremble. What kind of garbage did Doug tell her? I slipped from my seat and wrapped my arms around her, feeling like I had to protect her. At that moment, she appeared frail, almost aging before my eyes. "Mom, nothing's going to happen. I promise."

"I'm just being a silly, old woman. Forgive me."

She patted my face then straightened in her chair. "Let me ask you something. Did Doug show you a card with some markings on it?"

"A card?" A twinge of guilt went through me. I hated lying to my mom.

"Never mind. I didn't understand it. Neither did your father. Doug said to be on the lookout for that symbol on the card. Your dad said it was the number twenty-nine. Does that make sense to you?"

I shook my head. "Nope."

"Me neither." Mom shrugged. "You probably have homework. I won't keep you any longer. We should both head up."

Arm in arm we climbed the stairs and parted ways at my bedroom door. My mom was the most trusting, sweetest person I knew. I clenched my hands into fists, upset that my brother scared her.

Tomorrow I planned on asking Lucas about twenty-nine, why it was tattooed on the arch of his foot and what the hell the number meant. Once I knew, the truth would be in the open. I could explain it to Mom. Everything could calm down and go back to normal. I could only hope.

CHAPTER SIX

Could I handle another snub from Lucas? Ignoring me yesterday broke my heart, but he assured me today would be different. I fixed my gaze on the floor as I moved down the aisle. I dared myself to look at him and connected with those beautiful, secretive eyes. He nodded. I got a nod so my spirit soared. After I sat, Lucas turned in his seat.

"I'll meet you after school by the main door. My granddad dropped me off today so I can ride home with you." He spun back and faced the front of the room. I didn't talk to him again, but that was enough. I could make it through the school day.

Rushing for the front door after the final bell, I had doubts. Would he be waiting? Only one more hallway to find the answer.

"Watch where you're going!" A male voice stopped me cold. After recovering, I discovered I slammed right into Josh.

"Josh! Sorry. Didn't see you."

"Obviously. You haven't been at your locker the last few days. I only see you in history. You barely look at me. Is something wrong?"

"Nothing's wrong. I just need to get going."

"I'll walk you to your car. We still need to talk."

"Don't bother, really—"

"It's no problem. I'm going to my car to get my gear for practice."

No matter how hard I tried, I couldn't lose him. We walked together, and I distanced myself. Lucas stood right outside the building. My heart leaped out of my body when I saw him. He waited just like he said.

We made eye contact, and he took a few steps forward. I raised my hand in a wave to let Josh know I saw my friend.

"Lucas!" I kept waving as he backed off. I turned to Josh. "I really need to get going."

Josh stuck right with me. "So this is why you haven't given me an answer."

We stood in front of Lucas. "Lucas, this is Josh Reed, a friend."

Lucas nodded but didn't speak.

"Well, I'll see you later, Al." Josh gave a salute and headed for the parking lot.

"That's the old boyfriend who wants you back," Lucas said in a monotone voice. "The one you couldn't stop talking about the first week of school."

"To the back of your head." I giggled. "Jealous?"

"Where'd you park?"

I gestured in the general direction of my car, and we strolled through the lot. A little odd he didn't answer, but I brushed it off. I hoped Josh had his gear and would be gone when we got to my car. I decided to make light conversation and see if I could get the other Lucas back, the one I got to know at the diner.

"Did you ever apply for a parking pass? I almost didn't get in. The second day of school I was told of an opening."

"Never applied. I'm happy with the way things are."

"Maybe I'm romanticizing this a bit, but riding a motorcycle to school and ditching it in the woods makes you seem like a lone wolf or something."

"Or something?" The laugh came. Lucas let his guard down, and I could relax. We hopped in the Jeep.

"Isn't it little hard to ride wearing sandals? How do

you do it?"

He shrugged and stared straight ahead. I decided to keep going. "What's up with that nine or I, X on the arch of your foot?"

The muscles in his jaw twitched, and he blinked a few times before he faced me. "It's not a nine." He crossed his right foot over his left leg, removing the sandal. Across the arch were the Roman numerals X-X-I-X.

I had to suppress a gasp. "What does it mean?" I swallowed hard, not knowing if I wanted the answer.

"Just a dumb thing I did in middle school. A group of us thought we were tough and wanted to make a statement."

"Like a gang?"

Lucas threw his head back and laughed. "Not really. Just some guys who thought they were tough."

"Guys? No girls can have the tattoo?"

"Nope. Men only."

"Wow, that's sexist." I crossed my arms.

"I was thirteen, what can I say?" Lucas took my chin in his hand. "It's one of the reasons my dad wanted to move to a small town."

"Oh." I wanted to know more. "You lived in a big city?" Nate mentioned Gene Montgomery was from Missouri. Maybe I could pry the name of a city out of Lucas.

"Yeah." He slipped his sandal back on. "Want to head out? I have a feeling you know where to go."

Defeated, I started the car and decided to try again later as I headed for the main road.

"I have to give you credit for following me all those times." Lucas broke the silence.

"You knew I followed you?" I gulped hard.

"Yes."

"And you didn't mind?"

"I knew I could lose you if I wanted to."

Now I had to laugh. "You have some great riding paths in the woods. How long have you been working on them?"

"Pretty much since I've been here. Don't need much sleep. I like to work at night."

"It must get dark in there. Do you bring floodlights or something?"

"I meant until it gets dark. Summer's the best time for working late."

"Yeah, I know what you mean. I love the longer days." I arrived at the turn-off and steered the Jeep onto the new road. "Now where?"

"Past the diner. I'll tell you when to turn."

"Really? I thought this was all woods."

We drove along in silence until we passed the diner. "You don't have to work today?" Silly question since he sat right next to me.

"I get days off."

"Does your granddad work at the diner?"

"Once in awhile. He stays home mostly. Someone has to be there when Jonas and Hannah get home from school."

"So your mom works?"

"Yeah, she's at the diner most days." Lucas put his hand on my arm. "Are we done with Twenty Questions?"

"Sure."

"Good because you need to turn right, pull in this driveway."

"Driveway? Where?"

The gravel drive wasn't visible from the street,

surrounded by over-grown bushes. The Jeep barely made it into the entrance without scraping against their branches. Finally the drive opened up into an area covered with trees and a small pond. We drove over a wooden bridge to cross the water and continued on for at least another half mile until I spotted a house and a few large outer buildings.

"Pull up there." Lucas pointed to a two story barn-like structure that looked like it could hold five semi-trucks. A small cottage sat next to it, perhaps his grandfather's home. "Granddad! We're here!" Lucas jumped from the Jeep before I came to a stop.

An older man with a full head of white hair emerged from the cottage. He went to the barn and pushed back the door with little effort. As I watched him, I saw a definite resemblance to Lucas. Both had the same body build and height. They seemed to get on quite well. I sat watching the interaction, almost forgotten during their banter.

"Allie, come out and meet the old geezer."

Surprised to hear Lucas call his grandfather an old geezer, I tried to cover the shock. "Nice to meet you." I stared into the same brown eyes as his grandson's.

"Call me Grandpa Gene or Gene. Everybody does 'cept this one." He tousled Lucas' hair. "Come on, this way. Heard you got an interest in bikes."

We filed into the barn. Gene flipped on the lights exposing a showroom. Bikes sat on shiny black oval display stands. Each one appeared brand new and shone under the single spotlight positioned above.

"This here is one of my favorites, a 1940 Triumph Tiger. Triumph turned all their efforts toward the war after that bike. The company was bombed in 1942 during the blitz of Coventry in England and had to rebuild. Managed to get up and running and pump out more bikes before the war ended."

"Was that bike used during the war?"

"I'm told it was." Gene patted the seat like an old friend. "You two look around, be my guest. Got to drive to the diner and wait for Hannah's bus."

I wrinkled my brow and looked at Lucas. "The diner?"

"Makes it easier for the bus. It turns around in the parking lot and goes back to the main road."

"Oh." Lucas and I stood side by side in this unbelievable showplace. Harleys, Yamahas, Hondas of all types and a few names I didn't recognize glistened in the light. I noticed a few dirt bikes and felt drawn to them.

"Did you know that dirt track racing was originally an American sport?" Lucas asked.

"Of course I do. I admit I start to zone out when Nate begins his history lessons on all things motorbike, but I've picked up a few things." I winked as I sat on the edge of a display platform and studied the room. "Your grandfather put a lot of work into this. All of it came with you when you moved?"

"Yeah, we moved it all."

"Who set this all up?"

"Me and my dad."

"That's it? No other relatives or help?"

"Nope, Granddad has one son, my dad Sam." Lucas reached out and took my hand. "Stay for dinner?"

After I recovered from the initial surprise of the touch, I nodded. I wished he'd kiss me, but instead he let go of my hand and started for the door. As I followed behind, I noticed a metal staircase going up along the side of the wall.

"Where does that lead?" I didn't want to be nosy, but curiosity got the best of me.

Lucas pointed upward, and I saw part of the barn had a second floor. "Storage. Nothing thrilling."

As he slid back the door, we heard a truck coming down the drive. Gene drove, and two people sat in the seat next to him.

"Lucked out and got them both at one time." Gene exited the truck, and the boy and girl slid out the passenger side. "Kids, meet Allie."

"Hi, I'm Hannah." A dark-haired little girl came up and shook my hand. A bit unusual for someone that age.

"And this is Jonas." Gene gave him a gentle push. Jonas, fairer than Lucas but had the family resemblance, shoved his foot into the gravel drive.

"It's Joe. Don't call me Jonas."

"Sure. Hi, Joe." He struck me as sullen and angry.

"She staying for dinner?" He cocked his head in my direction.

"She has a name, Joe. It's Allie." Lucas grabbed Jonas by the back of the neck in a playful way. "Won't it be nice to have company?"

"Have you run it by Mom?"

"I've got it covered." Gene waved for everyone to follow him to the main house.

"So what grade are you in, Hannah?" I asked as we walked behind Grandpa Gene.

"I'm in third and Joe's in eighth." She seemed proud of the fact, like going to school was the best thing she'd ever done.

"So next year, Joe joins us at the high school?" I turned to Lucas, hoping it might bring Joe into the conversation.

"If he makes it through this year." Lucas nudged his brother, and Joe faced him, finally smiling. Without a word, Lucas took off into the woods with Joe in pursuit.

"They might be gone for awhile," Hannah whispered to me and shrugged.

"I take it they've done this before," I said as she nodded.

The ranch home complimented the forest it sat in. A stone front blended into sides made from dark wooden logs. I stepped inside the spacious house, admiring the great room. It had a stone fireplace and over-sized leather furniture, reminding me of a lodge. The tour continued as we walked straight back to an enormous dining area with a large picture window. I stood and gazed out at a beautiful gorge filled with a sea of trees.

An oversized kitchen in the center of the home had two ovens, a refrigerator and separate freezer. My mom would kill for all that space. High top chairs sat around a large island in the middle of the room. The cabinets were a creamy yellow with handles that looked like tiny tree branches. From the kitchen I noticed sliding glass doors that led out to a back deck and ran the length of the house.

"Now onto the library," Gene announced. I followed him into the next room past the kitchen and, to my surprise, Lucas sat on the sofa.

"What took you so long?" He flashed a smile.

"How'd you—?"

"Granddad brought you in the formal way, through the front door. I came in next to it, through the screened-in porch. I can take it from here, Gramps."

Again the smile as if Gramps was an inside joke. Maybe Gene didn't like the name and couldn't protest in front of me.

We walked up two steps and into a short hallway with a closed door straight ahead.

"This is my parents' room." Lucas opened the door so I could peek in then closed it. They, too, had a lovely view of the gorge. I couldn't wait to see the view when the leaves changed color in the fall.

We turned and walked down the hall again, through the library and stopped at another entryway just before we reached the kitchen. It led to a hallway, adjacent to the one we were just in.

"That's where I came in." Lucas pointed to the right. I saw the screened-in porch with a door leading to this new hallway.

"I didn't notice the porch when we walked in the front door. Guess I was too busy admiring everything."

"These are the kids' rooms." Lucas gestured to the left. "Mine's first, then Joe and finally Hannah. See the door at the end of the hall? It leads to my parents' walk-in closet. The house is one big circle. Well, actually, an oval."

"It's beautiful. You must love living here."

"I do. I don't want it to end." I almost forgot their stay would be temporary until his father got back on his feet.

Grandpa Gene appeared around the corner. "Lucas, your mom's home and can't wait to meet Allie."

We headed back to the kitchen where his mom was unpacking a huge bag filled with take-out. "I hope you don't mind food from the diner. I was running late." She turned to greet me. I noticed how much she looked like Joe, fair with light brown hair and honey brown eyes.

"Anything's fine, Mrs. Montgomery. Is there anything I can do to help?" I hoped my nerves didn't show.

"Please, call me Stacy. You just enjoy yourself. It will be nice to have someone different at the dinner table tonight. Sam's at the diner until closing. He sends his regrets."

I bet he does. He's the one who doesn't want me around. He's the one who told Lucas he couldn't see me.

We gathered around the huge oak dining table with the wonderful outdoor view and passed around the foil containers of food. So many choices, but I only picked from three, turkey, corn and mashed potatoes with gravy. After dinner, I helped clear the table.

"Here let me help you, Allie." Grandpa Gene took some of the plates. "So were you overwhelmed by the family? Lucas tells me you're an only child."

A little surprised, I quickly recovered. I never told Lucas anything about my family. "It may seem that way, but I have two older brothers. I hardly know Doug, my oldest brother. He left home when I was two. I'm closer to my brother, Dean, although he's almost twelve years older."

"Glad to hear that. It's not always easy for an only child, so much expected of them."

"Doesn't seem that way with Sam."

"You're right. I never pressured him. We all have to find ourselves." Gene walked to the kitchen counter and sets the dishes down. "Kids, don't you have homework to do?" He gazed around at all of us.

"Sure, I better go." I fumbled for my car keys.

Stacy put her arm around me. "Don't take it

personally. Gene's a little rough around the edges. He's really a big softie inside. Come back anytime."

Lucas escorted me to the car. I felt everything had gone too quickly and didn't want it to end. When we reached the Jeep, he placed his hands on my shoulders and pulled me close. I gazed up and before I could take another breath, his lips found mine. A wonderful shiver went through me. I wanted to grab on and never let go. For some reason I wanted to protect him. I was afraid to leave. His family seemed fine, no cultist tendencies, no abuse, no signs of anything abnormal. Why did I feel this way?

"Careful driving home." Lucas disrupted my thoughts. His lips brushed mine again.

"I will," I whispered and couldn't resist giving him one more kiss. I climbed into the Jeep and watched him go back inside. My phone began to beep. I realized I hadn't paid attention to it all evening. I had new messages, all from Nate.

The first asked if I was still at Lucas', the next said to call as soon as I could and the one I just received said what the heck was I doing that was so important I couldn't text back. I pressed speed dial, and Nate picked up on the first ring.

"I'm calling to see what's so important," I whispered into the phone.

"I thought you'd like to know the blogger posted another article. I think this guy's obsessed with finding out all he can about Gene Montgomery. Little does he know we could fill in the blanks."

"But we're not going to, are we, Nathan? Gene had a reason for walking away from that world. We have to respect it. Besides, he hasn't left it completely. He has an awesome collection of bikes."

"Really? Get me an invite."

"Let's get back to the reason for this call. I need to get on the road."

"You still there? Can anyone hear?"

"No, I'm in the car."

"Okay, wait till you hear this. Let me bring up the site. I'll read it to you." I waited in silence until I heard his voice again.

"The blogger says: *Don't know what happened to Gene Montgomery. He was destined for greatness and had ideas for bike upgrades that will never be known to the racing world. Who knows where that world would be today if those inventions had been shared? Gene's become my personal obsession. I've scoured antique stores and trade shows looking for any old bike magazines to see if I can find more about him. Finally I hit pay dirt when I came across the article in my last post.*" Nate paused. "The article he's referring to is the one I read to you before. You know, the one about how Gene retired and moved to Missouri."

"Okay, get on with it."

"He continues on. Blah, blah, blah, and then says he started looking for articles in any type of magazine or newspaper. He found an interview in a sports magazine with a popular biker who knew Gene. He was asked if he'd ever seen Gene since he left racing. This is where it gets interesting. Listen."

I heard Nate take a deep breath. "Read it to me!" I shouted.

"*I ran into Gene one time with his boys. He introduced me to his sons—Lucas, who seemed about nine or ten and a toddler, Sam. That's the last time I ever saw him.*"

"What? Read that again." I listened carefully as he repeated the information. "Nate, something strange is going on. Lucas told me Gene has one son. Sam. He didn't mention a Lucas."

"Well, maybe we finally found something, little one. They're on the run, and it has something to do with the disappearance of Lucas Sr. Odd that Lucas Jr. would never mention him."

"We don't know that for sure. We won't judge until we find out more. I got to go, Nate. It's getting late."

I hang up and stare at the house. The Montgomery home looked innocent enough. Soft lighting glowed through the windows, making the house look inviting. I recalled having a good time. Could the whole family be hiding a deep, dark secret? Could Sam have killed his brother? Was that the reason he wanted everyone to stay away from his family? And if he didn't kill his brother, what was the deal? Obviously Sam named his first son after his brother.

What happened to Lucas Sr.? Jail? On the lam? Drug dealer? Starting the car, I pulled away not wanting to believe any of this and wondered if I could look Lucas in the face without giving away my suspicions.

CHAPTER SEVEN

The next day I waited for Ashley, pacing back and forth in front of her locker. "Where have you been?" I called out when I spotted her.

"Rob couldn't get his stupid car started. I wish we could have talked last night, but my mom didn't get home till late. I had to give Emma a bath, read her a story—"

"Ash, it's fine. This is important. We don't have much time." I filled her in on the events of last night. "What do you think?"

"Let him explain."

"What? Did I hear you correctly?"

"There might be a reasonable explanation about Lucas Sr."

"So I should tell Lucas we've been searching the internet for information about his family and found a suspicious article about his grandfather."

"Well, don't put it like that. You can do it subtly."

"Thanks for the advice." I sounded sarcastic but didn't mean to be. "Sorry, it's not your problem. It's mine. You're great. Thanks for hearing me out."

"Allie, I'm worried about you. I don't like you getting mixed up in this."

"It could be nothing."

"True. Did I tell you Nate kissed me?"

"No, but I figured he would after that pillow fight."

"I might like him."

"Good."

"Don't tell him."

"I promise."

"And Allie?"

"Yes?"

"Be careful. And good luck. I'll see you in English."

As I walked away, my head hurt from trying to sort through everything I learned. Ashley could be right. I needed to find the truth. In my mind, I made it a big deal. It was probably nothing. I daydreamed through homeroom, and when the bell rang, I shuffled down the hall in a daze.

"Allie, wait!" Josh appeared out of nowhere.

"What do you want, Josh?"

"We haven't had time to talk. How about tonight? After dinner?"

"She's busy." A voice came from behind us.

I twirled around and almost collide into Lucas. "I am?" I looked at Josh. "I am."

"Fine, whenever you can spare the time. I can wait." Josh shot Lucas a dirty look and continued down the hall.

"Actually I hoped to steal you right after school. How would you like to go for a ride through my woods?"

"Oh, so now they're your woods?" I laughed and almost forgot my covert mission. "Sure, I think I'm dressed for it." I looked down at my t-shirt and jeans. "I don't have a helmet."

"No problem, I brought one."

"You're pretty darn sure of yourself, Mr. Montgomery. How'd you know I'd say yes?"

"I was hoping, Ms. Sanders. Meet you same time and place?"

"Yeah, same time and place." My heart pounded against my chest, this time for all the wrong reasons.

* * * *

The end of the day couldn't come fast enough. I wanted no distractions, just to make it out the door without anyone stopping me or trying to talk to me. I had a plan and wanted to put it in motion.

"Allie!" The smile that made me think of no one else spread across his face. "Let's drive your Jeep over to the field and go from there."

He placed his arm across my shoulders. We looked like the typical couple leaving school at the end of the day.

"How was your day?" Those dark brown eyes searched mine.

"Lucas, you confuse me."

"Why's that?"

"Well, some days you're normal and friendly and others you're standoffish, untouchable."

"Sorry, I'll try harder."

"And what are we? Friends? A couple? What?" I sounded almost angry.

"Definitely a couple." The smile briefly made an appearance.

I started the car and maneuvered through the crowd of people walking through the lot. I pulled onto the main road then back into the farthest parking lot from the school. We ran past the soccer field and headed for the woods, making sure no one paid attention to the students on the wrong side of the street. All we needed was for the school crossing guard to start blowing her whistle and wave us across to the other side.

The woods were a good distance from the main crossing, but I didn't want to take any chances. We jogged through the tall grass, reached Lucas' handmade path and slowed to a walk. I headed for the pile of brush. Lucas began to clear the leaves, exposing his bike. An extra helmet, strapped to the back, peeked through the leaves. Lucas undid the cord that held it in place.

My hands shook as I tried to snap the chin strap. I couldn't believe that in a few minutes I'd hold onto Lucas and fly through the forest. As I slipped behind him, I wrapped my arms around his waist. I took in his scent, reminding me of the fresh outdoors mixed with spice. My hands felt his chest muscles, hard and firm. His heart beat fast under my palm.

We sped off for a path I hadn't explored with Nate. It started off simple, a few twists and turns, and then wove its way through obstacles of trees and well-placed boulders. Just when I thought we'd hit one, we glided in the opposite direction. Before I wanted, the ride ended. We taxied down the main trail back to the pile of brush.

"That was quite a ride!" I pulled off my helmet and shook out my hair.

"Has anyone told you how beautiful you are?" Lucas slipped from the bike. His body came so close I could hear his breathing, see his chest rise and fall with each breath.

Where did that come from? I turned a rich shade of red and stared at the dirt floor of the forest.

"Allie?" Lucas cupped my chin in his hand and lifted as our eyes locked. I saw no evil lurking behind them, only pain. His face came closer, and his lips were just an inch away. I felt his breath then his mouth on mine; kissing me as if for the very last time. His mouth moved against mine, and I responded in kind. I didn't want it to end, that one perfect moment in our woods.

When it did, I felt a tug on my heart. How could I ruin this moment with what I knew? We sat on a grassy patch of land, holding hands. I didn't want to break the spell but knew I must.

"I really like your family."

"They like you."

"Joe seems a little angry at the world."

"Aren't we all at thirteen?"

I laughed. "Yeah, I guess we are. Hannah's sweet."

"And a little too trusting."

"Why would you say that?"

"She still sees the world through rose-colored glasses, like most kids."

"Your grandfather's very nice. He has the coolest bike collection."

"He's proud of it. Did you know they're in working order? You can ride any one of them."

"Wow, does he ever let you take them out?"

"Sometimes."

"You said your dad is Gene's only child?" I cringed.

"Yeah, why do you ask?" Lucas crossed his brow.

"It's probably nothing. You know my friend, Nate? He's a real motorcycle fanatic. When he heard about your granddad's collection, he started researching on-line." I played with my hair, trying to think how to word the next part. "I think I failed to mention he's a computer geek, too. He could be wrong, but he told me that when Gene retired from racing he returned to his home state of Missouri with a wife and two sons." I fibbed a bit on the information, but it made sense to present it that way.

"The writer misquoted or got it wrong, Allie. Sam's an only child," Lucas said as he looked straight into my eyes.

I studied his face for any ticks or twitches. "Here's the strange part. It said Gene's sons were named Lucas and Sam."

Lucas shifted position and pulled me close. "Everyone makes mistakes. I'll ask Granddad. He may have had a friend or neighbor with him."

"Yeah, that's probably it." He gave a reasonable explanation. The racer got his facts wrong.

Lucas drew me into another kiss. I pressed my mouth to his as he wrapped his arms around my waist. He kissed me back with more passion, a kiss filled with desire. He pulled back and gazed into my eyes. I forgot all my fears. "Trust me, Allie."

"I will." I felt hypnotized in the moment.

He gave me another quick kiss. "How about a soda at the diner on me." Lucas hopped up and helped me up. "I'll have you back in time for dinner and your date with Josh."

I playfully pushed him as we walked along. "I'm not meeting him. He just wants an answer about something. No big deal."

"Seems like it is to him. Let me guess, he wants you back."

"He cheated on me. I can't have someone like that in my life."

"I don't blame you." Lucas stopped and took me by the shoulders. "I'd never do that. Cheat on you. You know that, right?" He was so serious I just nodded. "Good."

We emerged from the woods and jumped into the Jeep. In no time we arrived at the diner. As we stepped inside, Stacy was wiping down the counter. "Hi, Mrs. Montgomery!" I gave a little wave.

"Allie, I told you to call me Stacy." She brushed a wisp of hair back from her face and continued working. "Lucas." She leaned over the counter, and he jumped over a stool to kiss her cheek.

"Hi, Mom. Thought I'd bring Allie in for a soda."

"You need more than that! I made fresh chili, have a cup."

"Soda's fine, really." I didn't think I could eat. My stomach needed to calm down from the stress of the day.

Lucas returned with two sodas, one bowl of chili and two spoons on a tray. "In case you change your mind." He slid into the seat across from me.

The chili smelled divine and had grated cheese on top. The plate under the bowl held a pile of taco chips. I reached out and stole one.

"Dip it in, go ahead." Lucas was so cute, I couldn't resist. We ate and talked until I realized I ate too much and stayed too long.

"We have to get back." I glanced at the clock on the diner wall.

"Sorry, I wasn't paying attention to the time. Having too much fun." Lucas waved to his mom. "Going with Allie. I'll be back to help you with the dinner rush."

I forgot we came together, and Lucas left his bike in the woods. The days grew shorter as we headed into fall, so we needed to hurry. I'd hate for him to stumble around the woods looking for his bike.

I pulled into the school parking lot, and Lucas leaned over for a goodbye kiss. It all seemed so sweet and normal, but I had mixed emotions. I watched him until he disappeared into the woods.

My phone rang. I glanced at the screen, revealing

Nate's name. "Hey, Nate, I'm on my way home. I think I'm late for dinner. What's up?"

"Are you alone?"

"Yeah."

"I've got some news."

"Not again!"

"I wanted to add more information to my Gene Montgomery search before you came over tonight and guess what?"

"What? Get to the point."

"Everything's gone, the articles, the blog, everything. There's no sign of the blogger. I can't even find his registration on that site. His blog's wiped out, every post gone."

"Strange."

"Did you ask Lucas about his grandfather?"

"Yeah."

"How long ago?"

"Probably two hours ago. Why?"

"Allie, I don't think you should see this guy anymore."

"Nathan Kalas, you're scaring me. Tell me why."

"Come on, you're smarter than that. Think! You tell Lucas about the blog, and two hours later it's wiped off the internet—gone, vanished."

"He was with me the whole time."

"My point exactly."

I trembled as I started the car. "I'm heading home. Call Ash and tell her about this new development. We'll meet later."

I glanced around the parking lot. All the teachers had left for the day, and football practice was over. Not one car left. As I pulled out, I swore I heard a motorcycle revving its engine. That didn't make sense since I dropped Lucas off over five minutes ago. He should be long gone. The noise faded away, and I decided my imagination was working overtime. No matter what Nate found out or told me tonight, I wouldn't—I couldn't—stop seeing Lucas. I was falling in love with him.

* * * *

Ashley and Nate took turns grilling me about the last two days I spent with Lucas.

"Just take Josh back, and end it now." Ash grabbed her hair and pulled.

"Wait, Josh wants you back? When were you going to tell me?" Nate looked shocked.

"I thought I told you. You probably forgot."

"Stop changing the subject." Ashley pushed Nate into his computer chair. "We have bigger fish to fry than old Joshy."

"Hey, you started it!" Nate stuck out his lower lip. He grabbed Ashley's hand, and they locked eyes.

Here we go again. If only I had that superpower of invisibility. And it was over. I should have excused myself and gone to the bathroom so they could be alone, but they'd never let me out of their sight. They wanted answers. I should just go ahead and break up their romantic moment with the announcement.

"I love him," I whispered.

"What did you just say?" Ashley spun around, hair flying. "You hardly know him! He could be a freakish stalker for all you know."

"But a cute one." I gave her a half smile.

"I'll give you that."

"Not as cute as me though, right?" Nate mugged for the invisible camera, and Ashley gave him a poke. He pulled her onto his lap.

Oh, no, they're having another moment. This shouldn't be happening with me in the room. I stood, ready to leave and give them some privacy.

"Where you going?" Ashley jumped off Nate's lap and blocked the door.

"Home. Got things to do."

"No, you're staying right here. We got together to help you solve a problem, and that's what we're going to do."

"Look, Allie, I can't believe I'm saying this." Nate took a deep breath. "Maybe Doug's right. Something could be happening in town that we don't know about. He's got major intel that we don't."

"You're siding with my brother?"

"No way. I'm looking at all sides. You said he asked you questions about kids at school. That wasn't a random conversation. He knows how to interrogate someone without them knowing."

I never told Nate Doug's real motive for coming home. I couldn't tell him about the tattoo, not yet.

"I know you're leaving something out, Allie. You're protecting Lucas."

"No, I'm not. Doug's just being Doug. He had no real reason to question me." I thought back to that conversation. Should I take it more seriously? I needed more facts. "Nate, keep searching. Please?"

Nate started typing on his keyboard, staring back and forth at his three monitors. "I'll try again. Maybe that blogger had some glitch on his computer, and he's back on the site."

Ashley sat down next to me. "You have to admit it's strange. There seems to be a secret in that family."

"Maybe once Lucas trusts me, he'll tell me. It might be something dumb, and we're making a big deal out of nothing."

"I'm the greatest! I found him!" Nate's arms shot up in the air.

"Gene Montgomery?" I asked.

"No, the blogger. He's on another site. He's written one post about motorcycles, but it's very general. This guy knows his stuff, and he's writing the basics. Someone got to him."

I looked at Ashley for reassurance. She couldn't really believe the Montgomerys were capable of tracking someone down and make them remove their posts from the internet. Or did Gene remove it himself? Why did the blogger pop up somewhere else and not tell the world what happened to him? My phone rang, and I lost my train of thought as soon as I saw Lucas' name. "It's him."

"He probably knows what we're up to and is calling to tell us to stop. There are spies everywhere!" Nate's eyes grew wide as he wiggled his fingers in the air.

"Hey," I whispered into the phone.

"Just calling to see how you are and find out if we can do the same thing tomorrow."

"Ride and go to the diner?"

"Yes."

"Sounds great, I'll see you tomorrow."

Ashley stared at me with eyes of steel.

"What?" I asked as I hung up.

"I'll never get to ride home with you again, will I?"

"Sure, it won't be like this every day."

"And we won't be hanging out that much either."

"Will you stop it? Of course, we will."

CHAPTER EIGHT

Ash was right. I met Lucas every day after school. We rode in our woods or went straight to the diner. If he had to work I'd sit in an out-of-the-way booth doing homework while I watched him work. Sometimes I'd stay for dinner, and Lucas would take his break to join me. Other times, we'd head for his house. Gene let us ride the bikes from his collection or we'd just hang out. Hannah and Joe would come home, and we'd play board games. The Montgomerys treated me like family. Even Joe warmed up to me.

Lucas eventually met my parents and stayed for dinner once or twice. We'd hang out with my friends at the Kalas'. For some reason Lucas acted nervous around Nate. They had so much in common. It puzzled me why they couldn't get along. We rode dirt bikes once in the backyard but never again. I couldn't expect my best friends and boyfriend to become the best of friends, I could only hope. Everyone needed more time to get to know each other.

The end of October came too quickly. The leaves changed to their fall colors. Shades of gold, red and orange painted the trees. Lucas and I strolled through his yard, making our way to the gorge to enjoy the view. We climbed the stairs to the back deck and settled in two chairs.

"I don't want this month to end. It's been special." I reached for his hand, and he wove his fingers through mine. "I haven't told you, but my birthday's coming soon. November fourth. Can't believe I'll be seventeen."

"That's not old." Lucas smiled at me.

"So when's your birthday?"

"March second."

"I'm older than you?"

"I'm afraid so."

We both laughed. "Doug's always telling me 'listen to your elders', so I guess you have to start listening to me. Ooh, that makes me sound old, doesn't it?"

"Not at all." Lucas kissed my hand. "What would you like for your birthday? Any special wishes?"

"For you to come to dinner. I asked Mom if I could have a few friends over, and she's fine with it."

"Let me guess. She's going to make her famous pulled pork."

"Ashley would eat it every day of the week." We laughed again. I stared out over the gorge as the autumn sun grew lower in the sky. "I better get going. I've stayed too long."

"My mom would have you stay for dinner every night if she could. She doesn't like being outnumbered by the males in the family."

"That's sweet, but I'm sure she's tired of having me around all the time."

"Not really." Lucas helped me up. "Come on. I'll follow you to school."

"You don't have to keep doing that. I can find my way out of here." Lucas always followed behind on his bike until I made it closer to town, past the school.

"I don't mind. Indulge me?"

"Fine." I melted into his arms, and he folded them tightly around me.

"I love you, you know." Lucas had been telling me that for a few weeks.

"Yes, I do, and I love you back." I found it easier to say when I didn't look at him. I'd stare into those eyes, see that smile and fumble over the words.

He drew me into a long kiss. They'd become full of yearning and hunger, like he was searching for someone and finally found her. I sank into his chest as he drew me so close I felt as if we were one. The sun began to set as I laid my head against his chest, both of us staring out at the golden sky. It reminded me of an ending to a wonderful movie, although I knew mine had just begun.

* * * *

"Hey, Allie, wait up!"

I hadn't talked to him in over a month, and was sure he'd gotten the message. I wasn't taking him back. I would never be his girlfriend again. "Hi, Josh, haven't seen you around."

"Try noticed, Al. I've been around. We do have a class together. It's like you look right through me."

Josh continued to walk next to me. A few more steps and I'd arrive at my classroom door. I'd ditch him then.

"Al, did you hear me? I just wanted to say happy birthday."

"Oh." I searched the hallway. "Thanks." *Almost there.* A familiar figure leaning against the wall caught my eye.

"… anti-social. Everyone says so."

I only caught the last of what he said, but the words stung. "What did you say? Who says I'm anti-social?"

"Hey, I said too much. It's your birthday and all, have a good day." Josh faded into the crowd.

"What did he want?" Lucas sound aggravated.

"To say happy birthday and tell me I'm anti-social."

"That's a stupid thing to say on your birthday. And

you're not, by the way. He's jealous."

"Thanks." I wanted to snuggle against him and say we should cut school, but the inner good girl told me to go to class. The bad girl wanted to say, "Let's hitchhike to New York City."

"Can I give you your present before the party?"

"I promised my mom I'd come straight home, but she won't mind if I'm a few minutes late."

"Great! I want to give it to you in our woods, if that's alright."

"I'd love it."

The rest of the day I wondered what my gift could be. Lucas gave no clues, and I never told him what I wanted for my birthday. We never shopped together, went to the movies or did things like other couples. We had our own special life, one that only we understood.

I raced down the hall as soon as the dismissal bell rang and out into the sunny, fall day. Still warm enough for no coat, I knew the days would be cooling down soon. Finding Lucas in the crowd, he grabbed my hand and ran for the Jeep. We became experts at dodging people and staying out of the crossing guard's vision. I pulled out of the school parking lot and into the soccer lot without anyone noticing. As we sped for the safety of the woods my heart pounded until we reached the shelter of the trees.

At the brush pile, Lucas pulled out his bike and dug around in the back saddle bag. He pulled out a long box tied with a bright blue bow and handed it to me. "Happy birthday."

I opened the slender black velvet box. A beautiful silver bracelet, dotted with pale blue crystal stones, glittered inside.

"Do you know what those are?"

I shook my head, taken back with the beauty of the bracelet.

"Blue topaz." Lucas took the bracelet from the box. I held my arm out so he could put it on my wrist. The sunrays poking through the trees made the square-cut blue topaz and diamond accents sparkle.

I threw my arms around his neck. I kissed him over and over. "I love it! I've never had anything like this."

I had the usual golden topaz jewelry, but nothing like the bracelet. My parents bought me a birthstone necklace that I hardly wore. When I was younger, Ashley and I bought each other cheap gemstone rings.

"Lucas, thank you so much." I hugged him with all my might. "I really should go," I whispered in his ear.

We walked to the edge of the woods, and Lucas waited until I pulled away. I waved as he disappeared into the forest. I couldn't help staring at the bracelet on the drive home. More than I expected, I just wanted Lucas to come to dinner. I hoped he didn't spend too much money on the gift. How could he afford the real thing? Still, the tennis bracelet was gorgeous, my first gift from Lucas.

I pulled in the driveway and found an unfamiliar car in my parking spot. My heart began to pound as I hurried into the house. *Who's here on my birthday? Bad news? Doug in disguise?*

"Happy birthday, sis!" Dean popped out from the living room.

I let out the breath I held when I saw him. Mom probably had him drinking tea, and he was looking for any reason to escape. His bright blue eyes shone, his long brown shaggy hair and scruffy beard fit him perfectly. We met halfway and hugged.

"Can I join in?" I heard a light laugh and spotted Autumn behind us. Blonde and willowy, she was light on her feet and ever so graceful. A ballet dancer at one time, she gave it up to live with Dean on the Outer Banks of North Carolina. I was a gangly twelve year old when we first met, and she quickly put me at ease. Our family called her Dean's muse. Without her, his painting career would never have taken off.

"When did you get here?" I crossed my brow. "I didn't recognize the car."

"We were in LA for my show and flew straight into Richmond. That's a rental." Dean wrapped his arm around Autumn and pulled her closer.

"How was the show?"

"Great, I was just telling Mom I sold everything except two photos." Dean grinned from ear to ear. When he talked about his paintings and photography, he became a little kid sharing his prized possessions.

"By the way." He took me by the shoulders and guided me into the kitchen. "I have something for you." He handed me an envelope.

Inside I saw cash, lots of it. "Dean!"

"Happy birthday, kid. We tried to find something in LA but were pressed for time. Don't spend it all in one place. Do like dad always told us when we were young, save it for a rainy day."

I had no idea how much money filled the envelope as I gave Dean a bear hug. "Whoa, what have we here?" Dean examined the bracelet on my arm. "What do you think, Autumn?"

"Someone has a generous boyfriend." She took my hand to study it better.

"Are you saying it's real?" My head spun with the news.

"Yep." Dean nodded. "Bet he paid a couple hundred for it. How long have you two been dating?" He closed one eye as he studied me.

"Almost two months."

Dean didn't respond.

"It's not like that!"

"I wasn't accusing you of anything, Allie. Just checking." Dean started to poke me in the side. I had to retaliate.

"Alright you two, enough!" Autumn intervened. "You're like an oversized kid around your sister, and I love it." She wrapped her arms around his neck and gave Dean a kiss.

"I'm taking this upstairs." I held up the envelope of money. "And put it in a safe place. Tell Mom I'll be right down."

As I skipped into my bedroom, my phone buzzed. I had a text from Lucas. *Be there soon.*

I dumped the money on the bed to see twenty dollar bills staring back at me. I piled them in stacks of five. Counting the piles, I had to check it twice. Ten, ten piles of bills. One thousand dollars. Dean did very well during his LA trip. I scooped up the money, stuffed it back in the envelope and slid it into a dresser drawer.

I heard Ashley's voice as I bounded down the stairs. "You made my favorite, Mrs. Sanders, thank you!"

"Hey, Ash!" I hugged her when I got to the bottom. Nate stood in line, waiting for the next embrace.

"Happy birthday, Allie." He gave me a quick squeeze.

"Why don't you take your friends in the family

room while we wait for Dad and Lucas?" Mom ushered us down the hall. "I can spend more time with Dean and Autumn until then."

I held out my arm so Ashley could see my bracelet. She let out a small gasp. Nate glanced at it and gave a sarcastic "lovely" comment. We settled in the family room to wait for Lucas.

"I have to ask you guys something," I said. "Josh tells me, *on* my birthday, that I'm anti-social. Do you believe that?" I stared at my friends waiting for them to come to my defense.

"Well, you have been ignoring your friends a bit, but that's to be expected," Ashley said as she broke eye contact.

"Expected? What do you mean by that?"

Ashley turned her head to look at me again. "Lucas doesn't seem to have any friends, Allie. He's a loner. Of course he wants all of your time. He's isolating you from the rest of us." She hit her head. "I've said too much."

"No, that's okay. You should've said something sooner." I didn't behave that way last year. Josh and I had tons of friends and went out with groups of people. We hung out at each other's houses or met friends at a fast food restaurant. In spite of that, I still had time for Ashley. "I'm sorry, Ash. I'll be a better friend, I promise."

"I offered to pick up the slack," Nate said. "Be as anti-social as you want."

Ashley gave him a playful push, and he pretended to fall into the couch. "Thanks, Allie, but I do understand, really." She turned to Nate and patted his face. "I'm getting used to hanging out with this one."

"Hey, guys, am I interrupting?" Lucas stood in the

doorway of the family room. He wore a black t-shirt and tight jeans. His dark hair fell over his eyes, and he shook his head back to remove the strands from his vision. He could be my only birthday gift, and I'd be completely happy.

"You're here!" I jumped up from the recliner. His hands went around my waist and pulled me toward him. One sweet kiss was shared. Nate cleared his throat.

"Sorry!" I pulled Lucas into the room. We shared my seat, snuggling in the recliner, waiting for Mom to call us for dinner.

We ate in the formal dining room which had more room and used for special occasions. Dad sat at the head of the table. Mom ran back and forth to the kitchen bringing out more plates and bowls.

"Mom, will you please sit down?" Dean got up and guided her to her seat. "There. Isn't that much better? We're all at the table now."

Dean sat back down and asked us about school, wanting to know if any of his former teachers still taught there. When he heard a few familiar names, he told hysterical stories about them. "You have Mrs. Greene for advanced placement English? She's the prim and proper one, isn't she? She always finds a favorite. I think I was it."

"And it's Lucas this year." Ashley pointed her fork at him.

"So everyone hates you, I take it?" Dean asked, as everyone laughed.

After dinner, we helped clear the table, taking plates, glasses and silverware into the kitchen. A loud rap on the front door interrupted our work.

"I'll get it." Dean rushed down the hall. I heard him say, "Well, aren't you formal. Don't you have a key?"

"Forgot it, little brother. How the hell are you?" Doug answered. The same Doug who told me back in August he wanted to see me more often and wanted to get to know me better. This was the first time he'd come home since then.

The last time he showed up for a birthday, I turned ten. My parents told me he was stationed far away and couldn't come for the others. I still cared about him then and felt hurt he couldn't make the parties. The tenth birthday changed all that. Stationed in Washington D.C., I waited on pins and needles until he arrived. He could come every year now I told myself. Well, the joke was on me, he never came again until this year.

"So where's the birthday girl?"

I heard Doug and Dean talking and laughing as they stepped into the kitchen. They had a great, easy relationship, one I couldn't understand, and felt left out.

"There she is." Doug walked up to me and gave me a hug. He wore his uniform as usual. He smelled of too much cologne or after shave. The hug he gave me made it difficult to breathe. When he let go, he handed me a box. "Just a little something."

I lifted the lid on the tiny, white cardboard box, which had no bow or wrapping paper. A tiny angel pin lay on some cotton. In the center of her dress was a yellow stone.

"Your birthstone." Doug pointed at the gem. "Here, let me." He pulled the back off the pin and stuck the sharp end through my shirt, attaching the back carefully. "There you go, for my little angel."

I wanted to gag but remembered my manners. "Thanks, Doug." I longed to add, "And Dean gave me a thousand dollars."

"Remember to wear this so you'll always be safe." Doug whispered so only I could hear. He put his arm around me and led me to a quiet spot in the kitchen. "You're lucky I'm your brother and here to protect you."

"I am? Thanks … I think."

"You think? You should be grateful we're family. I could squash you like a bug if I wanted." His voice stayed low, but the tone changed.

Where did that come from? His sinister smile said it all. I froze in place even though I wanted to pound my fists into his chest. What made him say that? As I studied his face, he didn't flinch. His blue-gray eyes cut through me like two cold stones. He blinked a few times and gave me another smile.

"Mom! Did you hear what Doug said to me?" I wanted a witness for future reference. Proof positive my oldest brother didn't like me. She must have heard what he said. She stood a few feet away.

"Oh, Allie, I'm sorry. I wasn't paying attention. Too busy talking as usual. What do you want, dear?"

"She wants you to see the gift I gave her." Doug gestured to the tiny angel clinging to my shirt.

"Oh, so thoughtful, Doug! A guardian angel." Mom embraced him. "That's what you are to the family, our guardian angel. I know you'll always look after your sister, even if I'm not around."

"Mom!" She made it sound like she'd die any minute.

"So where's this new boyfriend I heard about?" Doug glanced around the kitchen, completely changing the subject. No real hug for Mom in return, no promise that he'd protect me.

"I sent the kids to the family room. I need my space." Mom smiled and pushed us in the direction of that room.

Ash and Nate sat on the couch in deep conversation. "Where's Lucas?" I asked as we entered the room. I rolled my eyes hoping they saw the frustration and noticed Doug hot on my trail.

Nate shrugged. "He left."

CHAPTER NINE

"What?" *Strange*. Why did he pick up and leave so suddenly? How was I supposed to get through the rest of the evening without him?

"His phone rang then he split. Told us to tell you he'd call later." The look on Nate's face said it all. He didn't trust Lucas.

The party ended early since it was a school night. Dean and Autumn planned to stay overnight and leave in the morning. Doug said he had to head out. Relieved to see him go, I pulled the pin off and slipped it in my pocket. I'd throw it in a drawer later.

Dean saw my actions and followed me upstairs. "He tries, you know." He leaned against my doorframe, hands in his pockets.

"I feel like he only showed up to help Mom and Dad judge my boyfriend. He's probably running a background check as we speak."

Dean chuckled and came over to sit next to me on the bed. "How'd you like to get away for awhile?"

My spirits lifted. Suddenly I realized a lot of pressure had been placed on me. Dean understood that. Josh kept pressuring me to go back to him then accused me of being anti-social. Ashley said I neglected her, and Nate was suspicious of Lucas. I was tired of the drama. "Come to Duck?"

"Yeah, that's what I'm saying. How about this weekend?"

Duck—the quiet part of the northern Outer Banks. Dean's house, built on the beach, faced the Atlantic Ocean. He converted one of the upstairs bedrooms into a studio where he did his work. Great restaurants and shopping filled the village. It might be just what I needed.

Only one problem, how would I get there? Dean usually drove up to get me. Mom and Dad would drive down and pick me up. "I don't think Dad would want to drive this time of year. Do you think he'd let me drive the Jeep myself? It's only a three hour drive."

"No, I don't. There's no way I can get you. I have a commitment in New York City and a show in the village."

"That's okay, Dean. It was a nice idea. Unless—"

"Unless what?"

A great idea struck me. "Would you mind if Lucas came along? I won't have to drive alone. I'm sure Dad will say yes if you do."

"I have plenty of bedrooms." Dean raised his eyebrows.

"Dean! I'm not even thinking like that."

"Alright, I'll arrange with Mom and Dad for you to leave Friday after school. You can come back on Sunday whenever you like."

Happiness overtook me. "Thanks, Dean." I gave him a giant hug, immediately feeling better.

"Sleep well." He hugged me back and walked down the hall to his old room.

I couldn't wait. I had to call Lucas. He answered quickly.

"Is everything okay?" I asked. "Nate said you had to leave."

"I'm sorry I left so abruptly, but I got a call from Granddad. They couldn't find Joe. He didn't come home from school."

"Is he okay?"

"He's fine."

"Where did you find him?"

"He showed up at the diner an hour ago. I think he's trying out his independence. He doesn't want people telling him what to do, especially Mom."

"Glad to hear he's alright." I breathed a sigh of relief. "Hey, I have something to ask you." I told him about the weekend plans. "Will your parents give you time off from the diner?"

"I'm sure they will. This sounds like the perfect trip."

So you think you can come?"

"I know so."

"I can't wait. It's two days away but feels like forever."

"You have no idea what forever feels like." Lucas laughed. "Sweet dreams, Allie."

I kissed the phone and hung up, hoping to hold on to this feeling a little longer. I found out I was anti-social today, and it didn't bother me. I got a beautiful bracelet from the boy I loved and would wear it proudly every day. I had a great dinner party with friends that even Doug couldn't spoil. I didn't have to count the days anymore until I left this small town. All in all, it had been a good birthday, and Dean just made it a little bit better.

* * * *

As the sun set, my hands tightened on the steering wheel. We'd been on the road for hours and were nearing the end of the trip. Lucas sensed my fear of the looming bridge ahead and offered to drive. I pulled into a parking lot so we could trade places.

I felt safe in his hands as we crossed the Wright Memorial Bridge. I stared out at the Currituck Sound as we traveled over its shadowy waters. The Outer Banks lay on the other side, and we'd soon reach our destination.

"It will probably be dark when we get there," I said. "We can still walk the beach after dinner."

"I'd like that." Lucas excelled at driving. Everyone my age had been driving less than a year, but he seemed so sure of himself behind the wheel.

"Turn here. Duck Road." I pointed out Dean's house as we drove down the street.

Lucas whistled. "Very nice." We parked under the deck. I jumped out as soon as the car stopped.

"Leave the luggage. Come on!"

We could enter on the ground floor, but I wanted to make a grand entrance. I climbed the wide, white front steps leading to an outdoor deck that wrapped around the entire house. The cream-colored home, trimmed in brown, was lost to the dark. He'd have to wait to see the full effect tomorrow. Warm light came from the windows. Dean had the house looking its very best. I knocked on the door, and Autumn answered.

"Dean, Allie and Lucas are here," she called over her shoulder. "Come in. Dinner's ready, but can wait."

I glanced around as I stepped inside. Everything still looked the same. The open floor plan was so different from the traditional look of the family home. Golden oak hardwood covered the floors. A soft cream leather sofa with overstuffed yellow, brown and cream patterned pillows was the focal point of the living area. The gas fireplace had a large flat screen TV mounted above. A brown, short shag rug in front of the sectional sported a glass top coffee table.

An expansive modern glass table with seating for ten sat across from the living area. The kitchen, located directly behind the dining room, was only separated by cabinets. To the left were the stairs and guest bathroom. Dean and Autumn reached the master bedroom through a door past the kitchen, overlooking the ocean.

"I'll show you to your rooms." Dean motioned for us to follow him up to the next level. Three bedrooms and two baths shared this floor with Dean's studio along with another outdoor balcony.

"This is Allie's room." Dean had let me choose the color palette when I was younger. I wanted bright colors, but he talked me into more subdued shades. Relieved he didn't listen to me, the room had been decorated in creams, pale yellows and aqua, quite different from the bright yellow and neon blue I had wanted at twelve.

"Lucas, you can have your pick of one of these two and use this bathroom. I'll give you time to unwind." Dean disappeared down the staircase.

"Allie, you never could have described this. Thanks for bringing me here." Lucas swung me around, lifting me off the ground. The joy on his face made my heart melt. I hadn't seen that look in all our time together.

After dinner we headed down to the ground level. Pool table, mirrored wall with ballet bar for Autumn and workout equipment dotted the space. We used the private boardwalk to the beach and strolled hand in hand until we could walk no more. Sitting a few yards out from Dean's house, we watched the waves roll into shore. Tired but happy, we headed back inside. I fell asleep as soon as my head hit the pillow.

* * * *

Saturday was ours. Dean didn't care where I went because I knew the island. The Outer Banks were divided into small towns, and we easily drove to our destinations.

"Wright Brothers National Memorial is our first stop. The brothers left their home state of Ohio to test their flying machine in North Carolina." I told Lucas as we drove along. "The winds are good here."

We left the town of Duck behind, driving through Southern Shores then Kitty Hawk.

"I thought this would be where the museum was located." Lucas pointed to the Kitty Hawk sign.

"Actually they did most of their testing in Kill Devil Hills," I said as if I was the expert and had to giggle. We arrived at the site and spent a half hour at the visitor's center and outside finding the granite markers that showed where the brothers landed after their first four flights.

"Enough history," I said when we got back in the car. "It's time for some fun. Let's go to Jockey Ridge State Park. You'll see the tallest sand dune in the eastern United States."

Lucas laughed. "You're well-schooled in all things Outer Banks."

We bought a kite and ran on the beach. The dunes rose up from the sand, blocking our view of the ocean so we tried climbing as high as we could with the kite fluttering between us. Sliding back down, we looked at each other and said at the same time, "Dune buggies!"

We walked along the beach and ate ice cream cones and fish and chips in no particular order. Lucas searched for a dune buggy rental shop on his phone while we ate. "There's one not too far from here."

We found the shop and rode for an hour on the beach. The wind whipped through my hair as I made my way along the water. I glanced over at Lucas. He seemed relaxed, almost carefree, finally looking like a teen boy instead of a serious man.

Dean greeted us as we climbed the stairs at the end of the day, sun-kissed and happy. "Hey, you two ready for dinner? I'm grilling tonight."

"Sure, can I help?" Lucas offered.

"You just relax. This is your vacation."

Autumn was preparing a large salad in the kitchen when we walked in the house. We sat at the island, telling her of our adventures.

"Lucas is a really good driver," I said.

"All those years of riding bikes, right?" Autumn winked at Lucas. "Would you mind taking those steaks out to Dean?" She pointed to the plate on the counter.

"Not a problem." Lucas disappeared out the front door.

"So you really like him, I can tell." Autumn continued chopping vegetables.

"Yeah, I do."

"Well, just be careful. I know what first love can do to a girl."

"Did Dean tell you to talk to me?"

"No. I told him I would. I saw that look in your eye when Dean asked if anything happened between the two of you."

"It didn't! It hasn't!"

"But you want it to."

I had to think it over. It crossed my mind. If I considered sleeping with Josh, how could I not with Lucas? "Don't worry, nothing will happen. Lucas is a complete gentleman."

"Good to hear. Now go put this bowl on the table."

We ate at the dining room table, grouped at one end, instead of sitting on the stools in the kitchen. It felt cozy even if the table had six empty seats. Dinner ended later than I realized. By the time we cleaned up and put everything away, my phone said eight o'clock. I wanted to watch the sunset from the beach, even if it didn't set over the water, but couldn't complain. Our day had been magical. A night walk on the beach still could be a romantic way to end the day.

"Do you mind if we take a walk?" I asked Dean. "We'll be going home tomorrow, and I don't know when I'll be back."

"You can visit whenever you like now that you can drive." Dean winked at me. "Bundle up, the temperature drops fast at night."

Lucas and I started for the stairs to change into warmer clothes. We met in the hall and took the two flights down to the ground floor. Outdoor lights along Dean's private boardwalk showed the way to the beach, but it grew dark as we stepped onto the sand.

The ocean looked so different at night, lit only by the moon and stars. The water appeared to be a gray blanket, barely visible from where we stood. Only the white foam of the waves and their crashing against the shore reminded me it was still there.

We placed a quilt on the sand, settled in on a small dune in front of the house and listened to the sounds of the night. I lay back, and Lucas slid in next to me. He whispered my name, kissing me over and over. Time had no hold on us, we stayed in each other's arms, kissing, dozing, talking, not caring about the world around us. Just two souls on the beach. It felt as if we were the only people left on earth. I wanted to bare my soul to Lucas, tell him everything.

I turned my head, gazing into his eyes. "Before I knew you, I had to call you something." I giggled. "Last year, you were Loner, and this year I named you

Heathcliff."

Lucas bolted upright, clasping his hands around his knees, not the reaction I expected. "I'm nothing like him."

I sat up and wrapped my hands around his tense arm, leaning my head against his shoulder. "Lucas, he was a tragic figure. I guess I saw you that way when I didn't know you."

"His actions were deplorable. I could never do what he did."

"He was a wounded bird, devastated after realizing he could never be with Catherine. I agree Heathcliff could be mean and manipulative, but he had his reasons."

Lucas shuddered and faced me. "I love you, Allie," he said, his expression way too serious. "Because of that you have a right to know something. I'm going to tell you what this tattoo really means." He motioned to his right foot.

Surprised by the turn of events, I couldn't imagine what he might tell me. What he said could change everything. "I know what it means. Twenty-nine. You already told me the story. Middle school boys acting cool." I shivered. My stomach tightened, and I became nauseous as I realized the story was a lie. But I had accepted it. Now he wanted to tell the truth. I wasn't ready. In fact, maybe I didn't want to know at all. I held up my hand. "Don't tell me. Don't ruin … us."

But right there, sitting on our little sand dune, Lucas revealed his story, everything about his life. I sat motionless, barely able to fill my lungs with air as he spoke. His words floated through the darkness, slipped into my mind, turning and twisting my thoughts. At that moment, I realized I was his Catherine.

Unattainable. I could never be with him. Then it hit me. It was even worse than Catherine. I was the enemy.

CHAPTER TEN

I didn't remember going to bed, but woke up tangled in my sheets. I dozed fitfully, tossing and turning, until I gave up. The clock taunted me—five a.m. I tried to focus on what happened a few hours ago.

Twenty-nine. The number stood for something beyond middle school antics. The tattoo represented a secret society that mainstream America knew nothing about. I rolled on my side and rubbed my hand over my face. Lucas told me his birthday fell on February twenty-ninth. All males born on that day had special qualities, different from other men. Too much to process, it seemed more like make-believe.

Secrecy kept these boys and men alive and safe throughout the years. They possessed skills beyond the ordinary man. Lucas could see in the dark. It now made sense why he felt so comfortable at night. He could find his way when darkness settled in. I never worried about the time of day because Lucas' strong hand would always guide me. His one-handed strength had always impressed me. Add that to the list of talents—super strength.

I tried to keep my breathing steady. I focused on the intake of air going into my lungs, and the sound as it left my body. My brain spun out of control and back to reality.

Keen hearing. Lucas could hear conversations in the next room or beyond, even the quietest footstep. I searched my brain to see what else I remembered from last night. I got a little hysterical and must have passed out from the sheer exhaustion of sobbing my heart out.

Lucas confided he turned twenty last Leap Year so

that made him eighty years old. Eighty! He only aged once every four years on his real birthday. He had been living longer than I could process. I needed to wrap my mind around the fact that I was dating an eighty-year-old man. If we stayed together, I'd become an old woman, and he'd still be a young man. I wanted to start crying all over again.

The most shocking news concerned Doug. My brother headed up a special task force in charge of looking for these men called Niners, a shortened version of twenty-nine. The military had a special interest due to their heightened senses, strength and longevity—perfect military qualities. I was sure the army would love to dissect their brains for answers.

I shuddered at the thought of Lucas being tested— blood drawn, CAT scans, brainwaves being monitored then trained to be part of the STF 3-2-9, the name of Doug's special unit. Lucas already knew about them *and* Doug before I met him.

Lucas' Granddad wanted to meet me in person to check his facts. He'd already run background on me. When they confirmed I was Doug's sister, his family wanted Lucas to end things. He couldn't do it. Lucas said the more I came around, the more the family fell in love with me. Sadly I needed to end the relationship for everyone's safety.

As I lay staring up at the ceiling, something hit me. Doug had been born on February twenty-eighth. I swallowed hard and tried to do the math. I had trouble calculating in the predawn hour, but quickly figured out that my brother was born during one of the leap years. I sat up, clutching my neck. *Could it be? Was he actually born on the twenty-ninth? No way. He couldn't be like Lucas.*

A photo album of Doug and Dean came to mind. I

recalled pictures of them as children. It confirmed Doug wasn't a Niner. He grew older each year. Relief flooded through me.

A tap on the door startled me. I glanced at the clock, six-fifteen. I threw on a hoodie and zipped it up before I answered. Lucas had to be the one on the other side. I opened the door and stared at him for a moment, our eyes locking. Then I fell into his arms.

"Since we missed the sunset, I wondered if you'd like a sunrise?" I felt his lips move in my hair.

"Did you get much sleep?" I asked.

"Don't need much."

"Forgot."

He only needed two or three hours at the most to refuel his body, another perk for the army. I took his hand and guided him down the hall next to my bedroom out to the upper deck.

I turned on two patio heat lamps for warmth. The sky began to lighten, and flashes of bright pink skipped across the gray waters. As we sat and watched, the wispy pink clouds suddenly grew more intense in color, turning a dark shade of orange. The top of a reddish-orange globe appeared on the water's horizon, slowly rising out of the gray mist.

The sky above the rising sun now glowed as if on fire. The orange ball burst into a golden yellow. The sun rose above the horizon. Instinctively, I reached for Lucas' hand. We finished watching the show in silence.

"I want to tell you more. I need to finish the story." Lucas looked over from the lounge chair he perched on. I reclined back trying to soak in the last minutes together. He nervously shifted on the edge of the seat and squeezed my hand. "Does it bother you that I'm so much older?"

"Twenty isn't that old."

Lucas let out a sarcastic laugh. "You know what I mean."

"When you're thirty, I'll be fifty-seven."

"That's not a big difference."

My turn to laugh. "You're thinking with your heart, Lucas. You need to be practical. You know reality says this has to be our last day together."

"Hopefully I can convince you otherwise. But if you feel that way then I better get started. First, a history lesson." Lucas managed a slight smile. "Males born on the twenty-ninth showed little physical growth their first year. In reality they only aged three months. Their first birthday wouldn't be until the next leap year. We age three months a year." He repeated it again as if he wanted to make sure I understood. I nodded, wanting him to continue. "Long ago, people had their superstitions. They thought it was a bad omen if a child didn't grow properly and sometimes killed them."

I gasped. I couldn't imagine doing something like that. "That's terrible."

"Remember it was different times. They thought something was wrong with the child. They'd let him die or waste away if they didn't outright kill him. After a year, a baby would still look like a three-month-old. You can imagine the fear the family felt."

"That's so sad. How could anyone let a baby die?" I shook my head.

"Fear and ignorance. They didn't know the mind developed at a much more rapid pace. But Niners are unable to communicate that fact. We're very smart. I'm not bragging, just stating a fact. The only drawback is speech patterns. Those are the slowest to develop."

"So you're saying these babies were at genius level

but unable to tell anyone?"

"That's right. The ones who survived often had to fend for themselves, unsure why they didn't age like everyone else. If they did stay with family, their relatives died off, leaving them alone. Eventually these boys and men found each other and lived in groups, protecting one another, and looked for others like them." Lucas stared out over the water.

"They became a band of brothers because they knew if their secret was found out, they could be hanged or imprisoned for being wizards, warlocks, sorcerers or even vampires just because they were different."

"Well, you *are* different. You live longer, stay young longer. You're kind of like a vampire. Lots of my friends love vampire stories. Endless love."

"So now you're calling me a vampire?" Lucas leaned back and smiled.

"Without the teeth." We were teasing each other, and it needed to stop. Lucas might think I changed my mind. "When the Niners became a secret society, they came up with the idea of a tattoo. Right?"

Lucas shifted again in his chair, facing me instead of the glorious sunrise. "It was a secret code. All we had to do was show the arch of our foot to a fellow Niner."

"Not a gang." I couldn't help myself, I had to giggle.

"No, we're not a gang. Quite the opposite. As the centuries rolled on, this team of men grew in numbers and established communities worldwide. The symbol tied them together. One thing they learned quite quickly. They were smart, smarter than people of their time. When Leonardo De Vinci dabbled with flight, they perfected it. Ben Franklin experimented with electricity, they already had it. The group had Morse code for centuries before it was developed in the 1800s. With all that knowledge, they could stay hidden from society and yet have a life within it because they were ahead of the times. The Niners could monitor the world through their network. You think computers are a recent invention? We've had them for more than two centuries. The Niners are a loyal group, sharing their knowledge amongst themselves."

I had longed for an escape from the monotonous existence of a small town for as long as I could remember. I found this information oddly fascinating, but knew I couldn't be a part of Lucas' life. "So there's a Niner community in Montana?" I knew he grew up there after last night's conversation. Missouri was just a cover, not where the family really lived.

"Yes, the Niners found my family shortly after my birth. They explained to my parents what would happen to me. Of course, they didn't believe it. The Niners are an understanding group and offered their assistance whenever my family needed it. Their mission is to find and protect others like them. They've done it for centuries and have experience dealing with new parents."

"You said you grew up in the Montana compound. Your parents eventually realized the Niners were right."

"It took a little more than a year before they accepted the truth and realized they had to protect me. We moved to the compound and learned their ways. My family lives to protect me, something I find unfair. It's voluntary, don't get me wrong, but sometimes I feel I'd be better off on my own. There are many places I could live. I really could become the Loner."

"Oh, Lucas, that sounds awful. I have a feeling

your family wouldn't let you. Last night you said Gene's really your brother who's acted as your father for years."

"My parents became my grandparents, and Gene was my father. We tried to live away from the compound so Gene could continue his racing career. I always stayed home with my parents and never left the house much. As a nine-year-old, I acted my age and complained. Now I know I should've been grateful. Gene was a great racer who gave up that life to be my dad. We moved back to the compound so I could have more freedom. We found out Gene's wife was pregnant with Sam, and that helped lift everyone's spirits. Gene's dedicated his life to me. It's hard to call him Grandpa or even Granddad in front of people."

All the teasing between Lucas and Gene now made sense. Gene was his brother not his grandfather. No wonder Lucas called him an old geezer and gramps in a joking way. "So that article was correct. Gene had two children with him the day he ran into the racer. You were the boy with Gene and Sam all those years ago."

"Yes. Gene never thought he'd see anyone from the motorbike circuit in Montana. We were shopping in town when they saw each other and never knew it was part of an interview until you tipped us off."

"And you immediately removed the blog from the internet."

"Wiped it clean. We do daily security checks from our home computer base, but somehow that blogger got by us."

"You're aware he showed up the next day on another site."

"With our blessing."

"How'd you keep him from talking?"

"We have our ways." Lucas smiled and kissed my hand. I stared at him until he gave in. "Alright! It takes cash and a lot of it. Sometimes we have to threaten a lawsuit, too. The Niners have a fund for those sorts of things."

I felt relieved to hear how they had taken care of the situation. I imagined all sorts of scenarios, most ending badly. "Okay, back to your story. Gene's your father, and Sam's your brother until when?"

"Sam met Stacy in high school. He went to the local high school in town while I was homeschooled at the Montana compound. Well, not exactly homeschooled. There are schools for everyone to attend in the compound, but sometimes I studied from home. We're allowed to choose. Niner education is one of the top priorities.

"Well, anyway, they fell in love and married after college. They lived in town like a normal couple. Sam trusted Stacy. She knew everything. Stacy's the one who felt sorry for me and said I needed a high school experience, even volunteering to be my mom during that time. She wanted me to come and live with them. Gene would have no part of it. He felt we were safer in the compound than anywhere else until—"

"Until what?" I sat up almost fearing what came next.

"Doug's task force developed an intricate system of tracking down our compounds. We had trouble disabling it for the very first time. The Montana compound had to shut down for safety reasons to keep from being compromised. Everyone dispersed to safe houses or other compounds across the country. We're waiting for the all clear to be given. Then we can head back to Montana or stay where we are. Again, our choice."

"Oh my God! The Special Task Force almost found you. You came to Virginia to hide."

"Yeah, a few safe houses had already been established there. The diner was our cover story. We'd live in the community and run the diner. Sam became my father. Stacy, my mom, and Gene would be the grandfather of the family. Well, he really is grandpa to Hannah and Joe. I'm the only one playing a part. I'm the ringer of the family."

"Don't say that." I took Lucas' hand. "I can tell Stacy and Sam love you like a son."

"Thanks," Lucas answered. "I know they do, but I should be the one protecting them. Sam's my nephew. I should help him, not the other way around."

I didn't have an answer for that. Lucas had strayed from his story so I got him back on track. "You said the task force almost found the Montana compound. How could that happen?"

"The STF made great strides in the 21st century. Technology's moving faster than ever. It's getting tougher to stay ahead of advancements made in that field." Lucas held up the slim phone I'd seen him use many times. "This is not just a phone or a connection to the internet. It connects me to all the Niner facilities in the world and all their technology. I can also track anyone I want without putting a device on them or using an app."

"So the times you followed me home, you didn't need to."

"I could always find you on my phone. Early in our relationship I scanned you. I could see you were home, but I needed to *see* with my own eyes."

For some reason, that sounded romantic instead of

feeling like I had a stalker. I shook my head.

"What?"

"Nothing."

"It is something." Lucas locked eyes with me.

"When you said you always knew where I was, I thought you sounded like a stalker. That's all."

"No!" Lucas hit his forehead. "I would never do that. It's just that we have so many capabilities beyond what you have."

I held up my hand. "No need to explain. Let's get back to the discussion."

"What else do you want to know?"

"Is it safe for you to return to Montana?"

"Not yet, although it's close. The Niners created a virus to attack the task force's program. The compound still needs to remain shut down until they're sure it worked. Stacy wants me to finish high school before we go anywhere. Plus there's Hannah and Joe. Sam's grooming Joe to take over one day."

"So that's why he's so grumpy!"

"Not at all. He wants to graduate from brother to father one day. I don't want that. I plan on disappearing the day he thinks he's taking over. My family's made enough sacrifices for me. Now it's my turn. I got the whole high school experience and will hopefully make it to graduation."

"That's right, you told me you were here freshman year. I never saw you."

"I was good at blending in with the crowd." Lucas smiled.

"We could've been together longer." I blinked back the tears. "Or I could've been a threat to you sooner. I'm so sorry. I hate Doug."

"Doug's doing his job, Allie. He's convinced we'd

make good soldiers."

"I can save you, Lucas. We have to end it. You need to stop seeing me. My brother may have his suspicions, but I won't let him use me to find you. Your secret's safe."

"He already tried."

"What?"

"The angel pin, the one he gave you for your birthday is a tracking device."

I pictured the day Doug pinned it to my shirt like I'd want to wear it forever just because he put it there. He came home to investigate, not wish me a happy birthday. I tried to remember where I put the pin and envisioned it in a drawer. "When I get home, that thing's going in the trash!"

"Don't be so quick to get rid of it. You never know when you may need it."

"So I don't get the pleasure of having Doug trail after the garbage truck?" I laughed.

"Feeling better?" Lucas stood and pulled me up from the chair. He wrapped his arms around me. "I can't let you go, Allie. This is the first time I've been truly happy in my life."

I stopped smiling. I had given him false hope. "I'm sorry, Lucas. I just can't. I won't be responsible." He saw my resolve was serious, and the dark, brooding eyes appeared. I began to cry, sobbing into his shirt, gripping the fabric in my fists. I didn't want to let him go, but it had to be. My heart ached, I felt it might explode. I wished for the pain to leave my body. "It's over," I whispered. "Please accept it."

His arms tightened around me, and he whispered back, "Never."

CHAPTER ELEVEN

"So you broke up with the boyfriend?" Doug smiled at me across the Thanksgiving dinner table, filled with turkey, stuffing and all the foods I loved. I could barely eat, but forced down a big bite of cornbread, shoving it in my mouth so I couldn't talk.

"Doug, can't you see Allie doesn't want to talk about it?" Mom passed the gravy to him. "Is that hot enough? If not, I'll go warm it up in the kitchen. Just say the word."

"Well, maybe just a little hotter." Doug handed the dish back to Mom.

I wanted to scream out, "Do it yourself!" and watch the crumbs in my mouth explode in his face.

Dad cleared his throat. "Doug, we're happy you could share the holiday with us. So many times it seemed you couldn't get away from work."

"There's no such thing as a day off at my job, Pop."

"Well, we're thrilled you're here. Maybe we can get the old chess board out after dinner."

"You're on. One game though. I have to get going after that."

Doug walking out the front door in a few hours would let me finally relax. I could hardly wait. He had watched me all afternoon as if waiting for the right moment to pounce. I felt like a cornered mouse looking for the escape hole in the wall.

Although I felt trapped in my own home, Thanksgiving vacation was a welcomed relief from school. I felt like a pinball there, bouncing everywhere, trying to avoid Lucas and Josh and anyone else with prying questions. The countdown of Escape Small Town was back on. I hadn't spent one cent of the money Dean had given me for my birthday. I opened an account at the bank instead and tucked it away for that rainy day Dad always talked about. Or maybe it was time to go on an awesome spending spree. It looked like perpetual rain to me.

To keep busy, I cleared the table. We usually had a bigger group of people for the holiday, but for some reason, this year was just the four of us. I had no one to talk to besides the three people sitting in the dining room. Nate promised to call me as soon as he got home from his aunt's. I'd make an excuse that I needed help with homework and head over.

I ran the garbage disposal and scraped plates, placing each one carefully in the dishwasher. Mom dashed back and forth packing leftovers, and Dad set up the chess board in the family room. As the food swirled down the drain, I saw my life going down with the scraps. The happiness I felt a few short weeks ago had been replaced with a constant tug on my heart and a feeling of dread in the pit of my stomach.

The disposal snapped off. "Hey!" I saw a hand on the switch. A chill went through my body. "Doug! Turn it on. I'm not done."

"Oh, I think you can take a break, little sister. Why don't we sit at the table and cut the pies for Mom?" He took me by the arm and guided me to a chair. I watched as he picked up a knife with a long blade and cut into the apple. "My favorite. Piece?"

I shook my head. "What do you want, Doug?"

"To talk."

"You're never around long enough to talk. You don't even know me."

"Well, let's change that." He waved the knife in front of my face. "Mom's informed me if anything happens to them, I'm your guardian."

I swallowed hard. "Like legally?"

"Yes, legally."

Why was he bringing this up now? I was almost out of high school and would turn eighteen next November. I wanted to run into the family room and beg my parents to change the document to Dean. But Doug had them convinced. They'd do whatever he said. I assured myself my parents were fine, but my stomach squeezed into a ball of nerves. "Do you know something about Mom and Dad that I don't?"

"Oh, no, it's nothing like that."

Relief. "Well, I'll be eighteen next year so you won't have to worry about me."

"But I promised to always protect you, Allison, no matter your age."

"Why do you dislike me so much?" The conversation had gone from bad to worse so I blurted out the question I'd always wanted answered.

"I like you." Doug's face froze in a fake smile.

"No. You don't."

He leaned forward, both elbows on the table. "You *are* a little spoiled." He dropped his arms down and folded his hands. "There. I said it."

"That's not it." I stared at him hoping to break him down.

"I didn't feel the need for another sibling. One was enough."

"You weren't in charge of telling our parents how many children to have," I snapped. His arrogance confused me. Or was he manipulating me? Catch me off-guard?

"True." Doug looked away. "But they owe me," he said under his breath.

"Who? Mom and Dad? Why?" That sounded strange, even cryptic.

"Don't mind me." Doug pursed his lips as if he regretted I heard. "Now let's get back to you. I have a question. This ex of yours—Lucas—is he new to your school?"

"He's been around for a year or two." I mentally slapped my forehead. I fell into his trap and gave away too much information. Doug knew exactly when the Montana compound shut down.

"Interesting. Is it a year? Or two?"

"Not sure. I saw him last year for the first time." Ugh, I did it again. I squirmed in my chair and wondered if Doug sensed my nervousness. "I've got homework, Doug. Are we done here?"

He grabbed my arm. "Not until I say we are."

"You're hurting me." I wiggled away from him, not wanting another bruise.

He squeezed tighter then let go. "Sorry. I don't know my own strength." His tone changed back to false sweetness. "Please don't leave yet."

I decided to use his tactics. "I'll stay if you tell me one thing. Who owes you? And why?"

"Now that's the million dollar question, isn't it? Don't worry your pretty little head about it. The only thing I want you to be aware of is this. There are people out there ready to take over this country. I have to be prepared, ready to go at a moment's notice. If you want to help—if you're a patriot and loyal to this country— you should want to do your civic duty."

"I ... do, I guess." Was Doug talking about the Niners? He thought they wanted to take over the country? It didn't make sense after what Lucas told me.

"Then watch for that symbol I showed you. If you ever see it, call me immediately."

"Okay. Is that all I have to do?" I hoped Doug would think I sided with him, and his patriotic speech had worked.

"Yes." He took another bite of his pie. "Damn, that's good." He walked to the fridge, whipped open the door, and grabbed the jug of milk off the shelf. I watched in disgust as he chugged it down, draining it to its last drop.

* * * *

"Doug's on a mission to make my life miserable." I flopped on Nate's bed and rolled on my stomach, one hand under my chin. "I hate him," I said as I rubbed the arm he had grabbed.

"That's an understatement." Nate pushed his computer chair to the end of the bed and stared at me. "He thinks you know something. Do you?"

I couldn't share anything I learned from Lucas for everyone's safety. I shook my head and tried my best to look confused. I met his stare. "No idea. Doug's obsessed with this twenty-nine thing. Have you ever seen it written anywhere? Bathroom walls? On a desk? It's always written as Roman numerals."

"I thought you said Doug was looking for a tattoo."

"Yeah, right. A tattoo." I bit my bottom lip. "I should get one to drive him crazy."

Nate threw his head back and let out a loud hoot. "You know how to push his buttons, little one. I think I'll join you. We'll be the Twenty-nine Club."

"A club of two." I laughed. "Really, Nate, why is he all over me?"

"You're the only teenager he knows. Who else can he question? Think about it. He's far removed from that world. He's hoping you'll be stupid enough to help him. What did you tell me? He used the loyalty card? That may work on his recruits, but we're not impressed." He scooted back to his computer. "Let me do a search."

"On?"

"The number."

I grew nervous as I waited. If Nate found anything about the Niners he might connect the dots. I never mentioned Lucas had a tattoo, but with Nate's detective skills, he could easily figure it out. When I showed him the XXIX paper a few months ago, he didn't think much of it. Now, his interest level changed.

"Nope, nothing. Just that it's a Roman numeral and it's been a Super Bowl."

"Well, I guess whatever Doug's looking for is top secret. He didn't give me much information." I rolled over and sat on the edge of the bed. "What about the strange comment he made? Who do you think owes him?"

"From the story you told, I still think he's talking about your parents, or just one of them."

"He wishes I wasn't born. I took my parents' attention away from him. Could that be it?"

"He was sixteen, Allie. I thought he adored you when you were a baby."

"That's my mother's story."

"But your mom's a sweetheart, seeing only the good."

"Exactly." I rubbed my arm again.

"You've been doing that a lot." Nate gestured toward my arm.

"What?"

"Rubbing you arm, like it hurts or something." He sat forward in his computer chair. "Are you hiding something?"

"No!" I grew defensive. I could handle whatever Doug threw at me. "It's just brother/sister stuff. I'm sure siblings fight all the time, even leave bruises once in awhile."

Nate's eyebrows shot up. "Bruises? Did he hurt you?" His voice grew louder. "Damn, Allie! Men don't put their hands on young girls! He's sixteen years older than you. He should know better." He leaned back as if in thought. "Has he done this before?"

"Yes," I whispered. The memories came flooding back. Every visit home, Doug left me with a bruise. I showed my dad once, and he laughed it off. He said, "I'm sure he didn't mean it, sweetie. Doug doesn't know his own strength." I squeezed my eyes shut as I reflected back on those times.

Nate hopped up from his seat to sit next to me. "I knew I didn't like him for a reason." He wrapped his arms around me, and I buried my face in his shoulder. I tried to fight back the tears, but my eyes welled up.

"Hey, look at me." He brushed my hair back from my face. "Let's try to figure this out. Start from the beginning. The day Doug was born."

"He was born on February twenty-eighth." I sniffed and swallowed hard. Did all this tension have something to do with the day he was born? My heart raced as I realized I couldn't confide in Nate.

"Go on." He gave me a strange look. "Something weird about the day he was born? Dropped on his head maybe?"

I let out a small laugh. "Something like that. Three

years later, Dean was born and the boys were brought up together in a loving family. I dragged the photo albums out and found lots of pictures of Dean and Doug together. They went on family vacations and had big holiday celebrations. Nothing unusual. Except …" I bit my tongue to stop from saying it. One more day and Doug would have been a Niner. He would've been just like Lucas.

"Except what?" Nate crossed his arms and closed one eye. "Are you holding back?"

"No, but I have to get going. I've got a ton of homework." For some reason, I suddenly wanted to go home and find Doug's birth certificate.

"Okay, I'll be here for the rest of the night if you need me. We're hanging out with Ashley tomorrow. Don't forget!" he called after me as I rushed out the door.

I ran the whole way home, anxious to get there. Dad should be watching TV, and Mom could be reading the newspaper. I hoped they were distracted by their normal activities enough to ignore me.

"Hey." I stopped in the family room to find Dad trying to teach Mom how to play chess again.

"Clair, I keep telling you protect your queen," he said it gently, but I saw the frustration on his face.

"Mom's good at protecting the family, Dad. That's the most important thing." I walked over and put my arm across her back. "I'm going up for the night. You two behave."

"We always do, sweetie." Mom patted my hand and smiled up at me. "I told your father I'd give him an hour then I have some reading to do."

"Okay, have fun." I headed for the stairs, taking them two at a time choosing not to go in my room to the right of the steps. Instead I turned the other way and slipped into the guest bedroom, Dean's old bedroom. A fireproof safe held all the important family documents. Luckily, I knew the combination.

As I opened the safe's door, I saw neat stacks of folders and a few passbooks from banks. I searched for the one marked 'birth certificates'. The tabs had been carefully labeled so I found it in no time. My hand trembled as I flipped open the vanilla folder. Doug's sat on top. I skimmed through the details. Nothing unusual. My parents' names, the doctor, the hospital, place of birth all filled in correctly. Then something jumped out at me.

Time of birth. 11:59 pm.

I placed my hand on my neck to suppress a gasp. One more minute, and Doug would be a Niner.

I struggled with the urge to call Lucas and tell him what I found. But I couldn't make contact and break my promise. He needed the information. Then again, with all their technology, the Niners may already know.

"Darn!" I had no one to confide in. I straightened up, feeling lost and lonely. "Lucas, why couldn't you have been born a minute too soon?" I placed the folders back just as I found them. Tears filled my eyes as the answer came to me. "Then I wouldn't have known you." I shut the door of the safe and stared into the closet. "Are we destined to be together?" I sat back on my heels, breathing in and out to calm myself. "No, there has to be something more."

A few short months ago I only wanted to get through my junior year. I didn't know Niners and the STF existed. Now, they took over my thoughts to the point I didn't think about anything else. Should I be grateful I knew about this crazy secret world?

Sometimes, I wished I could be blissfully unaware—
that Lucas was just some teenage boy, and I was his girl.

CHAPTER TWELVE

January in Virginia had temperatures hovering around the freezing point. I shouldn't complain, other parts of the country had it worse. I always found the air bone-chilling cold and bundled up in layers and gloves with special fingertips, so I could use my phone.

I had a lot of time to think during winter break. I mulled over information from both sides—Doug and Lucas. Doug really believed in his cause. I hated to give him any credibility, but there could be a real threat to our country. How could I know for sure? I didn't have access to the secret intel. My head told me to keep an open mind.

I loved Lucas and trusted him, but I didn't know others like him or the Niner philosophy of life. They could be plotting to take over the world for all I knew. My heart believed in Lucas, and he'd win for that reason alone. I decided to hold off judgment on either side until I had more facts.

Instead of starting the car to head to school, I sat in the driveway daydreaming back to the day Lucas and I came home from the Outer Banks. We drove to our woods and strolled through the forest one last time. I grabbed a blanket from the car, and we sat near the brush pile to say our final goodbyes. We kissed and cried and kissed some more. Lucas told me if I ever needed an escape, I should come to our woods. He'd always find me.

My decision to end the relationship was validated during winter break. Doug came for three long days at Christmas. He grilled me about my life—where I went, what I did, did I have any new friends, what happened with the boyfriend—till I wanted to scream. I gave him the shortest possible answers without sounding too distant while hating him with all of my being.

He gave me some crappy presents, and I had to hug and thank him in front of the family. He could have given me a camouflage suit and canteen for all I cared. I did like one present, but would never admit it. In fact, I wore the gift now, a soft, pale blue hooded sweatshirt with hidden pockets for my gadgets and even a charger for my phone. Did the great gift soften my stance toward him? No, it made me more resistant.

I came close to telling Ashley everything during break but caught myself. Lucas trusted me with his secrets. I had to stay strong. Nate became my sounding board. He knew something was up with Lucas and his family but didn't question me. I never actually told him anything during our talks. He seemed to pick up on the hidden messages in our conversations. My silence seemed to answer his questions.

I started the Jeep and pulled the hood from my new sweatshirt closer around my head. Hard to believe Doug picked this out, probably had some help from Mom. I pulled out of the drive and traveled down our side street as slowly as I could, anything to prolong the trip to school. I planned to stagger my arrival times so Lucas wouldn't find me. What was I thinking? He knew my whereabouts at all times. He scanned me. If I went on a date, he'd probably pop up in the backseat of the car. I laughed at the thought as I turned into the school parking lot and found a space.

As I shut down the engine, a loud noise startled me. Someone pounded on the side of the car and slammed a paper against the passenger front window.

"Hey!" I screamed out.

I leaned forward to look past the paper to see who pulled the practical joke on me, but the message caught my eye. I read silently.

Don't say my name or anything out loud until I get in the car.

My heart went to my throat. The passenger door flew open. "Take it off! Take it off right now!" Lucas yelled as he jumped in the seat next to me.

"I have no idea what you're talking about." I tried to remain calm but having him in such close proximity made me lose it. My heart pounded faster. I swallowed a few times before I could speak. "What's wrong?"

"The sweatshirt."

"You don't like the color?" I asked in a sarcastic tone.

Lucas breathed out and took another breath before answering. "Did Doug give you that?"

How could I be so stupid? Doug realized the pin hadn't worked so he gifted me the sweatshirt. I should have known! Doug fooled me twice, and I vowed it would never happen again. I removed my coat and pulled the sweatshirt over my head, shivering.

"Here, put this on." Lucas handed me an identical sweatshirt with all the special features of the old one. "They'll think it malfunctioned or something. Are you alright?"

I didn't notice before, but Sam stood outside the Jeep. I pointed at him because my teeth chattered so much I couldn't talk.

"Oh." Lucas glanced out the window. "Dad came so he could disable and dispose of this." Lucas held the shirt in the air. He rolled the window down and handed it to him. "I disengaged the sound before I got in. Thanks, Sam." He turned back, crossed his brow, and pounded his fist into his knee. "I've got to stop doing that! I just called him Sam." He reached out and touched my cheek. "Are you okay?"

I sat with my mouth open, unable to process what just happened. Doug had turned me into a walking spy without my knowledge. He still thought I would track his victims without having a clue. Breaking up with Lucas hadn't stopped him.

"Lucas, this gives me one more reason to stay away from you."

"All the more reason *to* stick around. We can do great intelligence work." Lucas gave me that smile.

"I'll work with you, but that's all." I caved pretty quickly and put out my hand to shake on a deal.

"Great working with you." Lucas shook my hand and jumped from the car. "See you in class, partner."

What did I just do? I let Lucas back in my life. Not as a boyfriend, but he was back. I slid out of the car and headed for the main door of the school. I stepped inside, walked down the hall staring at faces but not really seeing them. Concentrating on schoolwork would be hard. Two factions of men in my life could be fighting for world dominance, and I had to go to AP English.

Lucas waited outside class like he used to do. I hope he didn't get the wrong idea from the deal we made. "What are you doing?" My eyes widened as I shot him a look. "I don't want anyone to think we're back together."

"Can't a friend wait for a friend?" Lucas grinned.

"No! We need to keep things as they were."

"Come home with me tonight after school."

"Can't."

"Yes, you can. I need to show you something."

I sighed. "Just this once, but we can't make it a habit. I have to go right home or my mom will think something's up."

"Then we'll come up with an explanation. We're study partners or working on a project together."

"You'll have to come to my house sometimes. It has to look good."

"I can do that."

"Lucas, don't read anything into this. We're not a couple." He reached out to brush my cheek with his fingers, but I jerked away. "I'll meet you by my car. Don't wait for me outside the school." I jabbed my finger in the air to make my point.

I entered class to see Ashley already in her seat and knew she had a thousand questions. I wrote a big "No" on a sheet of paper and held it up for her to see. That should satisfy the "are we back together" question.

After school, I took my time and headed for my locker. I slipped on my jacket and fixed my make-up in the small mirror attached to the inside door of the locker. *If this is so important, he can wait.* I finished up and started to close the locker door. As I did, I caught a glimpse of someone in the mirror.

"Hey, stranger." Josh seemed happy to run into me.

"How were your holidays?" I'd make small talk then slip away.

"Great. How about yours?"

"Same."

"You know, Al, we used to be friends. Can we start over? Friends?"

"Sure, why not?" I found myself shaking hands

with him. Out of the corner of my eye, I saw Lucas leaning by a water fountain farther down the hall. "I'll see you tomorrow, Josh. I've got to get going." Luckily he turned and went in the other direction.

"I thought I told you we'd meet by the car," I hissed as I marched by Lucas.

He reached out and took my arm to slow my pace. "Got worried you didn't show up. Don't be mad."

"I'm here now." I swung around to face him, eyes flashing with anger. "You have exactly one hour to show me whatever it is you want me to see."

Lucas held his hands in the air. "Hey, I thought we had a truce."

"We do." I softened my stance and sighed. Didn't he realize I had to protect us? "Where to?"

"My house."

I dreaded going to the place I loved so much. "Is this some kind of trick?"

"How?"

"To get me to let my guard down, kiss you on the deck when the sun's setting, to walk through the leaves with no one else around and feel so safe."

"All of that sounds pretty good." Lucas searched for my hand, but I resisted. I started down the hall with Lucas trailing behind.

"So let's plan what I'm going to tell my mom and dad," I said over my shoulder. "It has to be believable because they'll tell Doug."

Lucas passed me by and opened the school door, waving me through. "After you."

I rolled my eyes. "Well? Ideas?" I popped the locks of the Jeep, and we got in.

"Mrs. Greene did say we could do independent study this grading period—on your own, with a partner or groups. She's the answer to our prayers."

"True but won't my parents wonder why I'm working with you after we broke up?"

"Because I'm the smartest?" We both laughed as I pulled into the Montgomery driveway. "Drive to the barn." Lucas pointed to a place to park.

I jumped out and followed Lucas to the barn. He slid the door back and switched on the lights. I was blown away every time I saw the motorcycle display hidden behind that door.

"Up here." He pointed to the metal staircase against the wall. The vaulted ceiling gave way to a second level built in the back section of the barn. The steps ended at a small landing and we walked across an open walkway to a closed door. I stood at the railing and gazed down at the bikes while I waited for Lucas to open the door. He held his phone in his hand as he said, "Lights."

They automatically came on, and we entered a giant room with white walls. "Dagwood Five-Fourteen." I heard a beep and colored lights appeared on the wall in front of me. One by one, large display screens came into view around the room.

"How?" I knew my mouth hung open. My eyes opened wide as I shifted from screen to screen.

"The safe house has a direct connection to the main campus in Montana, actually to all the compounds worldwide. Our phones are linked through those connections and act as the conductors. We're working on mind commands instead of voice and eventually will give orders in our heads."

"And Dagwood?"

Lucas shrugged. "It's our family password. My father's birthday and his favorite comic strip character."

He faced the wall. "Diner." The inside of the diner instantly blinked onto the screen closest to us. Stacy and Sam stood behind the counter. Sam poured coffee and Stacy placed plates of food on a tray. "We're here, Sam."

Sam nodded as he continued to pour.

"He can hear you?"

"Yeah, but no one else can. Let me show you the Montana compound." Lucas stood in front of another wall and gave the command. I became mesmerized, spellbound. I couldn't stop staring, taking it all in.

The life-size screen flicked from empty streets with rows of cute Victorian gingerbread houses to a downtown area of shops, restaurants and a park. January guaranteed everything was covered in snow, except the streets and sidewalks, making me think of the North Pole. I felt like I could walk right into the magical winter scene.

"The Niners fashioned this compound on neighborhoods of days gone by. We named it Victorian Village." Lucas called out another command. "Headquarters." The Village melted away, replaced by a room filled with space age technology.

"Wow."

"We're all connected. I could show you compounds around the world. You could meet and talk to people who've been in your place. You can meet Niners, and they'd share their stories with you. You're seeing a world created by men ahead of their time and who would be the best weapon of mass destruction for any country. We don't want to be part of Doug's army. We have our own world. Can you understand why we have to stay hidden or hide in plain sight?"

"Yes, of course, I can. This is so wonderful, so

unbelievable. You must do everything you can to protect it."

"Then there's one more thing. Can I trust you?"

I nodded and whispered, "Of course."

"There's a leak. Someone's passing along intel on how to find me. It's coming from a person in this area. The Niners have pinpointed it to our region. We're working to finding the source."

"So that's why Doug's here. He's been given information."

"Yes. Do you think you can help find out who it is or how he's getting the information?"

I gestured around the room. "None of this helped?"

"No, we don't understand why. They're able to bypass the system. Do you see why I had to bring you here, show you this, ask for your help?"

I fell into Lucas' arms, sliding my hands around his waist. "I'm so sorry. I had no idea. Of course, I'll help." I lifted my head to look at him and saw his eyes glistened with tears. We kissed, ever so briefly, as if to seal our secret bond.

"I don't want anything to happen to you," Lucas whispered. "If for any reason you sense danger, stop and get out. Promise me."

"I promise."

* * * *

The next night Lucas and I arranged to study at my house. We devised a plan in case anything happened. Lucas would hide his bike inside Nate's storage barn if he needed a quick escape. We would work in the kitchen close to the back door.

I helped Mom clear the table after dinner, and as we worked, I heard a phone ring. She appeared flustered as she searched for her cell.

"There it is." She produced Doug's gift from her pocket. "Excuse me for a minute, sweetie." She disappeared into another room. Her strange behavior made me curious. I decided to follow and listen in.

"Thanks for calling back, Doug. Yes, you're right about that." She laughed, and I didn't know why. "No, Allie's home right now. She's studying with that boy, Lucas, tonight. Yes, here at home. He'll be here soon." There was a long pause. "Love you, too."

I raced back to the kitchen and pretended I had just finished wiping the table. Mom stepped into the kitchen, still drying her hands on the towel she grabbed on her way out. "Who was that?"

"Oh, just a neighbor from down the street." She sounded nervous.

"I'm going upstairs for awhile. Thanks for dinner." I kissed her cheek, and she seemed to relax, thinking I bought her story.

Almost running to my room, I closed the door and sat on my bed. Was my mother the spy? Did Doug give her the special phone for that reason? I dialed Lucas and relayed the message.

"Slow down, Allie. Let me think."

I tried to gauge his reaction. "Do you think my mom's the mole?"

"If she is, she's an innocent victim. I can't believe your mother would do that to you."

"We don't know what Doug has told her. He did show her the twenty-nine symbol. That's all I know."

"Let's see what happens. I'm leaving now. You let Nate know I'm parking my bike at his house?"

"Yeah, it's all set."

I paced in my room until I got the signal, two rings

on my phone, which meant Lucas arrived. Frantic, I ran down to open the front door and pulled him inside. "We're going to study after all of this?" I whispered.

"Got to keep up those grades." The smile appeared, and I suddenly felt calm.

After greeting my parents and making the usual small talk, we set up in the kitchen and began to work. An hour went by and the knot in my stomach started to fade. We made some progress and decided to take a break. I was pouring soda into glasses when I heard the doorbell.

"It's him." Lucas put a finger to his lips. I stood motionless. Lucas listened in on the conversation as he inched toward the door. "Let's go."

For some reason, I felt oddly compelled to grab my backpack as we headed out. I pulled up the hood of my sweatshirt as we ran out the backdoor, heading for the path between the houses. The bag slid down my arm and kept hitting me in the back of the knees, slowing my progress. I threw it down, planning to retrieve it later.

As we stood outside the Kalas house, I pointed to Nate's bedroom, the last window at the farthest end of the house.

"What was Doug saying?" I needed to know before we got to the bedroom window.

"He said, 'Thanks for calling, Mom. It was good to hear from you.'"

"That's it?"

"Yep."

"Then they've developed a code."

Lucas chuckled. "If that's true, your mom's deadlier than I imagined."

I poked him in the side as we stopped in front of

the window. We saw Nate sitting at his computer. I tapped on the glass. He didn't jump or appear startled but casually strolled over. He pulled the bottom pane up, popped the screen and pulled me in. Lucas jumped in behind me, and we landed on the floor.

"So what are you two kids up to now?" Nate stared down at us lying on the carpet, and glanced back and forth. "Skulking around in the dark? Very interesting. Trying to avoid someone?"

"Nate, cut it out. Doug's here and you know he never just pops over for a visit." I sat up and leaned back on my hands.

"Stand up." Nate instructed Lucas. Lucas nodded like he knew what Nate meant. I watched Nate look Lucas up and down, sizing him up. "So Lucas, you don't have to tell me, but I suspect there's something going on with you and your family. Nothing illegal or dishonest, but something you wish to protect. Little one here likes and trusts you. So do I ... to a point."

To my surprise, Lucas opened up, telling Nate just enough to make him understand. He didn't tell him about aging every four years, but did let him know he had certain abilities the task force would like to tap into. I explained how Doug's gifts to me were embedded with tracking devices.

"Do you have that pin on you?" Nate looked concerned. "You could be tracked right to my room."

"Oh my God, how could I be so stupid?" I hit my forehead. Then I remembered I dropped the bag in between the houses with the pin secured to the strap. I put the pin on the bag after the sweatshirt incident. I didn't want Doug getting suspicious. "No, it's not on me!" Relieved, I told them how I dropped the bag during the escape.

"Good! I have an idea." Nate started to tell us the plan when a knock came at his door, startling us. "Quick! In here," he whispered. Lucas and I slipped into his large walk-in closet.

"Nate? Nathan?"

"Come in, Mom."

"I have Mrs. Sanders on the phone. She wants to know if you've seen Allie. It seems that she and a friend are taking a walk in the backyard. Odd, it's very dark out."

"Nope, haven't seen her," Nate answered.

"Did you hear that, Clair?" Right, he hasn't seen her but I'll call if we do." I heard the door shut, signaling she left the room.

"That was close," I whispered as we slipped out of the tight confines.

"You guys go out back and hide in the storage shed. Wait a few minutes then it will be safe for Lucas to leave." Nate opened a desk drawer and handed me a slender pen. "Flashlight's on one end."

"Won't need it." Lucas took it from my hand and gave it back to Nate.

"Pretty dark out there." Nate tried to give the pen back to him.

"We'll be fine." Lucas lightly pushed Nate's hand away.

"Another one of your special talents, I take it." Nate nodded and waited for the answer he knew wouldn't come.

We slipped out the window, replaced the screen and snuck toward the back of the property.

"We're going into the woods. I hope you don't mind." Lucas had a hold of my hand. We only had the moonlight to guide us. "I don't want to be trapped inside the shed."

"Just go slowly, you know I can't see." I shivered and pulled my sweatshirt closer to my body. I felt my feet leave the ground and was swept into Lucas' strong arms.

"Is that better?" He whispered in my ear.

I rested my head on his shoulder until he set me down on one of Nate's bike paths. Another feeling washed over me as I clung to him. Fear. I was afraid I would lose him.

"I love you," I whispered and felt his hand under my chin, his lips on mine and I didn't push him away.

* * * *

Ashley stood on the curb, waving nonstop, as I pulled into the school parking lot. I rolled down the window and waved back.

"I have the best story!" Her eyes went wide. "You're going to love it! It's about Doug."

My blood ran cold when she mentioned my brother's name. We didn't have time so I motioned for her to get in the car. "Tell me what happened." I drove to a spot and parked.

"Nate and I had a date last night." She held up her fingers to make quotation marks. "He said he'd go to the bookstore with me. You know how much I love the bookstore, right? Did you pick your English project yet? Never was a fan of independent study, are you?"

"Ash, I know you love the bookstore. Lucas and I decided to work together, I hope you don't mind. Independent study is a good excuse for us to see each other."

"So you're back together." Ashley nodded. "No worries. Love trumps all. Beside, Nate's going to be my partner. I know he really can't, being a senior. Just hypothetically."

"He'll be a big help. Now tell me what happened at the bookstore."

"Well, for some weird reason, Nate told me to wear a blue hoodie under my coat and he wore one, too. I'm glad he told me to wear it because it was cold out. We both had the hoods pulled up on the walk from the parking lot."

"Ash! Get to the point!" I couldn't wait any longer. "Sorry. Go on."

Ashley rolled her eyes and continued. "The strangest thing happened. We heard this voice call out 'Stop'. The person grabbed Nate from behind and spun him around. Guess who it was? Doug! What's up with that?"

I wanted to laugh and cry all at the same time. Now I knew why Nate had measured his body type against Lucas'. He planned to get the pin off my book bag and wear it on his date with Ashley. He threw Doug off the trail and posed as Lucas. "So did Doug say what he was doing at the bookstore?"

"He apologized for startling us. He just wanted to say hi. I didn't buy the story for a second. Then he said he needed to get you a book for your independent study because you couldn't find your book bag. Then Nate looked at his bag and realized it was yours."

Liar, Doug, you are such a liar. I couldn't tell Ashley the truth so I said, "Bizarre story. Was he in uniform?"

"Yes! Now here's the crazy part. He never came into the bookstore. So I guess you didn't get your book."

"No, I didn't."

"Strange night."

"Yeah, very strange." I couldn't wait to tell Lucas

the story but had a feeling he already knew. We exited the car and headed for the school entrance. Lucas and Nate walked toward us. Certain that Lucas had Nate's version; I wanted to hear the real story.

Nate slung his arm across Ashley's shoulders as we met up. "Ash, do you mind if I stop off at the A/V room before I walk you to homeroom?" For a minute, happiness took the place of the anger I felt for Doug. Nate and Ash were finally a couple.

"Not at all." She gave him a quick kiss. They disappeared into the school, not giving us another thought.

"Well, come on. Tell me Nate's side of the story!" I tugged on Lucas' arm as he watched our friends disappear into the school.

"First, I need to know something. Are we a couple or not?"

"We have to be a secret couple. Is that alright?"

Lucas grabbed me and pulled me up against his body. I felt his muscles tense in his chest, his heart beat faster. He kissed me right there in the parking lot. I didn't care who saw. Being a secret couple suddenly didn't matter. He leaned back and stared into my eyes. "Let's walk. I'll tell you what Nate said."

Walk? My legs are mush after that kiss.

"After we left, Nate went outside to look for your book bag. He found it on the path and drove over to Ashley's. He was prepared for anything. When Doug approached, he remained calm."

"Thank goodness! Ashley said Doug grabbed Nate by the arm and spun him around."

"When Doug mentioned you couldn't find your bag, Nate looked at the one he carried and faked surprise. He blamed it on a mix-up. He's a good guy,

Allie. I trust him."

"He could be our decoy, Lucas. He'd take the pin whenever or wherever we ask him."

"It seems too easy, but we can give it a try. We want Doug to think we're two clueless teenagers, so we have to be careful."

"Don't worry. I'll make sure of it." I finally felt I had the upper hand. Doug thought he could outsmart me. Well, Mr. Mission Impossible, two can play that game.

CHAPTER THIRTEEN

Game on. For the next six weeks, Nate and I traded the pin back and forth with a wink and a nod. I passed it off to him at the end of the school day so Lucas and I could head to the Montgomery house without the fear of being caught.

Nate would then text me when he left school so I could leave at the same time, stop by his house and get the pin. Sometimes I stayed, and we strategized. I always made sure I got home well before dinner. Hopefully, Doug would come to the conclusion that I led a very boring life.

The plan seemed to work. Doug hadn't made an appearance in weeks. He could move on to his next victim. The more I thought about it, he was always on a Niner case. Even if I helped Lucas, someone else would be on his radar. We couldn't stop Doug or the STF, but I took pride in the fact I helped save one Niner from his clutches.

I couldn't take on the world so I focused on mine. I wanted to do something special for Lucas on Valentine's Day. Only the Montgomery family knew our real status so I enlisted Stacy's help.

After the diner closed that day, she stayed and waited for me to show up. Together we decorated a booth, lit candles along the counter and made a special dinner. Stacy headed home and told Lucas she forgot to turn off a burner to get him back to the diner. I'd be the surprise waiting for him.

Nate had the pin for the night. I lied to Mom and Dad and said I was going out with Nate and Ash so I wouldn't be alone and depressed on a romantic holiday.

I sat in the booth, excitement building, watching the candles flicker. It didn't take long before I heard the roar of a motorcycle then silence. Lucas stepped into the diner and spotted me in the corner. I couldn't resist, I ran to him.

"You weren't tracking me, I hope? Did my little white lie work?" I told him earlier I had to have dinner with my parents. "I didn't want to blow my cover and make Mom feel compelled to call to Doug.

"I wanted to track you. I knew I'd just stare at a little dot on the screen the whole night when you should've been with me." He took me in his arms. "Now you are."

"Happy Valentine's Day." After a long kiss, I dragged him to the booth and went behind the counter producing two plates of food. I slipped my gift under his plate.

"Hey, what do we have here?" Lucas lifted his plate when I set it in front of him. "I feel guilty. You went to all this work *and* you got me something."

"Go ahead, open it."

Lucas pushed the lid off the box to find a red foil wrapped chocolate heart on top of a framed picture of us.

"I love it." Then he reached in his coat pocket. "You didn't think I'd forget, did you?"

I gasped as I took the black velvet box tied with red ribbon. Tugging on the ribbon, I flipped the lid back and saw a silver open heart necklace. On the lower part of the heart were two gemstones, pale blue and purple, side by side. "Our birthstones?"

"Yes, the blue topaz is you and the amethyst is February's."

I slid out of the booth and back in next to him.

"Thank you." I gave him a quick kiss then another. "I'll never take it off." I said between kisses.

"I love you, Allison Sanders. This is a token of that love." Lucas held me close. We sat side by side just like the two gemstones on my necklace and ate our dinner.

"Lucas?"

"Yes, love?"

"How do I explain the necklace?"

"Say Ashley gave it to you, a friendship necklace. Didn't you tell me her birthday's in February?"

"You think of everything."

"I try. Now quit worrying so much and eat."

We finished, and Lucas cleared the plates, looking around behind the counter. "There's got to be dessert. Stacy had to leave something."

"She did. She said it's your favorite."

"Found it! Chocolate cake!" Lucas cut two pieces and brought them over to the booth.

"Lucas, your birthday's in two weeks. Do you celebrate every year? Has your family made any plans?"

"No, we don't want to drawn attention to ourselves buying cakes and decorations at the end of February. Plus why celebrate a quarter year? Doesn't make sense to me."

I decided to remedy that but saved the plan for later. "Speaking of birthdays …" Lucas' brow furrowed, and I grabbed his hand. "Are you aware that Doug was born on February twenty-eighth?"

"You mean a minute before midnight?" He chuckled.

"So you knew." I stared at him waiting for more of a response.

"It was a leap year. He could've been a Niner."

"I'm totally aware." I wrinkled my nose. "He's not

nice enough to be one."

"We are a great bunch of guys, if I do say so myself." Lucas laughed.

I squeezed his arm in agreement. "I never told you this but during one of my talks with Doug, he said someone owes him. I think he means my parents."

Lucas drummed his fingers on the table. "No, I think he just blames your mom. He's mad he missed being a Niner by a minute. So if he can't be one—"

"Then start your own personal army." I finished. I couldn't believe we talked about armies on Valentine's Day. Nate and Ashley were probably hanging out, listening to music and sharing mindless gossip. Lucas and I analyzed Doug and his strange obsession with the Niners.

"Still doesn't explain why he's mean to *you*, Allie. He can be mad at your mom for giving birth a minute too soon. Can't think of a reason he'd be angry with your dad."

At that moment, it became clear. "You're right. He's not angry with my dad. They have a great relationship. He's only angry at my mom. How was she supposed to know to hang on one more minute before giving birth? Mom waits on him hand and foot. She does his bidding, tries to keep him happy. Maybe subconsciously she knows he's mad at her and has no idea why."

"Okay, that explains why he said someone owes him but what about you?"

"I have no idea! Maybe he wanted me to be a Niner. That would make up for having to put up with another sibling. He could help raise and mold me." I tapped my chin. "Never mind. I'd have to be a boy for that to happen." I laughed at the thought and abruptly stopped. "He wouldn't know about Niners back then, would he?" A chill set in, and I rubbed my arms. "He was only sixteen," I said as if I needed to convince myself.

"That's a long shot, Allie, but I don't think he knew. We'll keep at this until we figure it out." He locked eyes with me. "I didn't want to bring this up today, but I might as well tell you now that we're on the subject of Doug."

"What?"

"We know the reason his task force has been so vigilant these past two years."

"Well? Don't keep me in suspense."

"Even though they never found our compound, they're aware a breach happened. They know we shut down a facility and have been monitoring the country for recent residents. They're particularly interested in students who enrolled in new schools the past two years, especially high schools."

"That's a lot of people to monitor. This is a big country."

"They use certain criteria to rule people out and narrow the search. We weren't on their radar until this year."

"When my mom became Doug's spy."

"Unknowing spy, if she is. I can't believe she's the leak."

"I can. She lies to me every time she gets a call from him and turns into a nervous wreck afterward. My mom's not very good at lying." I let out a huge sigh, and Lucas gave me a quick squeeze. I still had to find a way to get to Doug. I took a deep breath, and a plan came to mind. One I couldn't share with Lucas. I needed to get my hands on that special phone of hers—

the sooner, the better.

* * * *

"That's the stupidest idea I've heard in a long time!" Nate threw his hands in the air. "You can't trap Doug. He does the trapping!"

"But he thinks I'm clueless."

"Still don't like it."

"Nate, you have to promise not to say anything to Lucas." The two had become close and acted like best friends. They found out they had a lot in common just as I suspected.

"Not fair." Nate pulled on his hair, brown eyes searing through me.

"We need to find the leak. Doug's the only one that can lead us to him *or* her." I instantly thought of Mom.

"So let me get this straight. You want to steal your mom's phone, bring it to me, bug it and return it without anyone knowing."

"Right. But when you say it like that, the plan sounds dumb, like we'd never pull it off. I think the phone has some special system in place that Lucas can't hack into. If we can at least bug the phone, we'd be able to find out if my mother's passing along information."

"Look, Allie, I understand you want to clear your mom of any wrongdoing, but if this special force finds out what we're doing?" I tried to give him the saddest face I could muster. "Alright, fine! I give in. I'll take a look at the phone to see if it's possible, but that's it."

"Thank you, thank you, thank you!" I jumped up and hugged Nate giving him air kisses.

"Enough already!" Nate took my arms and placed them at my side. "To change the subject, have heard about the annual Leap Year Dance? I guess it doesn't come around once every four years," Nate said with a deadpan face.

"Very funny. No, I haven't." I joked. Everyone knew about the annual dance. At the turn of the century someone thought a Leap Year dance sounded like a good idea. Since it had been such a success, they decided to have one every year.

"Well, girls ask the guys to go to the dance. I want Ashley to ask me. You should ask Lucas. We'll all go together."

"Might be busy that day." I thought about Lucas' birthday, and the plans I made.

"I suggest you two go to the dance and make everything look as normal as possible."

"Okay, I think you're right. We'll go, but I need your help with one thing."

"If Ashley asks me, name your price."

"Birthday help."

"I can do that."

"Since I can't shop for Lucas, you have to do it for me."

"Done."

"You know it's Ash's birthday, too, don't you?"

"Of course. What should I get her?"

"Something romantic." I touched the necklace I wore.

"Jewelry?"

"I'll help. I can go shopping for her birthday without raising suspicion, but you'll be in charge of Lucas' gift."

"For the guy who has everything?"

Nate could be right. Niner technology far exceeded what I'd buy in a store. Lucas' grandfather, or should I say brother Gene, had all the equipment for motor biking. I was stumped. It had to be memorable for our first year together. Even though Lucas said he didn't celebrate birthdays in between the real ones, I had to do something.

"Jewelry?" I laughed, but Nate didn't.

"Might not be a bad idea. What if?" He proceeded to tell me his idea, which I loved.

I reached for my phone and called Ashley. We chatted for awhile. Finally I asked her about the dance. "Are you going to ask Nate?"

"And are you going to ask Lucas?"

"Already asked him," I fibbed. "I want to double with you and your date."

"Are you in Nate's room?"

"Uh, yeah."

"Hand him the phone."

"She wants to talk to you." I passed my phone to him. Their conversation turned into a marathon so I searched the desk for Nate's phone and called Lucas.

"What's up?" I heard Lucas' voice, and my heart began to pound like always.

"I want to ask you to the Leap Year Dance."

"Allie?"

"Well, it sure isn't Nate asking you to a dance!" I laughed. We talked for awhile then the conversation turned serious. "You have to agree that Nate's right about us going."

"Absolutely! Plus I get to take my girl to the ball."

"On your birthday."

"It's not really my birthday."

"Okay, it marks your quarter year."

"That's correct."

Nate ended his call so I finished mine. I had something important to tell him. "How late are you staying up tonight?"

"The usual. Midnight or so. Why?"

"I'm going to wait until my mom goes to bed then sneak in her room to search for the phone. She keeps it in her pocket at all times, but can't while she's sleeping. It's my best chance. I'll come over so you can install the bug."

"Are you planning on doing this tonight?"

"Why wait?"

"You think I have bugs lying around my room?"

"Yes."

"Okay, see you later." Nate stared at the floor for a moment then looked up. "And Allie?"

"What?'

"Be careful."

Now my heart pounded for a different reason as I ran across the backyards. I had to steal my mom's phone. When I slipped into the kitchen, she was loading the dishwasher.

"You left so soon after dinner you didn't get to have dessert." She looked up and smiled.

"I didn't want any, thanks though."

"You're spending a lot of time with Nate these days."

"I always do, Mom." *You'd probably turn him into the STF, too, if he didn't live here his whole life.*

"I guess you're right. Don't stay up too late."

"You always say that." I gave her a quick kiss and headed for my room, closing the door. Mom always knocked to say goodnight. Now I was glad she did.

It seemed like hours before the knock came. I quickly glanced at my clock, ten-thirty. I'd give her a half hour then go in. Dad usually stayed downstairs until the eleven o'clock news ended so I had time.

I needed to stop watching the clock. When I did check, only a few minutes had gone by. Finally the time arrived, and I made my move. As quietly as I could, I slipped out of my room and tiptoed to the master bedroom door. I sank down to my hands and knees after pushing open the door. Crawling on all fours, I slid across the carpet toward her bedside. Mom shifted position, and I dropped flat to the floor. One of her arms dangled off the bed inches from my head. *Close call.*

I held my breath and continued on. A nightstand, next to the bed, had to be the best place to leave a phone. I felt around the top until I found it. I wanted to scream with joy but knew I still had to get out of the room, rush over to Nate's and return the phone before Dad came up. He was a light sleeper. I'd never pull it off with him in the bedroom.

The escape from the master bedroom went smoothly. Out in the hallway, I let out a loud whoosh of air and breathed in deeply. Back in my own room, I picked up my phone and texted Nate to say I'd be there soon. I stole down the steps and into the kitchen. I opened the door and shivered as I stepped out into the dark night. I rushed along the path, hoping no one noticed me. His window had been left open, just a crack. I pushed it up the rest of the way and scrambled in, collapsing on the floor. As I rolled over, I gazed up into Lucas' eyes.

"Nate! You promised!"

"Uh, I don't think I did. Anyway, I need him. I don't have the kind of bug you want for this phone. It has to be undetectable, untraceable. I called Lucas after you left. He brought something over."

"Ooh, you two are so frustrating!" They both

appeared to suppress a laugh.

"Let me see the phone." Lucas held out his hand.

I wriggled into a sitting position and placed it in his palm.

"If I put it on the outside cover, it should be fine." He glanced at Nate for approval.

Lucas took a sheer piece of paper from his pocket, peeled off a half-inch clear square and placed it on my mom's phone. It became invisible. "This will pick up everything she says. We won't hear Doug's side of the conversation but this should help us figure a few things out." He handed the phone back to me. "Good luck."

Lucas helped me out the window. I had no time to spare. Dad would head upstairs in a few minutes. I glanced at the clock in the kitchen as I slipped in the door. I had ten minutes to get the job done.

"Oh, Allie, you startled me. I didn't know you were down here." Dad wandered into the kitchen seconds after I shut the back door.

"Just getting some water."

"Well, goodnight then."

"You're going up?"

"Can't watch the sports tonight. I saw the team lose once today and can't stomach seeing the highlights."

"Oh, then goodnight." I gave him a quick hug. Sitting at the kitchen table, my heart sank. No way would I get the phone back in the room now. I had to come up with a new plan.

* * * *

I set my alarm extra early so I would wake as soon as Mom went downstairs. I usually showered during Dad's breakfast hour and never saw him in the a.m. Since I didn't eat breakfast, I slept as long as possible.

Today would be different.

I heard Dad go downstairs and grabbed Mom's phone, hurrying down the hall to their room. I stood next to the bed looking for a place to hide it. *Under the bed? Behind the dresser?* She'd think she knocked it off in the middle of the night and didn't check carefully. *Perfect.*

I placed it close to the back of the table so it would be hard to see if she had searched for it and raced back to my room. Someone came up the stairs as I settled into bed.

"I'll take a quick look around, Clair, before I go to work." Dad walked past my bedroom. "You're up early."

"Hi, Daddy. Homework." I pretended to be immersed in my laptop.

I heard him grumble as he went into the bedroom and a few minutes later, Dad strolled to the top of the stairs. "I found it, Clair. Now can you relax?"

Mom's voice came from the bottom of the stairs. "Doug just bought me that new phone, Jim. He'd never forgive me if I lost it. I'm so relieved you found it."

Oh, I just bet you are, Mom. Special Task Force Doug would not be too pleased that his inside contact lost her link to him. Just think how mad he'd be if he knew his little sister outsmarted him. I smiled to myself, picturing his face slowly turning a bright shade of red and smoke coming out of the top of his head. *Sorry, Doug, make that one for the good guys.*

CHAPTER FOURTEEN

Tonight I was just a teenager getting ready for a dance. What a relief not to worry about spies, Niners or the STF. Ashley came over early. We hung out for most of the afternoon trying different hair styles and make-up. After changing our minds countless times, we were finally ready.

We both had the perfect dress and admired ourselves in the full-length mirror one last time. Ashley's dress had a sweetheart neck and A-line skirt. She positively glowed in the short, purple tulle outfit. Nate's birthday present, a teardrop birthstone necklace, was a great addition to the dress.

My ice blue dress was strapless with a v-shaped jeweled notch in the center of the top. The empire waist gathered at the bust line and cascaded down into soft layers. The bracelet and necklace from Lucas were made to go with the dress. We both twirled around and hugged each other. The doorbell rang, signaling the boys had arrived.

Their faces lit up when we reached the bottom of the stairs. My dad just shook his head at how short the dresses were, but I didn't care. He kept silent and took the required photos. I couldn't wait to get in the car and drive away. I expected Doug to jump out of the bushes any minute and wanted to get as far away from the house as possible.

Nate drove us to the high school. As I slid in the backseat next to Lucas, I decided I should stop worrying and have some fun.

When we pulled in the school lot, I felt like I should head for class, but instead we posed for formal pictures. Music blared from the gym, and the halls were decorated with gold and green crepe paper and balloons. Green frogs wearing gold crowns smiled down at us from the walls. The theme, *Kiss a Frog to Find Your Prince*, became a fun take on Leap Year.

"Have you found yours?" Lucas whispered in my ear as he pointed to one of the leaping frogs.

"Yes, I don't have to look anymore." I squeezed his hand. "I'll be kissing that frog later tonight."

"I'll hold you to it."

We stepped into the gym and made the rounds, talking to a few people from English class then bumped into Josh and Chloe. Her white strapless dress had a glittery silver band across the top. Much shorter than mine, my dad's eyes would pop out of his head if he saw it. Chloe looked like she had spent extra time at the salon getting a spray tan and a white-blonde dye job. I could tell Ashley tried hard not to say a word. I could already hear her questions in my head. *Isn't she a little tan for this time of year? Is her hair white or blonde? And your dad thought our dresses were short?* We looked at each other and shook our heads, reading each other's thoughts. We made small talk then excused ourselves.

We headed for the dance floor and pushed through the crowd to find a spot to slow dance. When the music ended, we walked to the refreshment table and had our obligatory glass of punch.

Nate motioned for us to go out in the hall to find a place to sit. The spot he chose kept us out of the way of most of the traffic.

"I'm enjoying the frog theme," Nate said. "Never thought of myself as one, but now I'll never be able to forget those things." He gestured toward the wall. We laughed, and I imagined him as a frog still having all the expressions of his face.

"You'll never be a frog to me." Ashley patted his face. She gave him a quick kiss. "Still a boy. Now?" She stared at me with a twinkle in her hazel eyes. "Allie, kiss your frog."

Lucas and I became self-conscious, and as he leaned over I kissed him on the cheek.

"Not good enough!" Nate called out so loudly I thought the whole hallway heard.

Lucas took the initiative and kissed me on the lips. "Is Leap Year officially sealed with a kiss?" He glanced around at the group. We held our plastic cups in the air.

"To Leap Year," Nate toasted. "And thanks to this dance, all the ones in between."

Thank goodness for Leap Year or I'd never have met this wonderful guy sitting next to me. I raised my glass in honor of Nate's speech.

* * * *

After the dance, Nate dropped Lucas and me at the end of my driveway and continued on his way.

"How are you getting home?" I didn't care if Lucas could see in the dark, was stronger than any man or could hear someone coming a block away. I worried.

"Well, if you must know, I put in a call to Gene. He'll pick me up like a good grandfather."

"It must be hard to call him that." I dug in my bag for the house key.

Lucas put his hand over mine. "Let's not go in. This has been a perfect evening. I don't want it to end."

The night temperature grew colder, and the wind picked up. I only wore a light sweater over my dress. "Alright, where do you want to go?"

"You're freezing, aren't you?"

Lucas removed his suit jacket and wrapped it

around me. He put his arm over my shoulders and walked me back down the drive. A black stretch limo pulled up and stopped right in front of us. Lucas opened the door and ushered me inside.

"You had this planned all along, didn't you?"

He smiled as the window between the driver and the backseat slid down. Gene was at the wheel. "Where to?" He gave me a quick grin and waited for the command.

"Just drive around, Gene. If I need you, I'll let you know." The window rose up and shut. Lucas turned to me and kissed me lightly. "This is not what you think. I'm not going to seduce you." He teased. "I've got something to tell you."

My heart began to race. I tried to imagine what he would say, but I didn't have a good feeling. Was he leaving town? Did the STF find out about his family? Were we being tracked or was there a new bug on me? I preferred the seduction.

"Don't look so upset. It's good news."

I relaxed and sat back, sinking into the comfortable seat cushion. I made up my mind to enjoy the ride.

"Your mom's not a spy," Lucas said.

I bolted upright. Joy washed over me then overwhelming despair took its place. Someone was still out there giving the STF information. "How do you know?"

"Gene's been monitoring her phone. He sent me a message an hour ago. She made a call to your brother after we left, maybe right before she went to bed. It seems like she hasn't talked to him in awhile and scolded him for not calling her. She doesn't understand why she has to call him all the time. Then she was quiet for quite some time and finally said that something was hard to believe. We think that comment was about me. She told Doug we went to the dance with Nate and Ashley, what we wore and said it all seemed very innocent to her. She saw no cause for alarm."

"That's it?"

"Yes, except we have no idea what Doug told *her*. That phone has top of the line security. We give the credit to the five Niners who work for him. I've been in contact with Julian. I hope he can help figure out how to hack into the phone."

"Julian?"

"Oh, sorry, I feel like you should know him. He's the commander in charge of the Montana compound, been around since the 1800s."

"Which makes him in his forties?"

"Something like that."

Reality hit me like a ton of bricks. Julian could be over two hundred years old. How could I ever expect to be with Lucas or have a life with him? He had lived for eighty years already, but was just a babe in the woods compared to other Niners. I sighed too loudly and gazed out the window.

"Did I say something wrong?"

"No, just the opposite, you presented me with the truth. The cold hard facts are we'll never be together long term."

"Don't say that. I can see it happening."

"Only if I can find a good plastic surgeon," I said with an edge to my voice.

"Hey, don't talk like that. You'll be beautiful no matter what age you are."

I decided to change the subject. "So your leak's still out there. Any ideas?"

"Julian's investigating that, too."

"Where is Julian?"

"In a safe house in Pennsylvania. He's living openly in the community with his wife and kids."

Why did I bring Julian back into the conversation? I knew I had to ask the question. "Is this his first wife?"

Lucas hesitated. "No, his second."

"Second set of children?"

"Yes."

"What happened to his first wife?"

"She died."

"Of old age?"

"Yes."

"And his first set of children?"

"One has passed, the other's still living."

"Thanks for being honest with me." I went silent then had to ask, "So I'd be wife number one?"

Lucas smiled. "No, you'd be the only wife I'd ever have." He kissed me passionately, like the second time he kissed me, when I felt I'd never see him again.

If only he was right, if only that could be true. I'd hide for the rest of my life in Montana or Istanbul if he wanted. Everything seemed too good to be true, but nothing was easy or simple as Lucas made it out to be. Nothing.

CHAPTER FIFTEEN

I searched the house for birthday supplies, and rummaged through the drawer in the kitchen that held the assorted household junk. When I found the number candles from long-ago birthdays, I grabbed the two and a zero and a 'Happy Birthday' banner Mom kept on a closet shelf. I hid the items in a bag under my bed.

The Montgomerys didn't have to lift a finger, I'd do it all. Nate even helped and bought some black birthday plates and napkins sprinkled with colorful confetti.

I didn't hide the fact that I planned to go to the Montgomery's on this cold, gray March afternoon. Although I hadn't said we were back together, my parents suspected as much after the dance.

As I started to load the car, Nate ran across the front lawns. "Hey, Nate, what's up?"

"Ashley and I were invited to the party. We'll be coming over later. I finally get to see the motorcycle shrine." His eyes shone like a little boy at the holidays.

"I'm shocked."

"Shocked we're invited or shocked we're going."

"I'm surprised they're inviting anyone to the—"

"I'm not going to tell anyone where they live," Nate interrupted. "The Montgomerys are an interesting bunch. I'd wish they'd trust me a little more."

"I trust you for all of us." I hugged him and jumped in the Jeep. I waved as I drove away, thinking about the invite. Gene had probably run a background check on Nate and Ashley, too. My phone buzzed, and I pulled over to answer. "Lucas, I'm on my way."

"Did you hear I invited Nate and Ashley?"

"Yeah, he just told me."

"Do you think they'd be insulted if we ask them to park at the diner? We'll get them from there."

"No, not at all."

"If we blindfold them, will they?"

"What?" I screamed into the phone then took a breath to think. "Nate won't, but what will you tell Ash?"

"I need you to call her and feel her out. Can you do that?"

"Sure." I pulled back on the road after ending the call. When I got to school, I turned into the parking lot. My hand trembled as I speed-dialed her number. "Ash, it's me."

"Yep, I figured that out. Aren't you supposed to be with Lucas? Isn't it his birthday or something? What did you get him?"

"I'll tell you later. I'm on my way, but I have to ask you something."

"Go on."

"How would you feel about being blindfolded and driven to Lucas' house for his birthday?"

Laughter came from the other end. "Is this a sick joke or something?"

"No, it's serious. There's a reason no one can know where he lives, more for your safety than his."

"I always thought there was something up with the Loner, and now you're giving me my first clue. Are his parents running from the cops?"

"No."

"Are they wanted in six states?"

"Nothing criminal, I can assure you."

"And you know what it is."

"Yes."

"And you're not going to tell me."

"Maybe someday, but not now. Trust me?"

"You know I do. Blindfold away. See you later."

"You're a gem. Love you."

"Love you, too. Be careful though, Allie. Promise me."

"I promise." I had the best friends in the world.

I pulled out of the school lot and headed for Gilbert Road. I couldn't wait to get to the Montgomery house. Hannah would help decorate, and Joe would just slump in a chair and watch. The ride went by so fast; I arrived early. Hannah ran out to greet me and helped me with the bags.

"Mommy made a giant chocolate cake. Lucas' favorite!"

Joe held the door open. "Hi."

"Where's the old man?" I asked.

His eyes danced with laughter, but I only got a slight smile. "He's getting all fancied up for you," he said with a straight face.

That young boy had the weight of the world on his shoulders and bore it well. He shrugged everything off. Maybe I didn't notice before. Joe wasn't mad at the world. He accepted his place in it.

Lucas made an appearance when we reached the library. "Allie!" He came up and hugged me in front of his brother and sister, something they were used to now.

Hannah unpacked the decorations and found the number candles. "I'm putting these on the cake!" She held them high in the air.

"Make sure you put them in the right order," Lucas called after her. "Don't want to be oh-two." He took my hand and led me to the kitchen. Stacy was frosting the cake as Hannah tried to set the candles in place.

"Doesn't Hannah think it's odd you're twenty?" I whispered to Lucas.

"She knows I was home schooled and thinks I'm behind because of that. Little does she know I've been pulling off fifteen, sixteen and now seventeen for years. Although, I'll be just the right age for college. I'll turn twenty-one while I'm there."

"You have this all planned out, don't you?"

"Yes. I started to look at colleges. That's when I plan to make my break from them." He nodded towards his family.

"They have to let you live on campus, won't they?"

"They can't follow me if I'm in a dorm."

"They could move to the town."

"I won't let them. Joe and Hannah are happy here."

"So you want them to stay in the safe house and not go back to Montana?"

"It's their choice. Knowing Sam, he'd stay for his kids. They like it here. Stacy would choose to move back to be closer to her family."

I watched Stacy put chocolate frosting on her daughter's nose with the spatula. She had made a lot of sacrifices for the family. I admired her for that.

Gene walked into the kitchen. I received a bear hug from him. We had grown closer over the months. I felt like he was a brother to me, too. Sam came in behind him and nodded, still not fond of the situation. I felt he saw me as a liability.

I wanted to give Lucas his present in private so I steered him back to the library where I left his gift. I grabbed the silver and black bag and handed it to him. We sat down on the caramel color leather sofa, and I played with my fingers as waited for his reaction.

What if he doesn't like it? What if he thinks it's stupid? I began to question my choice, not so much the gift but what I did to it.

Lucas pulled the tissue from the bag and reached in to find the box at the bottom. As he flipped open the top, I held my breath. He blinked as if to hold back tears.

"Do you like it? You think it's silly, don't you?"

"I love it, Allie. I'll wear it always." He slipped the silver ID bracelet from its holder and gazed at the engraving. "How'd you think of this?"

I had two initials engraved in the bracelet—LA, Lucas, Allison. I wanted to put our birthstones on either side but Nate talked me out of it. I watched as Lucas snapped it on his wrist, thrilled he liked it.

"Thank you." He kissed me, and I melted into him.

"Ew!" Hannah held up her hands in front of her face. "Grandpa says it's time to get your friends."

"Thanks, Han." Lucas popped up and pulled me up with him. He exited through the door leading to the porch, and I headed for the kitchen.

"Stacy? Anything I can do to help?"

"Talk to me, tell me about the dance. You know my son. He's a man of few words."

Not with me he isn't. I guess boys and their mothers don't share all their secrets. I happily recounted all the details—what we wore and the frog theme.

"That sounds so cute." She handed me a bread basket to take to the dining room. "Now I get to meet your friends in just a few minutes. I've been trying to picture them in my mind."

"Ashley has some pictures from the dance on her phone. She can show you."

"I'd love that."

The front door swung open, and Lucas escorted Nate and Ashley into the house. Ashley rubbed her eyes and glanced around, taking in the décor. Nate didn't seem to care. He strolled across the room and stared out the picture window, probably thinking about all those motorcycles in the barn.

"You made it." I ran to Ash and took her by the arm. I introduced her and Nate to Stacy and the kids.

"Everyone, dinner's ready." Stacy announced from the kitchen. Sam went to help, and Gene steered us to the huge dining table.

After dinner, I said, "Gene, you need to tell Nate about your bike collection."

"I can do better than that. I can show him." Gene got up from the table. "Stacy, wonderful dinner. I'll be looking forward to that cake." Gene motioned for Nate to follow.

"Dad, let's join them." Lucas tapped Sam on the shoulder.

"Jonas, you should go, too." Stacy urged him from the table.

He grudgingly followed, leaving us girls behind.

"This is nice." Stacy smiled at us. "I have three sisters back home, and this is a nice reminder."

We chatted as Ashley showed the pictures from the dance. Stacy stopped her when she reached the one of Chloe and Josh.

Stacy raised her eyebrows. "Skirt's a little short."

We heard the roar of motorbikes over our laughter. Getting up, we headed for the front porch and saw five bikes roll out of the barn. The caravan pulled up to an asphalt path in the woods.

"Well, Nate should be happy." Ashley chuckled.

"Do you girls drink coffee? Tea?" Stacy asked. "I'm going to get some ready to have with the cake. Gene has to have his mug of coffee with his chocolate."

"Coffee's fine," I answered.

The sun had just set when the guys came back from their ride. Nate was in a deep conversation with Gene as they walked into the house. It seemed as if his wish came true, to be accepted by the pack.

As we gathered around the table, Lucas insisted we didn't sing as he cut the cake. He passed around huge pieces. Everyone told him to make them smaller, but he sliced them bigger and bigger.

Hannah giggled, and even Joe had to smile, as Lucas gave him the largest piece. I loved this family. I looked at all the faces at the table and knew I could do this forever. Then I stared at my two best friends. They'd probably be erased from the picture if I joined the family. I had to ask myself, could I do it without them?

* * * *

Lucas and I sat alone in the great room after the party ended, and Nate and Ashley had left. A scowl crossed his face.

"What's wrong?" I asked as I reached for his hand.

"Nothing's wrong." He grimaced. "Everything's wrong," he growled as he pulled his hand back and punched the sofa cushion. I flinched and leaned away. "Allie," his voice softened, "I didn't mean to scare you. This has nothing to do with you or today."

"Then what?"

"I'm tired of pretending. The birthday reminded me of what I am, what I'm doing. Pretending. I've lived a long life and should be nearing the end of my years like Gene. But here I am, still young and kicking!" He half-laughed and rubbed his hand over his face. "Soon I'll lose everyone and be left on earth all alone."

"Lucas! That's not true. You have Sam and Hannah—"

"Then what? Their kids take over? Everyone I know will be gone. Don't you get it?"

I searched for the right words but none came.

"Allie, I can live almost six hundred years. Do you know how long that is? Niners are a healthy bunch. We don't get sick. The youngest recorded death was ninety-eight years of age. That's Niner time."

I did the math in my head. "In reality, three hundred and ninety-two years."

"Exactly. Can you wrap your mind around that? Picture how many generations of family I will see die."

"Lucas, try to stay in the here and now. You have me, your family. You're very lucky."

"If only we could stay young together." He wrapped his arms around me, pulling me closer.

My heart fluttered. "If only."

"Now that I've found you, I couldn't be happier. No, wait." Lucas raised his finger. "Make that the happiest I've been in my life. One giant obstacle stands between us. I'm a wanted man. I'll always be a wanted man."

"Because of my brother." I hung my head, tears filled my eyes.

Lucas' hand lifted my chin. "If not him, someone else. Don't blame yourself. The Niners can't easily hide in plain sight anymore. It's becoming more difficult. The advances made in surveillance, technology, and tracking are growing by leaps and bounds. I'm starting to think the only place Niners are safe are in the compounds."

I never heard Lucas talk that way before. To me, he was a teenage boy I met at school and suddenly it sank in how foolish I'd been. The seriousness of our situation overwhelmed me. "So what are you saying?"

"Part of me wants to turn myself over to Doug and be done with it. Maybe you and I could still be together."

I gasped. "No!"

"The other part of me wants to fight, and prove the good guys can win."

"Then let's fight. I don't trust Doug." I've been leaning more and more toward the Niner side. "I want the good guys to win. From what you've told me, the Niners are a great bunch of men who only want what's best for others."

"Yeah, for all the good it does. We need to toughen up. We've been sequestered for too long, manipulating our destiny from a safe haven."

"So in our world, it's good versus evil."

"That's one way to look at it. I'm sure your brother feels he's on the side of righteousness. Damn, Allie! What am I going to do?"

"Right now she's getting her ass in the car." Gene's voice boomed from behind us. I never heard him talk like that before. "I'm sorry, Allie. Just head for home."

My heart pounded as I scrambled for the door. "Why? Can you at least tell me that?" I looked back over my shoulder, confused as to what just happened. His reddening face said it all—concern, anger, shock.

"We just got word. The STF is in the neighborhood. I need to power down and engage the emergency safety system. Our cloak is always up, but I want to be safe. You need to be far away from here."

Rushing out the door, I pulled the night air into my

lungs. I tried to breathe slowly and calm down. My head ached. *How can I drive?* My hands trembled as I started the car and maneuvered down the drive. My foot pressed down on the gas pedal, and I flew out onto the main road. Faster and faster, I pushed the car to its limits. The diner went by in a blur. The three way stop at Gilbert Road came into view. My brain told me I needed to get home, the sooner the better. Doug would show up, and I needed to be ready.

Without thinking, I pulled into the school lot instead of passing by. I had to regain my sanity for the rest of the drive home. A streetlight shone above me. I gazed up.

"What just happened?" I asked as I rubbed my forehead. I closed my eyes and concentrated, going over the events leading up to this minute. "No!" I yelled. "It can't be." I slammed my hands on the steering wheel. I screamed and cried, pounding the wheel over and over. We trusted my friends and now one had betrayed us. It made perfect sense now.

"Nate! You traitor!"

* * * *

I rolled into a tiny ball on my bed sorting through the past hours. Nate had figured a way to pinpoint the location of the safe house and passed the information to my brother when he got home. That had to be it. When I put the final pieces in place I would contact Lucas. Gene had the house shut down, and I couldn't take the chance now.

My bedroom door flew open. "Allison!" The sound of that voice made my unwilling body sit straight at attention. Doug stood before me, eyes blazing. "Where have you been?"

"A birthday party?" I tried to sound sarcastic even

as my heart pounded so loudly I swore he could hear it.

"For who? The ex?"

"Maybe?"

He sat on the edge of the bed so we were face to face. I scooted away from him to avoid any bruising. "Allison, sweetie, this is for your own good. Tell me where you were."

I gagged on my words and couldn't speak. He called me "sweetie" almost like he meant it. My brain had stopped functioning, and I scrambled to find an answer. "I was at a diner."

"The one off Gilbert? That thing's been deserted for years. There's nothing out there anymore."

"Well, it's back up and running. Maybe you better brush up on your hometown, Doug."

"How many at the party? Anyone you never saw before?"

"Probably twenty kids, six aliens—I think they were green or maybe one was purple—and a couple vampires." I couldn't resist the vampire reference.

"Very funny."

"You should arrest those vamps. They only come out at night." My body fought exhaustion, but I could keep it up for as long as he could. Doug wouldn't break me, not tonight.

"Look, I'm going to tell you a secret." He edged closer. "Something even Mom and Pop don't know. You have to swear you won't tell anyone."

He played the good cop tonight. I almost bought the act, but stopped myself from saying anything. I waited for him to continue. "You know I work for a special unit at the Pentagon."

"Top secret." I placed my index finger over my lips.

"Right. But I'm going to share something with you. It's about The Bomb."

That made me sit up straighter. "*Thee* Bomb?" I had no idea what he was talking about.

"Are you giving me your teenage crap or are you really interested?" His mask began to slip.

"No, I'm serious. Do you mean the nuclear bomb?" I finally figured out what he meant.

"Yes. Picture having an antidote, being able to diffuse it. Our country would be safe. No one could threaten us again. We'd be in control of the world."

Doug had my attention. "Go on."

"There might be a way to do this. I ... we ... need all the help we can get. So you see, what I'm asking? You need to go beyond your civic duty, patriotism or family loyalty. You could help save many people's lives. It's not a bad thing I'm doing, Allison." He folded his hands in his lap. "Please help me."

I almost believed him except for the fact that Doug hadn't told me one thing about the Niners or what part they played in his scheme. "How?"

He pulled the card from his chest pocket. "Remember this?"

"Roman numerals can help you?"

"No, but the people with this tattoo can."

"Oh." I acted like I finally got it. "I'm supposed to frisk people at my high school looking for that symbol."

"Very funny. It's a little easier than that. It's always on the arch of their right foot."

"It's March, Doug. Everyone wears shoes."

"It'll warm up soon. Just be on the lookout."

"I still don't understand how they can help."

"Well, let's just say it's a mark of a highly intelligent group of people. Sort of like MENSA."

"What's that?" I wrinkled my nose.

"A society for people with IQ's over 130, only these men are much smarter."

"So because I'm in AP classes, I'll be able to spot them. Okay, I'll keep an eye out." Not really, but I wanted Doug out of my bedroom. Maybe he'd back off. What was I thinking? He suspected Lucas and hoped I'd turn him in.

"That's all I ask, little sister." He placed his hand on my arm. It felt cool to the touch. Maybe he was the real vampire. I shivered, but he didn't notice.

"Since we're being truthful here, Doug, why don't you tell me what you have against me? I never did anything to you."

Doug sighed and leaned back. "Well, if you must know, the year Mom found out she was pregnant, we planned a trip of a lifetime out west, hiking, camping, you name it. All the things guys love to do. We'd be gone for six weeks that summer, but of course, everything was cancelled because of you."

That still didn't seem like the real reason. "What about the next year, after I was born?"

"Take a seven-month-old on that kind of trip? Mom wouldn't leave you behind and Dad wouldn't go without her. Plus they used most of the money saved on girly baby stuff."

"Sorry, but that's the lamest excuse I ever heard. Don't you think you're way too old to hold onto that kind of grudge?"

"You're right. That was a long time ago. Over. Done." Doug stood and straightened his jacket. "Friends?" He stuck out his hand.

Mine trembled, and I fought to keep it steady. I looked at him for a few moments then decided to offer my hand. "Friends." I felt his grip tighten around my palm, almost too hard.

"Well, good night then." He strode toward the door, back straight, feet in precise movement. Before he closed my door, he turned and winked. "It was quite a productive talk."

I felt sick to my stomach, and my head hurt. "Productive talk?" I threw myself into the pillows. "What just happened? I think I'm more confused than ever."

CHAPTER SIXTEEN

March faded slowly into spring. The Virginia bluebell started to appear. Its sky-blue blooms dotted the forest as Lucas and I walked along the path to retrieve his bike.

"Spring vacation is two weeks away. Should we take another trip to the beach?" He squeezed my hand.

I shivered, remembering the only time we visited. "Not the best of times, if I remember correctly."

"We deserve a do-over, don't you think?" Lucas wrapped his arm around my shoulders and pulled me to him. "In a way, aren't you glad you know everything? It all worked out. Your mom's not a spy. I think she got Doug to back off. What more can we hope for?"

"To find the leak. The person's still out there." I couldn't bring myself to tell Lucas my suspicions. Nate had become his best friend. How could I hurt him? So instead, I planned to watch Nate's every move and prove myself wrong.

"We're no closer. I don't understand why. Julian's passing all his information on to Levi for another look. See if we're missing anything."

"Levi?"

"The regional commander for the western states. He lives in the Napa Valley compound. He's been alive for two-hundred years."

"So that makes him fifty." I'd grown used to dividing and multiplying everything by four but still had a hard time with all the numbers spinning in my head.

"He's like Julian's big brother. Just like Julian is mine."

Even if he seemed like a brother, Lucas called him

a commander. That sounded like an army to me, causing doubts to rise up. How could I ever learn the truth? Maybe another trip to the Outer Banks would help. We could discuss the chain of command and what the Niners' goals were. "I'll give Dean a call and see if he's going to be home. I haven't seen him since Christmas."

In front of family and friends, he had given Autumn an engagement ring on Christmas Eve. Whenever the marriage took place, I would be the maid of honor.

As we walked through the woods, I admired the spring scenery—flowering trees, wildflowers awakening, the leaf buds on the trees—the sense of a new beginning. Lucas took me on a short ride to enjoy all its wonders. He worked on the path ahead of time, checking for potholes that might have sprung up during the winter and removed brush and debris. We swung back onto the main path and out to the Jeep, parked in its usual spot.

"Two more weeks!" He held up his fingers. "Then freedom. We deserve it."

"I thought you liked school."

"I do, but I've had enough."

"You could complete all these classes in a week's time, Lucas. In fact, you could already be in college. Have you made your decision yet?"

"Wherever you go."

"Seriously, have you picked a college?"

"I have it narrowed down. I was thinking Yale or Harvard."

"Well, excuse me! You'll be going there on your own. I'll never get in."

"Don't sell yourself short. But if you don't get

accepted? We could get you in."

"We? You never told me you had that kind of power."

"Computers can do a lot of things if you know how to use them, Allie."

"What else haven't you told me?"

"Transporters."

"What?" My jaw dropped.

"Have you seen that old television show where they transport people from one place to another?"

"No, but I've heard about it from Nate. He's into sci-fi." I took Lucas' hand as we strolled along the path.

"In that show, they use a transporter. People materialize in a location set by the ship's computer and can be transported back to the spaceship the same way. I can't believe you never saw that show. It's a classic. How about the movies?"

"Okay, it's coming to me. I did see one movie based on the show." I never liked science fiction, but realized I lived in the middle of it now.

"We perfected sending objects through space. People are next."

"I wouldn't want to be that guinea pig."

We reached the car, and Lucas rested his hand on the hood as he continued. "I agree, but we have volunteers lined up to try."

I leaned back on the Jeep next to him, eyes wide. "Some people volunteer even when they know there's a risk?"

"Some old timers are making it known they'd be the first to try it out."

"I think no matter how long you live, you'd want to keep on living."

"When you've watched generations of family and

friends leave this earth before you, it can be hard. I've yet to experience the full effect. As you know, I'm dreading it. Some say you never know the feeling until you experience a few centuries. We're a healthy bunch, remember. We have to die of old age. The old timers are willing to take that chance."

"You said someone died at ninety-eight." I did the math in my head. "That was three-hundred and ninety-two years."

"We usually live longer. He was an exception. At the Montana compound one old chap just passed away at one-hundred and five. Still on the young side."

"He lived sixty years longer. So he was born in the 1600s?"

"Yeah, he migrated here when the Niners made their first voyage in the early 1800s. They knew they needed to start compounds to protect the boys born in America. Abraham was a very interesting, insightful man. He saw all kinds of things during his life span. His family lived in the Netherlands. When he was an infant his father commissioned a family portrait painted by Rembrandt."

"*Thee* Rembrandt?"

"Yep, he started out as an Amsterdam portrait artist. The Dutch had become famous for their work in that century."

"Does the portrait still exist?"

"It's in our archives museum. Abe donated it before he died."

"I can just imagine what else is in that museum." I always loved the arts and decided it would be my major in college.

"I hope you can see it one day. I can't begin to tell you what's there."

"So how did Abe end up with the Niners?"

"Word spreads, even back then. People noticed he wasn't growing properly and began to talk. Luckily, the Niners heard about him and came to the family. They suggested they say Abe had died. The Niners would raise him, provide for him. Of course, provisions were made for the family to still see him. Abe was like a real grandfather to me. He told me what to expect as I aged and how I would feel, always using his past as an example. His stories were fascinating. I could listen to him all day. He watched the world change for centuries."

I didn't know what to say. I tried to imagine what it was like to live over four hundred years and how I would change in that time. The world was so different than when Abe was born.

"I should be going. Thanks for sharing." I gave Lucas a quick kiss and jumped in the Jeep to head for home.

"Hey."

I stuck my head out the window. "What?"

"Just this." He ran around to the driver side and gave me a kiss. I took in the fragrance of the outdoors as our lips found each other. My stomach flipped over as I pulled away.

"I love you," he said as he patted the doorframe and strolled toward the woods. I had to watch until he disappeared from sight.

As I pulled in the drive, I saw the dreaded black SUV parked in front of the garage. *What's he doing here? It's no one's birthday, no holiday. Is it interrogation time again?*

I slid from of the car, debating whether to face Doug sooner or later. I walked through the garage and into the kitchen, hoping Mom didn't notice.

"We're in the family room, Allie!" she called.

Darn! Does she have super power hearing now?

It dawned on me that Mom had her phone in her pocket or nearby. Lucas or Gene listened to everything she said, which meant they also heard the people around her. I made a mental note to be careful what I said when we talked. But Doug, he had no idea. Maybe he told Mom something they could use.

I slipped out my phone and sent a text to Lucas: *Doug's here.*

Within a minute, I got an answer: *I know.* I felt a little safer walking into the family room.

"Hey, Doug." I gave him an air hug and grabbed a handful of cookies from a tray on the table. I settled in next to Mom on the sofa.

"Aren't you going to ruin your dinner eating all those?" Good old Doug couldn't resist reprimanding me.

"She could stand to put on a few pounds, Doug. Look at her." Mom defended me. I sat back to watch the show.

"Mom, I'm just trying to help."

I got a text: *How many cookies are you eating?* I couldn't help laughing and spit out some crumbs onto my shirt. Doug clenched his hands into fists. Irritating him was too easy, but I enjoyed every minute.

"Want me to get you a bottle of water, dear?" I could only nod my answer. Mom scurried into the kitchen. Doug glared at me but said nothing.

When Mom returned, she removed the top and handed me the bottle. I saw Doug roll his eyes. I would make this up to Mom. I felt bad using her but had to take advantage of the situation.

As I took a sip, I let some dribble out the corner of

my mouth. Mom handed me a napkin. Doug did everything in his power to stay calm in front of her.

"So just passing through, Doug?" I decided to stop torturing him.

"Yes, I stopped by to see Mom. She's having problems with the new phone I got her."

"When did you get her that phone? I don't remember you giving it to her at Christmas or even her birthday."

"Oh, Allie, don't you remember Doug's visit on your first day of school? He dropped it off then. He said mine was getting old, and I needed all these new features." Mom paused. "And I still don't use them, Doug. I don't know why you wasted the money."

I thought back to that day and remembered it felt strange that Doug had come for a visit. He had brought Mom the phone and tried to explain all the ins and outs to make sure she used it. He wanted to grill me next, but Ashley showed up.

"Not a waste of money, you'll learn how to use it, Mom. Allie can help you." Doug turned to me. "I can't believe you're almost done with junior year. It's gone fast. Have you made any new friends? Or is Lucas still taking up all your time?"

"I like to hang out with Lucas and my usual friends."

"Nate has good computer skills, doesn't he?"

"He's always been good, that's nothing new." *Why is Doug asking about Nate? If Nate worked for him, would Doug make it so obvious?*

"I might have to recruit that kid. Where did you say Lucas lived?"

What? "I didn't." Now I started to get nervous. My phone rang, startling me. "I have to get this."

"Thanks for the save." I whispered to Lucas as I headed up the stairs, closing my bedroom door behind me.

"He's still fishing, Allie. He asked your mom a lot of questions before you got home. He's got nothing, but I'm worried he's beginning to suspect Nate of something."

"I'll warn him," I said with mixed feelings, but my love for Nate won out. He couldn't be the leak.

"Tell him to stop whatever he's doing for the time being."

"Okay, talk to you later." I hung up and dialed Nate.

"What?"

"Nice greeting."

"Hello, Allie dearest, what can I help you with today? Is that better?"

"Knock it off and listen. Doug's here. He's asking about you."

"That was sweet of him."

"Can you be serious for a moment? Lucas said he thinks Doug's suspicious because you're doing something on that computer of yours."

"Go on. I'm listening."

"I finally have your attention? Good! We have no idea what Doug knows or how much he knows. We just want to keep it that way."

"Understood, I'm disabling now."

"Disabling what?"

"Never mind."

"Nate, you can be so frustrating at times."

"Done."

"Now be a good boy and lay low until this blows over, whatever *it* is. Have I told you I hate Doug?"

"Not in a couple weeks, Allison."

"Thanks, Nate. You know I love you like a brother."

"Same here. Only not as a brother. Well, you know what I mean."

Yes, I did know what he meant. We had to watch each other's backs. I felt better after talking to him. I didn't trust Doug. His visit meant he was up to something. Whatever it was, I didn't have a clue.

* * * *

Spring Break was just a week away. Dean gave us the green light to come to the Outer Banks. The excitement of a brief vacation kept me going through those last days of school. Ashley and I shopped for summer clothes and visited the bookstore so I'd have something to read on the beach. Little did she know, I had no intention of reading, I planned on spending every waking moment with Lucas. I let her pick out a few books for me, nodding in agreement as she held them up.

On Friday before break, the final countdown began. When the bell rang, I rushed for my car and sped home. I packed my bag and went over last minute details. Lucas wanted me to pick him up at the diner. I hadn't talked to him since first period, but he had last minute arrangements, too.

After kissing Mom and Dad goodbye and reassuring them I'd drive carefully, I ran for the Jeep. As I drove by the school, I felt relieved I didn't have to pull into that parking lot for a whole week. I drove past our woods and smiled as I recalled all the memories made there.

Gilbert Road felt like an old friend. I came to the three-way stop and made my left turn. My heart beat fast as I turned into the diner. I couldn't wait to see Lucas and get on the highway. A few cars were parked in the large gravel lot.

I felt like skipping, freedom felt so good. When I reached the door, I saw a large, muscular man, early thirties, behind the counter. Surprised, I thought only the Montgomery family worked at the diner. Maybe they hired someone to help out in Lucas' absence.

"Hi," I said to the burly man sporting a day's worth of beard and shaved head. He was handsome but scary at the same time. "Is Lucas here?"

"Who?"

"Lucas Montgomery."

"Never heard of him, missy."

My heart began to pound. I must be dreaming and would wake up to see Sam standing there in place of this man, and Stacy cooking at the grill. "His family owns this restaurant."

"That's news to me. This here is my diner."

"For how long?"

"Going on three years now."

I stood helpless, looking at him for any clue, any sign it could be a joke. His eyes gave me an empty stare. "Thanks." I gulped almost choking on the lump in my throat. "If Lucas shows up can you tell him Allie was here?"

"Sure kid, Addie. No problem," he said as he wiped down the counter.

"No, Allie."

"Whatever." He didn't look up.

Stunned, I walked back to the Jeep and sat in my car, staring at the diner. "What just happened in there? Where is everyone?"

I started the car and headed for the road, only I

didn't turn left, I went in the opposite direction. With a new found sense of urgency, I flew down the street and into the Montgomery driveway, speeding toward the house. There had to be an explanation. I would get one as soon as I reached the house. I parked by the barn, jumped out and banged on the front door. "Lucas! Lucas, are you in there?"

The house looked dark inside, and the door wouldn't open when I tried the handle. The screen door to the front porch was locked as well. Running to the barn, I tried to slide back the door but it wouldn't budge. Frustrated, I let out a scream.

I ran to the back deck and peered in the huge dining room window. The furniture was there but nothing else. No children's toys strewn about or jackets thrown on backs of chairs. The house seemed spotless, wiped clean. I sank to the ground and began to sob.

"Lucas, where are you?" I yelled, hoping my voice would soar out over the gorge and reach him. I pounded on the sliding glass doors, hoping to be let in. "Where did you all go?" My hand slid along the glass, leaving a smudged trail behind.

I leaned against the glass, staring out at the gorge in a trance. *Think!* My mind fought the command. I swiped at the tears that rolled down my cheeks. *Get it together!* My nose ran. I couldn't stop crying. I sniffed and grabbed my bag to find a tissue. *That's it!*

I dug for my phone, chastising myself for not thinking of it sooner. *Make a call, my last ray of hope.* My hand trembled as I hit the speed dial key. As I listened for his voice, I heard a message say the number was disconnected. That made no sense so I called Nate. He picked up instantly.

"Nate!" The whole story poured out.

"Slow down, Allie, I only got part of that. Where are you? I'm coming to get you."

"No, that's okay. I'm going home." I hesitated. "No, I'm coming over. Are your parents at work?" Despite my misgivings, Nate was still my best friend. I needed him.

"Yeah, you okay to drive?"

"I think so."

I wiped my eyes and nose on the back of my arm and stood. The sun shone brightly, and the gorge view would be beautiful on any other day. Instead I saw it through a haze of tears. I made my way to the car, drove out of the woods with no idea how I made it to Nate's house.

Nate had the garage door open as I pulled in. He was waiting in the kitchen, and I ran into his open arms.

"This makes no sense, Allie. You say his phone's disconnected? That phone is his lifeline."

Lucas could track people and had connections to all the Niners throughout the world. Nate was right. How could it be disconnected?

"Do you think he's trying to make me think there's no way to find him?"

"Maybe. I did an investigation of my own. I called him and got the same message. It makes no sense. He'd never give up his tracking device."

"That's it! Thank you, Nate." I threw my arms around him and gave him the biggest hug.

"What for? I didn't do anything."

"Yes, you did. You reminded me of something. Wish me luck!"

I ran to the Jeep and backed out of the garage and down the drive. I knew exactly how to find Lucas or should I say he'd find me. He told me once if I came to our woods, he would find me.

Not holding back on the gas pedal, I arrived at school in record time. I parked in front of the soccer field and ran faster than I ever had to the main path in our woods. I stopped at the brush pile to wait for his arrival. He would come for me.

I dug in the brush to check for his bike. He could be here already. It turned out to be just the pile of brush and leaves. I wandered up and down the paths looking for clues or signs of him. As I did, the day started to cloud over.

The forest no longer had rays of sun peeking through the leaves of the trees. A strong wind gust sent dry vegetation swirling around my feet. The temperature dropped a few degrees. I wrapped my arms around my body for warmth and continued to pace. A drop of rain hit my hand then another. Dark clouds rolled in, and a clap of thunder startled me.

"I can wait you out, storm!" I yelled up at the sky. The leaves seemed to laugh as they rustled louder in the stronger winds. Rain started to find its way through the canopy of trees. I wept as I got pelted by the large drops. The storm grew in intensity. Sheets of water poured down on me. Determined to win the fight, I huddled under a tree, shivering.

"Please, Lucas, please come for me," I whispered. I didn't know if I stopped crying or not with all the water running down my face. Exhaustion swept over me, draining me of my courage. I slid down the tree trunk and sat in a tight ball with my arms wrapped around my knees. A jumble of emotions swirled inside me as the surrounding elements pounded my skin—the howling wind, the relentless rain.

I had to blink the water from my eyes but thought

I saw a figure running down the path. My heart soared. I didn't feel cold or wet anymore. I knew he would come. He'd explain everything. The rain parka he wore hid his face, but I could picture his smile, the one I loved. He came for me, just as promised. In one hand he carried another parka for me.

"Allie! Are you crazy? What are you still doing here?"

I looked up into Nate's face and screamed. I couldn't stop the hysterics. I felt as if I was possessed. Nate gathered me into his arms as I pounded his chest, calling out Lucas' name over and over. He guided me back to his car and placed me inside.

The car's heater blew hot air full force. Its warmth helped calm me. I rested my head back, feeling water trickle down my back. My wet hair dripped onto Nate's car seats. I sat staring out the front window for the longest time. I could feel my heart slow and found my voice. "Sorry, I'm getting everything wet."

"Don't worry about it. Here." Nate handed me a cup of coffee, my favorite, caramel latte.

"How did you know I'd be here?" I sipped from the cup, trying to focus.

"It wasn't that hard."

"He promised he'd always find me."

"Sometimes we can't keep those promises."

"Stop being so profound." I stared at the cup in my hands, holding on tightly for warmth.

"Okay, then let's get you home."

"I'm not going home."

"Please tell me you're not going to look for him. Are you?"

"Nope, they're smarter than us and always one step ahead."

"Make that two steps."

"Nate, I'm not in the mood for jokes."

"Well, where are you going then?"

"To Dean's. I need time to think. I need to get away from here."

Nate took my chin in his hand and gently turned my head so we looked into each other's eyes. "Drive safely, little one."

The rain stopped as suddenly as it started. I jumped out of Nate's car and into my own. I headed for the highway and the safety of Dean's home.

CHAPTER SEVENTEEN

I sat in the Jeep staring at the high school, afraid to exit the car. I dreaded walking in today. Ashley and Nate promised to meet me in the parking lot and threatened to carry me in if they had to.

The week I spent at Dean's hadn't helped. I sat staring out at the ocean most of the time. He did run interference for me, calling Mom and Dad to let them know what happened. He also instructed them not to ask questions and let me talk when ready. I came to a conclusion on that beach—life would be simpler if I dated Josh again. Sure there'd be problems but they'd be typical high school couple problems. One underlying question remained. Could I jump into this relationship after being hurt by both Josh and Lucas? Was I crazy?

I sent Josh a text over break. His words made me feel better. He had been patient; reassuring me that he only took Chloe to the Leap Year dance as a favor. He ended things long ago. I made arrangements to meet him after English at my locker.

So why did I feel so nauseated? A panic attack set in as I clung to the steering wheel. I could sit in the car all day and not move. A tap on the window startled me back to reality. I saw Ashley's smiling face pressed up against the glass, her nose a little squashed.

"Come out!" She motioned to open the door. "Or we'll drag you in. Are you still going ahead with your plan to meet Josh?"

"Yep." I slid out of the driver's seat. A shiver went through me. Lucas met me here for the past three months. I coughed and pounded on my chest.

"You okay?" Nate grabbed my arm.

"Fine, I'm fine. Let's get this over with."

We walked to the school, Ashley on one side; Nate on the other. They took me to homeroom and deposited me at the door. Somehow I made my way to English. Lucas' empty desk mocked me as I passed by. Tears pricked my eyes. As class began, I couldn't stop staring at the desk in front of me. I had no idea what Mrs. Greene taught today. The bell rang and Ashley waited for me outside of class.

"Bookstore tonight?" She flashed a bright smile. "Walk you to your locker? Do you want me to wait until Josh shows up?"

"Sure." I hoped that answered everything.

Ash opened my locker and helped me put away the English folder. I stood numbly by as she found what I needed for the next few classes. "He's coming," she hissed. I wasn't sure if she approved, but her eyes said she was supportive. "Hey, Josh."

"Ash, good to see you. Al, you're looking good after your visit to the beach."

"Thanks." I made eye contact with Ashley giving her permission to leave.

"So, you think you want to try again?" Josh seemed nervous. I found it kind of cute. He could be the new and improved Josh, except for calling me Al. I had time to work on that.

"Let's see where this goes," I said.

"Fine with me. How about if we meet here all week? Then I'll see you in history. And you have to promise to save Friday and Saturday nights for me."

I watched his lips move without really absorbing what he said. It seemed like we had just been in a race car and zipped around the track full speed. My head spun as I said, "Okay."

"You pick a movie, any movie you want, for Friday," Josh said.

"So!" A booming voice came from behind us. "You finally got him back. You've been trying all year to steal him away, and you finally succeeded."

We both turned to see a raging Chloe standing in the middle of the hall with three other girls who also had the look of mock outrage on their faces. Chloe held up one hand, wiggling her finger at us. It brought out an inner fire, and I couldn't hold back.

"Yep, that's what I was trying to do, Chloe, and it worked." I slammed my locker and walked away. One of the dumbest confrontations I had in high school yet. How could she think I stole Josh when I was with Lucas? Was Josh lying to me about breaking up with her months ago? I needed some answers and planned to get them this weekend.

* * * *

"Good to see you again, Josh!" My father's voice traveled up the stairs.

"Nice to see you, Mr. Sanders." Josh looked up when he spotted me on the steps. "Al, you look … beautiful."

A rush of warmth rose up my neck and into my cheeks. *Argh! I'm blushing. I don't want to!*

Josh wasn't hard on the eyes either with his blonde hair cut to perfection and sparkling blue eyes. Everyone said we made the perfect couple. Even though he looked great, I felt nothing.

"You kids have fun!" Mom called from the family room.

"Did you pick a movie?" Josh helped me into the car, a first for him.

"Yeah, some comedy. Is that alright?"

"Comedy's are good."

I didn't remember much about the movie but recalled laughing a few times. Josh reached for my hand, and I let him. I listed pros and cons of the relationship in my head as I watched the screen, trying to convince myself I did the right thing. My parents were thrilled, Ashley accepted it, kids at school commented it was just a matter of time and even Doug put his two cents in. He said he approved during one of Mom's phone calls.

After the movie, we ended up at a fast food restaurant where all the high school kids hung out. We sat in a booth, and occasionally someone came over to visit. I swore I saw Chloe on the other side of the room making out with some guy.

"Is that?" I pointed to the couple in a corner booth.

"Chloe? Yeah, she's trying to make me jealous."

"Are you?"

"Not in the least. Ready to go?" Josh hopped up and helped me on with my coat. As we headed for the door, I thought I saw Chloe push the guy away and cross her arms, staring daggers at us.

Josh made small talk on the way home. I barely heard what he said. I kept feeling as if I made this all happen. It didn't feel right. He turned in my drive, quickly shifted into park and pulled me over to him. "Remember how many times we wished I could drive and have a moment like this? Well, now we can."

He kissed me, and it felt familiar. I responded by returning the kiss, holding my breath until it ended. Afterwards, I reached for the car door handle. He placed his hand on my arm. "Don't go in yet. Let's make up for all the time we missed."

Not really sure what he meant, I didn't move. He slid me closer and began to kiss me again, over and over until I placed my hands on his chest and pushed away.

"Josh!" I wanted the night to end. He let go and looked in my eyes. I saw my friend from middle school, my boyfriend from high school, but I saw it as part of my past. This wasn't going to work. How did I tell him? "I'll see you tomorrow. You can pick what we do."

"Are you up for some bowling?"

"Sure, I'll see you then."

"Al?" He took my hand and kissed the top. "Thanks for giving me a second chance."

I scooted over and opened the door. "Goodnight, Josh."

Walking to the front door, I felt an empty void inside. The pain in my heart grew, a pain Josh couldn't fix. The only person capable of doing that was someone I couldn't think about or let his name pass my lips.

* * * *

Ashley and I never made it to the bookstore. She had to baby-sit, and we didn't needed the book until the following week. So we waited for the weekend. On Saturday we made plans to spend the day there.

As we swung open the doors, the wonderful scent of books hit me. I took in a deep breath, wanting to escape for a few hours. We planned to start reading the assigned book, have our coffees, grab a little lunch. We established the routine many years ago. The round table by the check-out held the school's required reading. We both reached for *Fahrenheit 451,* a futurist novel where reading was outlawed and firemen burned books. No romance, just book burnings, I hoped.

I wandered the aisles for about an hour noting Ashley's growing pile. Mine stayed the same, one book, so I walked over to the café and ordered my caramel latte. As I flipped through the book, my thoughts drifted back to the first day of school and the bookstore when I sensed Lucas was there. I tried to zone into that feeling now. Closing my eyes, I imagined opening them and seeing him across the table. When I did, a confused Ashley stared at me.

"What are you doing?"

"Making a wish. One that won't come true," I said as I shrugged. "But trying just the same."

"You were trying to turn me into Lucas, weren't you?"

"Something like that. And don't say his name."

"Where are you going on your date tonight?" Ash brilliantly changed the subject.

"Bowling." A great idea struck me. "And you and Nate are coming, too."

"We are?"

"You are." I grabbed my phone and texted Nate then sent Josh a message. "It's no fun bowling alone."

"I take it you don't want to be alone with him."

"Maybe. I feel like I'm forcing this to work."

"So tell him! You don't seem happy at all. If you're using him to forget you-know-who it's not fair to Josh or you."

When Ashley mentioned *him*, I felt his eyes on me. I glanced around but saw no one.

"See, you think he's here, don't you?" Ashley waved her hand toward the store.

"Yes," I whispered, hanging my head. A tear dripped from my eye onto my pant leg. I stared at the tiny spot until another joined it.

"Aw, Allie, don't cry. Lucas is a bum, but maybe he didn't have a choice. Did you ever think of that? You said his family was here temporarily until his dad got back on his feet. Maybe he got a great job offer, and they had to leave in a hurry."

"Thanks for trying to make me feel better. At least you didn't say they were running from the law this time."

"I was thinking that." Ashley tried not to smile, and I joined her with a slight grin.

"Don't know what I'd do without you, bestie."

"You don't ever have to find out."

* * * *

Loud music, bowling balls dropping to the floor and the shouts of success as the pins crashed onto the wooden lanes greeted us. The scent of the bowling alley, smelly feet, old carpet and food rolled into one played havoc on my senses.

We rented our shoes and bowling balls and chose a lane at the far end. I wasn't a great bowler. My dad had taken me a few times. Dean and I would hang out here on some Saturdays, but I didn't keep up. Josh had his own ball and shoes since he was a great athlete at every sport. The three of us pulled on our rented shoes. I tried not to think how many pairs of feet had been in them before mine. Nate and Josh went to the snack counter to get sodas.

"Are you going to tell him?" Ashley waited for them to leave before she started her questions. "Did you plan what you'll say? Want to practice?"

"I'll tell him when he drops me off tonight and, no, I don't want to practice. There's something I need to find out first. I told you about Chloe having that outburst at my locker this week. I have a feeling Josh isn't being straight with me about their relationship. I want him to tell me the truth."

"Will that make a difference?"

"No."

The boys returned, and we began the game. I pretended to be interested but when Josh's turn came, I got distracted by the other bowlers. Every boy with dark hair could be Lucas. If he returned, it might be undercover. Acting like a casual bowler made perfect sense.

"Al! Snap out of it! It's your turn." Josh stood in front of me pointing to the alley.

"Oh, sorry," I jumped up and took my last shot. "You two guys play the next game. Ash and I need a break."

I grabbed her by the arm and dragged her to the ladies' room. If Lucas was here, he might get a signal to me, and I could slip away. We walked as slow as possible, but made it to the bathroom without interruption. The place was empty except for one girl standing over a sink, holding onto the sides with both hands. I didn't know if she was sick or going to be sick but didn't want to be there for either. She raised her head, and I saw her face in the mirror. Mascara ran down it, lining her face with black streaks. Her red and swollen eyes stared back at me.

"Chloe!"

"Well, if it isn't Miss Boyfriend Stealer."

"She didn't steal your boyfriend, Chloe." Ashley came to my defense as she took a step toward her.

"Don't, Ash, I can fight my own battles." I put my hand up to stop her from charging. "Chloe, let's talk, okay? I have a question for you. When did Josh break up with you?"

"Why?" she sputtered.

"Please? Just answer?"

"During spring break."

"What?" Both Ashley and I said at the same time.

"Well, I knew he'd end it whenever you'd give in and take him back. He told me as much. I can't blame you, really. He's dreamy and handsome and awesome." Chloe began to cry again.

"So you kept dating him even though you knew he'd drop you for Allie?" Ashley turned to me. "Sorry, couldn't help myself."

"It's fine." I waited for Chloe to answer.

"Yeah, I kept dating him because nothing happened. Allie was with that hot guy, Lucas. I hoped Josh would eventually forget about you. That all changed when Lucas left town, didn't it? You just had to have Josh back, and you probably don't even want him." She took a step forward.

Chloe struck a chord. I decided to be truthful. I could see she was hurting and really cared about Josh. He should be with someone like her, not me.

"You're right."

Her eyes widened, and she froze in place. She probably didn't expect that answer. "I'm just casually dating Josh to see if I wanted him back, and I don't."

"Really?" she gulped. "That's the best news I've heard all week!" Chloe wrapped her arms around me, pinning my arms to my sides. She stepped back, smiling.

I suddenly had the strength to end this charade. "Why don't you clean up and go back to your friends? I have a feeling Josh is going to need someone to talk to later tonight."

"What just happened in there?" Ashley could hardly contain herself as we left the ladies' room. I steered her outside the bowling alley.

"I was afraid she was going to punch me for a minute!" I laughed with relief. I almost created a false life for myself and hurt someone in the process. "I need to end this sooner rather than later."

"Let's go back in and tell the boys we're ready to leave." Ashley tugged on my arm, but I waved her away to say I needed a moment. She went back inside, leaving me alone.

Not ready to go in, I sat on the stone wall surrounding the building's landscape. Breathing in the night air, I felt rejuvenated.

"I'll wait for you, Lucas. I gave up on you without a fight and won't do that again. Wherever you are, you're there for a reason. Maybe I'll find out some day. For now, just know I love you." I realized I'd been talking aloud when some boys came out the door and gave me a strange look. "Guess I better get back inside!" I said, making a goofy smile.

I saw Ashley talking to Nate when I got to the lane. She must be telling him what happened during our bathroom trip. Josh had his ball and shoes packed up so they knew we wanted to leave. Josh seemed a little too eager when I approached him.

"You had enough, I heard." He teased. "That's okay. We can come back any time you want." He stroked my cheek. "I'd like to have you all to myself anyway."

A shudder shot threw me. I turned away, making a big deal of saying goodbye to my friends. We parted ways, and Josh took my hand, guiding me to the exit. He didn't notice Chloe as we passed by her lane, but I gave her a nod. Still looking dejected, she gave me a slight smile.

"Al, I can't wait any longer. I've been waiting to do

this all night." Josh dropped his bag to the ground and gave me a long kiss right in the middle of the parking lot. He pulled my body so close I felt his heart beating.

"Josh, stop." I gently pushed him away.

"I don't care who sees us, I want everyone to know how I feel about you."

Before I could say another word, he kissed me again and again, then walked me to the car and helped me in. He ran to the driver's side, started the car and held my hand for the drive home.

"This has been a great weekend, Al. It's our new beginning." Josh parked in my drive and turned in his seat to look at me. "I was so stupid last year. I've learned my lesson."

"I'm glad to hear that, Josh, but I have to tell you something. This isn't working for me. I thought it could, but it isn't. It's too soon or maybe it never should have happened."

Josh's eyes showed surprise then hurt. "Oh, I see. Well, I can wait."

"No, don't wait. You have a very nice girl who really cares about you. She's waiting for you to come back to her."

"Chloe? Is that what this is about? I told you it's over between us."

"It's not about her. It's about you and me not working. We can't force something to happen or bring back what we had. Too much has happened. I want to go back to being friends. I'm sorry, Josh."

Josh scooted me closer and held me in his arms, kissing the top of my head. "I wish you the best, always have. If that guy hurts you again—"

"A little hard to do when I don't know where he is."

"True."

I leaned back and gave him a peck on the cheek. "Thanks for being so understanding."

"Who knows? Maybe someday?"

"Maybe." I slid out of the car and watched him pull out of the drive, hoping he'd go find Chloe. As I walked to the front door, I got a sensation someone watched me, just like at the bookstore. I heard a rustling in the bushes, but figured it must be an animal or the wind. I waited for another minute, hoping to see Lucas come around the side of the house. What would I do if I saw him? I'd run into his arms and never let him go.

CHAPTER EIGHTEEN

Sleepless nights. Never-ending days. I went through the emotional wringer and made a conscious decision to stop feeling sorry for myself. I didn't need a man in my life to make it complete, never did. After last year's break-up with Josh, I had decided to be an independent woman. I made the choice to be with Lucas. Now a new chapter in my life was about to begin.

The rumor mill had started up. Whispers that I broke up with Josh flew through the hallways. A few sideway glances came my way, some talk behind my back. A clear conscience helped me through the day. I knew I made the right decision. Josh belonged with Chloe, and I belonged with? No one.

I wanted to stick to a routine so I could finish the year under my terms. The plan started now. Ashley met me in the parking lot, and we walked into school together. In English, I focused on the teacher, the white board, other students, anything but the seat in front of me.

Afterward, at my locker, Josh and Chloe stopped by. Chloe smiled like the Cheshire cat in *Alice in Wonderland*. Josh seemed okay. We talked for a few minutes. I hoped we could remain friends.

After school, Nate took me to my car before heading back inside to finish up his A/V duties for the day. I drove straight home, had a snack and headed to my room. Simple, but it worked. Each day got better. I focused on the future. My future plans had been on hold, and now I researched colleges and places to live after graduation.

For the rest of the week, I fell into a routine. Ash waited in the parking lot with Nate. When he saw my car, he waved as he headed into the school, to give us girl time. After I parked, I grabbed my things and jumped out.

"My, aren't we perky today?" Ash teased as we made our way toward the building. "Same schedule as yesterday?"

"Yep, it worked quite well. Mom was thrilled to have me home early. I'm okay, Ash, really." I squeezed her arm as we parted ways at my locker.

I wouldn't come back to the locker after English and give Chloe a break from having to see me. I rummaged through it, looking for books to get me through the next few classes, slammed the door and went to homeroom. If I focused on my schoolwork, it would distract me from thinking. I had so much time on my hands I already finished reading *Fahrenheit 451*.

At the end of the book, cities across the country burned to the ground. One of the characters compared it to the legend of the phoenix—the bird's long life, death in flames and rebirth from the ashes. Then he and a group of people set off to rebuild the city just like the phoenix rose from its ashes. I identified with the phoenix. I planned to rebuild and create a better me. Maybe I wouldn't burn down so easily next time around.

The bell rang, and I started down the hall looking for Ashley along the way. She caught up, and we walked into class. "A new week," she said. "You made it through the last one. Each day should get better."

"Thanks for your support, Ash. I don't think I could make it without you." I squeezed her arm as we stepped into English class.

I ambled down the aisle, not really looking at the people as I passed by. My book bag slid to one side and hit someone in the head. Odd, no one should be in the seat in front of me, unless we got a new student.

"Ooh, sorry." I slipped into my chair and tried to organize myself. Gazing up so I could apologize again, I made contact with a pair of familiar chocolate brown eyes.

"Apology accepted." Lucas smiled, but I didn't. In fact, I didn't say a word and stared right through him until he turned around.

How dare he! He can show up in class but can't contact me? I refuse to talk to him. He can beg all he wants. I glared at the back of his head during class trying to make a getaway plan. Lucas could easily block me from walking down the aisle.

Darn him! The broken pieces I thought I put back in place scattered all over the classroom floor. I didn't want to pick them up and start over again. As class continued, I got my resolve back. *Be strong, make your own decisions.*

End of class brought me to my senses. I glanced at Ashley hoping for advice on my escape. She saw my dilemma and shrugged.

"Can we talk?" Lucas stood and blocked my exit just as expected.

"No."

"Please."

"No!" I searched his eyes and felt my resolve begin to weaken. "Maybe."

"I'll wait for you after school, like always."

"It's not 'like always', Lucas," I said as sarcastically as I could.

"I won't let you down ever again. Please. Let me

explain."

"Alright but I'm not going to our woods, the diner or your house." I pushed past him and hurried to catch up with Ashley. "Do you believe that? He goes missing in action for three weeks and shows up in class like nothing's changed."

"He wants to see you?"

"Yeah."

"You should hear him out." Ashley waved as she went down another hall.

I stood with my mouth opened, shocked by her answer. But maybe she was right. I had the whole day to cool off and think rationally. I prepared a list of questions, and if I didn't like his answers, I'd walk away.

The day went by in a blur. I wondered how I managed to keep up my grade point average. When the final bell rang, I took my time going to my locker. I planned to make Lucas squirm. I had no clue where we'd go since most places were off limits. As I threw a few things in my book bag, I sensed someone watching me. A glance down the hall confirmed my suspicions. Lucas.

"This is our new meeting place, isn't it?" he asked when I reached the water fountain.

I didn't answer and kept walking through the hallways to the main door. Finally I found my voice. "So where do you want to talk?"

"You made it kind of tough, but I have just the place. Your house."

"My mom's there."

"No, she isn't."

"What did you do to her?"

"Nothing." Lucas laughed. "Her hair appointment was moved. She left you a note or maybe sent you a text." He jumped in the passenger side of the Jeep.

I pulled out my phone and saw I missed a message. She would be late, color and cut, and could I put the casserole in the oven?

"Fine." I started the car and headed for home.

As we stepped into the house, I felt his hands on my shoulders. He spun me around to face him, and the next thing I knew, I kissed him. I clung to his shirt like he would run out the door if I let go. Then I started to cry and pounded his chest. "You left me! You left me all alone here!"

"You were never alone, Allie," Lucas said as he guided me into the family room. We sat together on the couch. I leaned against him as he wrapped his arms around me. "You were at the diner then went to my house when you couldn't find me. You tried to call and got the disconnect message. Nate's house was next then the woods."

"You were supposed to come," I whispered

"I did in a way. I sent Nate."

It all came back—Nate finding me in the rain, warming me up in the car, handing me a caramel latte. Lucas had sent him. "Why didn't *you* come?"

"We were too far away. I was already in Pennsylvania. We had a false alarm at the house but no time to figure that out until we reached Julian's. Gene woke us in the middle of the night and said there was a breach. We had to leave. After what happened at my party, Julian instructed us to come straight to his home in Pennsylvania and work from there. Everything was shut down at the safe house as a precaution. Sean stepped in at the diner."

"Who's Sean?"

"A Niner. He lives nearby. We call him a

freelancer, never married or had any children. He goes wherever he's needed and likes it that way. He's part of the security team stationed at the Montana compound."

I pictured the handsome man behind the counter who helped protect the family. It began to make sense. I would put Lucas' safety first over anything else. "But why didn't you just tell me?"

"I wanted to, but Julian thought it best if you were truly shocked and upset so your family would buy it. My phone was never disconnected. The message you heard was programmed to play only if you called. I stayed in contact with Nate the whole time. Once we got the all clear, I couldn't wait to come back. I wanted to call you, but Gene thought it best to give it some time before we told anyone."

"So you were here? At the bookstore and my house?"

"I had to see you. When my phone showed you were at the bookstore I had to go." He paused and took a breath. "You had a busy weekend, didn't you? You're back with Josh? The movies, the bowling alley—"

"I went out with Josh as friends. Nothing happened. He knows I won't be going back to him, ever again."

"I was at your house, Allie. I saw you in the car."

"You and your night vision! We were saying goodbye. I'm sure you heard the conversation."

"Parts of it, I wasn't close enough to hear everything."

"So you're jealous."

"Of course, I'm jealous! I'm also mad at myself. I put you in that position."

"So if you heard me tell him we had no future, why didn't you show yourself?"

"We were still testing the system. Julian said to wait a week to be sure. There was a possibility we wouldn't stay. I couldn't hurt you like that. If anything suspicious showed up, we were to fly to Montana immediately. I hoped to contact you from there."

"Montana?"

"Yes, it's safe to live there again. Stacy wants to go back and voted to head there from P.A. The rest of us want to stay here. She gave in … reluctantly. It's only one more year. I tried to tell her, but she wasn't buying it."

"Poor Stacy. She feels outnumbered by you men. She misses her sisters."

"She'll get to see them soon. We're sending her on a surprise visit this summer to Montana."

"She'll love that." The topic strayed, but it felt good to be in Lucas' arms. "So what was your excuse for missing two weeks of school?"

"I was so sick I dehydrated and had to be hospitalized for a few days. It's all documented."

"I bet it is. And Joe and Hannah?"

"They were on an extended holiday with family."

"In a way, I guess they were."

"Yeah, but it was hard on Hannah. She doesn't understand everything. She doesn't know about me. She just thinks I'm her big brother."

"Oh! I didn't realize. I assumed she knew since Joe knows everything."

"It's better that way. Some Niners never tell their extended family the truth. They just fade away from everyone's lives."

"That's sad."

"Sad, but protecting the ones you love is important."

"Don't ever protect me like that again. I want to know where you are, even if you have to leave me for awhile."

"I'll try my best."

"And one more thing," I gave him my most serious face. "I make my own decisions. You don't make them for me ever again."

Lucas held his hands up in surrender, and a slight grin crossed his face. "When has anyone ever made you do something you didn't want to do?"

I gave him a playful shove. "You know what I mean. This relationship has to be on equal terms. If not, I'm out."

"Ooh, Allie, you're scaring me!" Lucas threw his head back and laughed. "I love it. You're strong. Don't ever forget that. I won't either." He kissed the top of my head and bolted up. "Your mom's pulling in. I need to leave. You'll have to explain how I showed up in class today after a long illness."

"She'll ask why someone didn't call to let me know."

"Say my family thought I called you, and I thought they contacted you. It was a mix-up of communication. I love you!" Lucas slipped out the backdoor.

The sound of the garage door closing reminded me I forgot to start the casserole. I rushed into the kitchen and turned on the stove. My head was in the fridge searching for the dish when Mom came into the kitchen.

"Looks like dinner will be late," she said.

I turned and saw she didn't look upset. "Mom, you look great. Sorry about dinner but I have some good news." I told her Lucas' story and tried to gauge if she bought the lie.

"I thought it was strange how he just disappeared. Mix-ups can happen." Mom shrugged. "If he was in the hospital he shouldn't worry about anything except getting better. Glad to hear he's well now."

I hated lying to everyone, but it had to be. I'd hate it more if Doug ever got his hands on Lucas. I had to improve my lying skills so next time I could be trusted with all the Montgomery secrets.

CHAPTER NINETEEN

Anti-social became my name again. I made my own choices and wouldn't listen to gossip or be part of any high school drama. On the last day of school, I cleaned and sorted my locker before leaving junior year behind. I wanted to dump everything into the huge garbage can in the hall, but decided to stuff some remnants in my book bag.

"Here let me help. The sooner you get done, the sooner I can tell you my surprise." Lucas opened the pouch. He zipped it shut after I stuffed a few items inside and threw the bag over his shoulder. I made a final sweep of the area.

We took each other's hand and headed for the Jeep. My heart pounded with excitement. When we got to the car, I opened the trunk so he could throw our bags in. "I can't stand the suspense any longer! What's the surprise?"

"Just a few more minutes, not here." Lucas jumped in the passenger side, waiting for me to get in. "My house," he commanded. "I'll tell you on the back deck."

I wanted to speed down Gilbert Road and get there as quickly as possible. A voice in my head kept hoping for good news. It couldn't be bad. Why would Lucas call it a surprise then? "Surprise! I'm leaving." My heart sank to the pit of my stomach. *Just wait and quit torturing yourself.*

We only had a half day of school. The afternoon was ours. I pulled down the long drive, parked in front of the barn, racing Lucas to the deck.

"Tell me!" I yelled as I spun to face him.

"I will, but first," Lucas said as he pulled me

toward him. "We've finished the school year. Congratulations." His lips met mine. I wove my hands through his hair as the kiss ended. Lucas leaned back, staring into my eyes. "It's not like we graduated or anything, but it feels good."

"Yes," I broke from his arms. "One more and it's off to college. And freedom!" I whirled around on the deck, feeling the warm sun on my skin.

"Well, before that happens, how would you like to visit Montana?"

"What?" I twirled back to face him.

He crossed his arms, and a smile appeared. "I told you we're sending Stacy so I booked two more seats on the plane. Your parents won't have a problem, will they? After all, my mom's going with us." He winked.

"I don't think so. Where will we stay?"

"We can't stay in town or with Stacy. Her family thinks she lives with Gene, Sam and the kids. They don't know about me. Gene and I have a house in the compound. I thought we'd stay there."

"Alone?"

"Yep, I'll be a perfect gentleman."

"I know you will be." I took a couple steps to reach him. I longed for him, wanting more than the kisses we shared. This twenty-year-old man was really eighty and surely had different values than kids of my generation. "I'm sure my parents will let me go. If not, I'll just throw a tantrum or something." I teased.

Lucas laughed and slid the door to the kitchen open. He disappeared and returned with lunch. We sat at the outdoor table, eating turkey sandwiches, and discussed the plans.

"What about Doug? Do you think he'll go into high alert when he hears Montana?" I reached for my soda.

"You keep telling me you'd lie to protect us, so I'm asking you to do that. Remember we never say Montana. You have to say we're going to Missouri. Can you do that?"

"Okay, but all Doug has to do is check the airlines, the flight plans—"

"And we'll be on a plane to Missouri."

"I should've known. So tell me what will we do in Montana?"

"The compound's located near Yellowstone National Park. We could visit if you like. I want you to see where I live, meet some people, hang out in our village."

"I'd like that. Why aren't Gene and the rest of the family coming?"

"Someone has to stay here. Gene's more than willing. Sam feels if Hannah goes back she'll start talking about her brother Lucas. That could be a problem. He decided to stay here with the kids and let Stacy have time with her sisters."

"So when are you going to tell Hannah the truth?"

"Not before we have to, probably when they're ready to move back. Or maybe never."

"When you moved here, Hannah was five. Did you suddenly come into her life as her brother or did she already know you?"

"Sam and his family would visit the compound so she knew me. He realized he couldn't say I was his uncle or even a brother so he never said who I was. When we moved here, we just told her I chose to live with Grandpa in the village, but now we could all be together."

"And Joe knows the truth?"

"Yeah, it's so unbelievable. For some reason he seems to understand. He knows I'm his great-uncle."

I helped Lucas clean up and daydreamed about leaving for Montana. I couldn't wait to see his home in Victorian Village. "How long will we be gone?"

"A week. Stacy doesn't want to be away from the kids any longer than that."

"Makes sense."

I curled up on the couch in the great room and fell asleep. When I woke, I found Lucas next to me watching something on the flat screen TV.

"Look at this." He pointed his phone at the television. A travelogue came on and showed the mountains, valleys, streams and sweeping vistas of Montana.

"How'd you find that?" I blinked a few times, surprised.

"Not a channel."

"Oh, Lucas TV."

"Exactly. Now choose a topic. I worked hard on this."

Looking over the subjects, it became hard to pick. "It's between *Arts and Culture* or *A Day in the Life*. Which I feel is about you."

"Then why don't we watch both?"

I checked my phone for the time. "Ooh, I've got to go. Mom made a special dinner for the last day of school." I couldn't leave without stealing a few more kisses from my boyfriend.

"When is the trip?" I asked as we walked out to the Jeep.

"In two weeks. It will give you time to shop." Lucas gave me a poke in the side.

"Great. Wish me luck." I kissed him again. He held

on tightly as if he never wanted to let me go.

I hopped in the Jeep, rolled down the window and we kissed again. I waved as I went down the drive.

I smelled dinner cooking when I stepped in the house. Mom was usually in the kitchen, but not today. I snuck up to my bedroom hoping for a few minutes alone, but I heard her voice as I reached the top stair.

"It would be nice if you made it home for Allie's dinner. It's her last day of school, Doug. We could celebrate together as a family. I invited Ashley and Nate, too." Silence for a minute. "No, I don't know how to get a hold of him or he would be invited. Allie's always at their house so I haven't seen him." Silence again. "I don't know why you're so distrusting, Doug. New families come to the area all the time. Yes, I would love for her to end up with Josh or even Nate but that isn't how love works. The family may seem a little unusual, but everyone's different. I've got to go. Allie should be here by now. I wanted to surprise her. I'll give her your best. I love you."

I inwardly celebrated when I heard Doug couldn't come for my dinner. Pretending I just got home, I called out. "Mom, are you up here?"

"Allie! Hi, sweetie!" She came out of her bedroom. "We're having a little dinner party for you tonight. Do you think you can invite Lucas? I have no way of getting in touch with him, and hope it's not too late."

"I'm sure he can come. Thanks, Mom." I searched for the phone in my back pocket and saw I had a message: *I'll be there.*

"Go look in the dining room, Allie."

I headed back down to the dining room. Mom had decorated the room with balloons and her good china. Candles already had been lit, and a present sat on my plate.

"Mom!" I called to her. "I didn't graduate or anything."

She appeared in the archway. "You've had a rough year. I thought you deserved something special. Go ahead and open it. Your father won't mind if he's not here."

I froze. *Did Doug help pick it out?* I couldn't hurt Mom's feelings so I pulled colorful wads of tissue from the bag. A gift card to my favorite store lay on the bottom.

"Surprised?" Mom looked so eager to please. Did I neglect her that much? "Maybe we can do some shopping together?" She looked like someone expecting rejection. My heart melted.

"Sure." I came around the table and gave her a big hug.

"I have lots to do before everyone gets here." She gave me a quick kiss on the cheek. "Go relax until then."

"Sounds good." I started for the stairs and grabbed my book bag off the back of the chair. "I'll clean this out in my room."

"I'll leave you to it." Mom waved her hands in the air as she disappeared into the kitchen.

I paused when reached the top of the stairs. I glanced to my right and stopped at the doorway to my bedroom. Something inside urged me *not* to go in. I placed the bag down on the floor next to the entryway. Dean and Doug's rooms were farther down the hall. Dean's had become the designated guest room, but Doug's remained untouched. I glanced up and down the hall, sure I'd be caught. I inched closer to Doug's doorway, holding my breath.

Maybe I can find something to satisfy my curiosity in his room. I took a few more steps. *Dad likes to say 'Curiosity killed the cat.* The knot tightened in my stomach. *Well, let's hope it doesn't kill me.* I rarely went in the bedroom or even looked inside when I passed by. Now I carefully examined the room from the doorway.

The walls had been painted a creamy off-white. The dark wood furniture stood out against the walls. The bed, covered with a navy quilt, had white and navy checked pillow shams sitting precisely side by side. The hardwood floor shone as the sun from the window bounced off it. A red, white and blue braided rug lay by the bed with a larger one in front of the closet. Everything was pristine, orderly. Mom must dust and clean every day in fear of him coming home and finding it less than perfect.

"What am I looking for?" I whispered as I found the courage to step into the room. I gave a sigh of relief once I made it inside. *What am I afraid of? This is my house, too. I can come in here if I want.*

I strolled around the room, wiping one finger along the top of the dresser checking for dust. "Do I expect a flashing neon sign announcing 'here's the clue, Allie'?" I came in here to learn something about Doug, and I had to be the one to figure out where to look.

I pulled open the double doors to his closet. My stomach tightened, and I could barely breathe as I pushed them back as far as they could go. I almost expected an alarm to go off. When no alarm sounded, I relaxed.

A few shirts and pants hung on hangers. Shoe boxes were neatly stacked below. *If I was a teenage boy, I might keep something in a shoebox other than shoes.* I sank to the floor and sat cross-legged in front of the pile. *Let's start at the bottom.* I opened a few boxes and found shoes.

"Yuk. Why is he keeping those?" I placed them back just as I found them. Something caught my eye as I leaned further in the closet.

Shoved back against the farthest corner, under a duffle bag, was one more shoebox. I crawled into the closet and dragged the container from its hiding place. Doug's hidden treasures had to be in there. If anything, maybe I'd get to know him better, get inside his head and see what was important to him. As I lifted the top, I prayed I wouldn't find another pair of shoes.

"Thank you, Doug." I held the lid over my head in triumph as I stared into the box of hidden gems. Typical boy stuff filled the container—an arrowhead, Boy Scout badges, an old baseball. I examined each item as if I found a prize, trying to picture Doug as a boy.

A folded piece of notebook paper lay at the very bottom. "Do I dare?" Hands trembling, I opened the worn piece of paper that appeared to have been unfolded and refolded many times. Written in beautiful, flowing cursive, a message stared up at me.

Doug,
After what I saw you do to your sister, I can no longer be with you. I wish you well in life and your career in the military.
Kimmie

A lump grew in my throat until I could hardly swallow. Short, ragged breaths escaped as I read the words over and over until I had them memorized. "What did you do to me, Doug?" I carefully folded the paper and replaced it in the box with all of Doug's prized possessions. I slid the box under the duffel bag exactly where I found it.

My heart pounded with the fear of being caught as I closed the closet doors. I tiptoed toward the door, glancing up and down the hall. I made a dash for my room, throwing myself on my bed. My eyes closed as I tried to process what I found. "That's it!" I sat straight up. "You hate me because you lost your girlfriend, the love of your life." I examined my body, checking my arms and legs for any telltale signs of abuse. *A scar? A burn mark? What did he do?*

The doorbell rang, interrupting my thoughts. "I'll get it," I called as I rushed down the stairs. The mystery would have to wait.

When I opened the front door, Nate and Ashley stood on the porch, holding hands. Lucas followed soon after. When Dad got home, Mom called to us, announcing dinner was ready. Once seated, a brilliant idea struck me.

"Mom, Dad, thanks so much for this dinner and inviting my friends. I have some exciting news. Lucas is going to Mu—mu—Missouri with his mother and has invited me to join them."

An awkward silence followed, and Lucas finally broke in. "Of course, we'll be staying with my mom's family. She hasn't been home in three years. It's been a long time."

My dad cleared his throat and looked at my mother. He knew I put them in an uncomfortable position. "Well, Clair, should we discuss this later then let them know our decision?"

"I don't see the harm in letting her go, Jim. She's never seen that part of the country."

"Clair." My father appeared defeated and stared at me. "How long?"

"A week."

"I guess you can go as long as you call home everyday."

"Thanks, Daddy! I promise I will."

Ashley's face wore a look of surprise. She bit her bottom lip as she stared at me. We continued eating, and the conversation turned to Missouri. Lucas answered all the questions thrown at him about the state. Nate didn't let up until I shot him a look that said cut it out.

After dinner, the four of us headed for Nate's house. Lucas and Nate carried on their good-natured jabs. Ashley appeared frustrated as she grabbed me by the arm. "What's going on? I feel like I'm being left out of something."

"You're not." I wiped the smile from my face. Ashley's eyes told the story of how she felt. "We're just having fun. I guess I've been encouraging it a little. Nate's starting to like Lucas. I wanted them to become friends. Sorry. I didn't mean for you to feel left out."

"You're forgiven. I can see it, too. I know how much you want the two of them to be friends."

I placed my arm across her shoulders. "Like us."

I watched the two guys banter and joke. Lucas and Nate had become close. Lucas sent Nate to save me from the storm. He never broke contact with him. He finally made a friend, and if it had to be anyone, I was happy it would be Nate.

CHAPTER TWENTY

The plane would soon land in Billings, Montana. I couldn't wait to see where Lucas grew up. I had so many unanswered questions. Stacy couldn't stop talking about her sisters during the flight. She kept parts of her life secret for so long I saw the relief in her face as she spoke freely.

"Of course, my family knows Gene, but I feel bad for Lucas. He's like the dark secret of the family. I wish I could bring him home and say he's a friend of the family or something."

"You sound like a protective mother."

"Thanks, Allie. I try."

"Just think of this week as a gift to yourself. Do what you want and don't worry about the rest of us. You'll video chat every day with the kids, won't you?"

"Yeah." She sighed. "Sam can track me if he chooses. I find that a little creepy though."

"I have to admit, I like it." I smiled, knowing Lucas kept track of me at all times.

"Their technology is so beyond what we know, it's a little scary," Stacy whispered.

"I can hear you, Mom." Lucas leaned across me and pointed to his ears.

"That, too!" Stacy laughed.

We landed and headed for the baggage claim. An oversized SUV sat ready and waiting at the door when we exited the airport. I had serious doubts it was a rental. Lucas knew where to find the key and loaded our luggage in the car.

We had a two hour drive ahead of us, dropping Stacy off in the city of Bozeman then a few more to the compound. We got the typical mother lecture in the car about not doing anything crazy when alone, and if we did, practice safe sex. I felt my face flush as she gave us "the talk" but thought it was kind of cute. She didn't know Lucas and I already had that discussion and *nothing* would happen. She reminded us to call and to have fun.

We soon pulled into Sam and Stacy's driveway. Julian had returned to Montana and had someone open and clean the house for her return.

Lucas helped Stacy out, took her bags from the back, and they disappeared into the house. I waited in the car for his return. My heart began to beat faster. What was I thinking totally immersing myself in his world?

Lucas hopped back in the car and drove away from the town toward the mountains. He glanced over, and took my hand. I had my answer. I could go anywhere with him. We drove on the open road, no towns or houses, just miles and miles of beautiful scenery. The mountains grew closer, and I thought we'd run out of road. Lucas made a hard left and guided the car onto a dirt trail. We drove through acres of pine trees. After traveling for a few miles, we suddenly came to a dead end, facing a wall of tall evergreens and shrubs.

Lucas looked over at me. "Now where?"

"I'm supposed to know?" My eyes widened as I shrugged.

He smiled and pointed. "Keep looking around. See if you can find the opening. Use your instincts."

After a few minutes, I gave up in frustration. "Nope, don't see it. Are we going to sit here all day?"

"I guess so. We can't drive in until you do this."

I didn't understand why he wanted me to find the

hidden opening so badly. I'd never come here by myself. It could be some sort of Niner test. Studying the bushes, I saw a place where we could drive through without hitting any of the larger trees.

"There, drive right through those bushes."

Lucas stepped on the gas and followed my command. If I was wrong, I saw a major accident in my future. Branches hit the windshield as we bumped along. Surrounded by greenery, I screamed for him to stop, but Lucas continued on. We broke through to the other side. He said a few words, and a paved road appeared among the trees. He sped along the new street. It swung to the left then right again, appearing to go nowhere as we continued to drive though a forest of pine.

Finally, we came to a clearing. A huge concrete wall over ten feet tall, stretched for miles across the countryside. A steel door, wide enough for two cars to come and go, blocked us from going any further.

I studied the landscape and said, "I know the area is covered by a cloaking device. If anyone flies overhead, they just see trees. If someone finds that opening, they'd just see grass and trees. So why the wall? The doors?"

"Good question." Lucas leaned back in his seat as he came to a stop in front of the doors. "Safety is the easy answer. We can make the average person think there's nothing here. But what if they decided to explore further? We needed a way to stop them."

"If I made it this far, I'd want to know why these walls are here."

"Look over at that sign." He gestured next to the doors.

Privately owned testing facility, Trespassers will be

prosecuted.

"Makes sense. That would keep me away. But what about that part of the population with the need to know?"

"A squad of scary looking security guards would meet them at the entrance if they got that far. No one ever has."

Lucas got out his phone, punched in a few numbers, and the door lifted. He continued to talk to the phone. "Lucas Montgomery, program 508, guest Allison Sanders. Please assign number 509 and activate her account."

We drove through the opening and were greeted by more trees and grassy fields. A four story building reminding me of an office building or a giant outlet store magically appeared before my eyes. "That wasn't there before." I pointed straight ahead.

"It was." Lucas chuckled. "Only you couldn't see it until I activated your account."

"You mean I … it …" I slapped my forehead. "How?"

"The wonders of technology." Lucas smiled. "You'll still have to be scanned before we leave headquarters. The computer needs to know who you are so it won't mark you as an intruder. It's always on high alert for any security breaches."

"Oh." I blinked. Headquarters was this sand-colored rectangle, windowless building in front of me. The place had the look of a testing facility.

The door opened on the first floor of the building, and we drove in. The ground floor looked like a giant parking lot. Lucas drove to a spot and parked the car. "Come on." He ran around to my side and took my hand. I followed him as we sprinted to an elevator.

"You still use elevators?" I teased. Then I realized we left the luggage. "Lucas, aren't you forgetting something?"

"Don't worry. It will be taken to the house."

"By the luggage robot?" I joked.

"Something like that." Lucas had a twinkle in his eye. We got off on the next floor filled with futuristic-looking cars. "Pick one." He swept his hand around the garage.

So many choices. Drawn to a two-toned sienna red and silver model, it reminded me of an old-fashioned VW Beetle, only sleeker in design.

"This one." I glided my hand over the exterior, sliding smoothly from the back of the car to the roof and down to the front.

"Fine choice." Lucas told his phone the car's number. The doors automatically popped open. We slipped in, and the car began moving without a sound. Lucas looked over and stroked my hair.

"Hey, keep your eyes on the road!" I laughed.

"Don't need to, the car knows where we're going." We traveled down a ramp and out the other side of the building, zooming toward Victorian Village.

"Hey! I wasn't scanned." I looked over my shoulder as we left the building.

"You were scanned the minute you stepped out of the car." Lucas winked. He pointed to the street leading us into town. "Think of the village as a giant grid. The middle of town has shops, restaurants and places for socializing. The residential streets spread out from there. It's an easy walk to the middle from anywhere in the village or you can drive as some prefer. Usually it's the people who live on the outskirts who do the driving."

We approached the main street and Lucas—or the car—hung a left at the third side street. I saw the village on the webcam, but it didn't compare to seeing it in person. Red brick paved the streets. Each home had a well manicured front yard.

The Victorian-designed houses had been painted all the colors of the rainbow. We rode past pale yellow, then forest green, deep blue and even pink. The homes had towers and turrets and gingerbread trim. White seemed to be the chosen color for porches and trim, but some had other colors as accent.

We made a right turn and drove past five more houses then a left into Lucas' driveway. I noted the directions in my head in case I needed them. His home looked gorgeous, barn red in color, with a white two-sided wrap-around porch traveling from the front of the house around to one side. In each peak of the house, the siding changed color from dark gray at the bottom, pale gray, a strip of white and finally red again. A white triangle of gingerbread decorated the inside of each peak.

"I bet it was hard to leave," I murmured as I slipped out of the car and gazed up at the home.

Lucas took my hand and led me up the steps and inside. "I wouldn't have found you, if I didn't." He squeezed my hand.

The interior of the house came as a shock to the senses. I expected to find a Victorian-themed décor instead of ultra-modern. An expanse of oak hardwood floor greeted us. The floor plan opened up to a huge great room that took up most of the first level. A see-through fire place showed a kitchen on the other side. The dining room sat overlooking the front yard.

"Come on," Lucas walked me back down the hall

into the front foyer and up a grand staircase. "There are three bedrooms with their own baths up here. My parents, Gene and I lived here for many years."

I was busy admiring the architectural design when it came to me that Lucas had actually lived here. He wanted me to see this as his family home.

"Gene and I had our own bedrooms. My mom and dad had the largest room across the back of the house. I let Gene have it after their passing. He's the head of the family now."

"Do you miss your parents?"

"Very much. I regret they'll never see me grow up, marry, have a family like they did for Gene. My biggest regret is they didn't meet you."

I couldn't help myself. I fell into Lucas' arms, and the house tour ended.

"I love you, Allie." Lucas gently pulled back from me. He kissed my forehead. "I'll show you to the guest room."

"The guest room? Can't I stay with you?'

"Let's see what happens."

My luggage sat against a wall in the room. "How did …?"

"Just like you said. Robots." Lucas laughed and wrapped his arms around me. "We're going to have a great week, just you and I."

"I like the sound of that."

"Come on, I'll fix us some dinner. You can do some shopping while I get things ready."

"Let's just stay in tonight, the two of us, after dinner."

"Oh, we will. Trust me."

Curious, I followed Lucas down the stairs. As he walked into the great room he said, "Fireplace, no heat." A fire appeared behind the glassed-in wall. "Display."

A huge screen appeared on the giant empty white wall opposite the fireplace. Now I knew why it looked so plain when we first arrived. No pictures or mirrors decorated the huge wall.

"Where'd you like to shop? Paris? Rome? Or somewhere closer? Rodeo Dr?" I must appear confused so Lucas chose for me. "I'll pick somewhere simple. A place you know well."

A familiar mall appeared on the screen, so life-like I felt I could walk around the place. "Is that?"

"Yep, your mall. Here let me show you how it's done. Just walk in place, and you'll move forward. Walk to any store you want to shop in. If it's to the left, swing out your left arm and same for right. You'll face the store and can walk right in. If you see something you like, let me know." Lucas disappeared and left me to make my own discoveries.

I marched straight for my favorite store, knowing I had a sizable gift card to spend. So realistic, I felt I could really be there. I had to practice staying in place. A few times I banged into the wall. After getting the hang of it, I started to browse. "Lucas?" I called to him. "How do I know this stuff's in stock?"

"You're in real time," he answered from the kitchen.

Silly me, I should've guessed. "Size?"

"Don't worry about it."

The time flew, and Lucas returned to the great room. "Dinner's ready. Did you have fun?"

I nodded. Everything I touched was listed on the side of the wall.

"So you want all this?" He swept his hand down

the wall.

"No! I didn't realize the computer kept track of it!" I covered my face, embarrassed.

"Okay, so look at the wall and tell it which ones to remove. Then give sizes to the ones you keep."

Each item had a number so I was able to do it quickly. "There, now how do I save until I get home?"

"Well, you're not saving the list. I'm buying it for you."

"No, I have my gift card."

"Let me do this one thing for you." Lucas gave me that smile so I couldn't resist.

"Where will it be delivered?"

"To your house after you get home? You can tell your mom you shopped on-line, which you did. Come on."

He steered me to a high-top table surrounded by multi-colored leather bar stools in the kitchen. No pots or pans sat on the stove.

"Lucas, I have so many questions. I don't know where to start."

"Start anywhere."

"How'd you make dinner?"

"See that microwave-looking contraption over there? I place my order on the phone, wait and it's delivered right inside there. A recent invention, I might add."

"So you didn't cook, but someone did?"

"Yes, and sent it through that food transporter." He gestured toward the appliance.

I remembered Lucas telling me the Niners had worked on a transporter for people. That must be the first step. "Really? A food transporter?"

"Yeah, not a microwave. You have to admit it

looks like one. We found food easy to send and used a similar look." Lucas took a bite. "And it's still hot. We had to work the kinks out on that. Food would arrive cooled off, and you had to reheat."

After dinner I began to yawn. "I don't know why I'm so tired. It's only seven o'clock."

"Tack on two hours. It's nine o'clock back home."

"I still shouldn't be tired!"

"It's been a long day, Allie. Let's curl up on the couch in front of the fire and see if that helps. You can keep asking your questions there."

That sounded inviting, but I stared at the dishes left on the table. "Is there a robot for this, too?"

"No, but all we have to do is place them in here and they'll be cleaned." Lucas pulled out drawers from his dishwasher and we placed everything in. "Discard Garbage. Clean."

The dishwasher started up. He escorted me into the great room and placed more orders to the house—music, low light, drapes pulled, house locked.

"House locked?"

"We could leave the door open, but it's more a safety precaution than anything."

"In case Doug finds us?"

"Exactly." Lucas stroked my hair as I leaned against his chest. I tried to picture Doug storming into the house. I shuddered at the thought.

"You okay?" Lucas rubbed the sides of my arms.

"If Doug did anything to hurt you or any of the Niners, I don't know how I'd live with myself."

"He won't, Allie. I promise. I'll always keep us safe." He stroked my cheek, and I tried to relax. "I don't want him to hurt you."

"He might already have."

Lucas bolted upright, taking me with him. He took me by the arms, staring straight into my eyes. "What did he do? Tell me. If he hurt you, he's a dead man." The calm Niner personality dissolved into a raging inferno. I felt his body tense. His eyes went wide, his teeth clenched. The muscles in his jaw twitched.

"No, he hasn't hurt me." I wrapped my arms around him. Seeing his anger, I decided to leave out the bruising stories for now. "I haven't had a chance to tell you about something I found. I searched Doug's room, hoping to find a clue why he's always been so mean to me. I think I found one. That's all I meant."

Lucas relaxed a bit and leaned into the sofa. "You scared me for a second. If Doug hurts you because of me, I'll never forgive myself. Then I'll kill him with my bare hands."

"He won't hurt me." I assured him even if I wasn't so sure. "He did something to me when I was a baby. His girlfriend broke up with him because of it. I found a note she wrote. It said she couldn't be with him after what he did to me."

"What did he do?"

"That's just it. I don't know."

"Has anyone in your family ever talked about it?"

"No. Mom never mentioned I was hurt or had an accident when I was little. She always said his girlfriend broke things off because she was going to college and Doug enlisted. She said Kimmie thought it would be too hard to keep the relationship going."

"Not if they loved each other." Lucas shook his head. "So he blames his baby sister for something *he* did."

"I think so." I held out my arms and legs out in front of me. "I've checked my body looking for scars but I can't find a thing." I scratched my head and came across the familiar one inch bump on the back and froze.

"What? What is it?" Lucas separated my hair. I felt his hand on the bump. "Looks like you had stitches when you were younger. It's a scar. Did you fall off your bike?"

"No ... no, I didn't."

* * * *

I woke up the next morning in the guest room, mad at myself for falling asleep on the couch last night. Lucas carried me up in the middle of the night. Disappointed, I wanted to sleep in his room. The bed felt comfy, and I had a hard time wrestling myself out of the cozy nest. I headed to the shower. There were no hot or cold shower handles, only a shower head.

"Now what?" I said to bathroom walls. "All I need is some water so I can take a shower." When I said "water", the shower turned on to the perfect temperature. Mission accomplished. I hoped I could figure out how to turn it off. "Water off" did the trick. I dried off, dressed and bounced down the stairs. I smelled coffee as I stepped into the kitchen.

"Caramel latte?" Lucas handed me a cup.

I backed away, holding one hand up. "Too early. Sorry. I don't do breakfast."

"One new thing I learned about you today." Lucas put the mug in the sink. "Not even coffee in the morning."

"I'll sit with you while you eat, and you can tell me what we'll do today."

Lucas placed a plate of eggs and toast on the table and a cup of black coffee. "How would you like to go back to school?"

"No."

"Well, today, you are. You'll learn all about the state of Missouri, the town I supposedly live in. You'll see the landscape, the area in general. You can say we spent most of our time with family so you won't have to answer too many questions."

"Are we using the giant screen out there?" I pointed to the white wall where I did my shopping.

"No, I'll show you." On the kitchen wall, above the fireplace, was a painting. "TV." The painting slowly dissolved, exposing a flat screen. "Missouri."

The program started. I felt as if I should be taking notes. When the show ended, I slapped my forehead. Not much sank in. "I need to watch that a few more times."

"Enough school for now. Let's go to the square. It's a beautiful day for a walk, don't you think?"

We stepped into the sunny June day. I admired the baby blue sky with its white cirrus clouds, thin and wispy, floating by. We crossed the street, strolled down the closest side street, until we came out on Main.

Main took us right to the square. Quaint shops lined the street along with cafes and restaurants. People milled about just like any other small town. Colorful outdoor bistro tables, painted red, blue or yellow, dotted the landscape. People enjoyed a cup of coffee or breakfast sandwich as they basked in the morning sun. A playground filled with children sat in the middle of the square.

No road ran through this section of town. Pedestrian walks wove their way through gardens, fountains and green space. A white gazebo perfect for concerts and weddings was at the far end. The old-fashioned square made me think of times gone by.

Although I said I wanted out of my small town, this gave off a different vibe.

"Lucas, I could live here forever."

"Happy to hear you say that."

"Is that why you brought me here? To see if I'd like it? To see if I'd live here?"

"One of the reasons. I just wanted you to see for yourself." He slipped his hand into mine and guided me to a table for two.

"So the Niners are satisfied to live in compounds? They don't want to take over the world?"

"Where did that come from?" Lucas held out my chair. "Oh. Let me guess. Doug."

"He insinuated that some group may want to take over."

"Deflection is the best ammunition." He shook his head. "No, Allie, we don't want to take over the world. We just want to help it."

"I know he's been trying to brainwash me. Sometimes I almost believe him."

"If anyone wants to rule the world, it's your brother."

"Do you think that's his plan? He is driven."

"I don't know. But enough about him." Lucas took my hand. "How are you feeling today? I didn't want to push you last night. I'd like to finish that conversation."

"I'm sorry I fell asleep. We were talking about my mom, and what she said about the scar. Then I woke up, and it was morning."

"Did you remember anything?"

"Only that my mom said I had stitches when I was a toddler. Maybe?" I touched the back of my head. "You don't think."

"That Doug did it?" Lucas glanced away. "Yeah, I do."

A small gasp escaped. "I can hardly remember the details. I asked about it once. Maybe twice. It's like my mom wants me to forget."

"Well, for today, let's forget." Lucas squeezed my hand. "No more talk of Doug. I want you to enjoy your time here."

I looked around at the children playing in the park. "Do you know which ones are Niners and which are family members?" I noticed two little girls swinging at the playground. "Well, obviously not them." I nodded toward the girls who were pushed higher into the air by a young boy. "But definitely him, their brother."

"You're right. I know everyone here, but we respect each other's privacy. They may want a family day, just them. It's understandable because one day they might be torn apart. Those aren't his sisters, Allie, even though he looks to be eight or nine."

"So in reality, he's thirty-two. I didn't think of that. Who are the girls?"

"His nieces. They're visiting for the day."

"Won't they want to help him?"

"You never know. I'm one of the lucky ones. Of course, parents want to protect their children, but siblings, extended family don't always have the same desire. Sometimes the Niner makes the choice to go off on his own, visit when he can. The family makes up lies to those who don't know him, say he's a long-lost cousin or something."

"You make it sound so sad, so tragic."

"Don't you dare say like Heathcliff." Lucas placed his head in his hands.

"I won't. I wasn't." *Well, maybe I thought of him.* "I

don't want to make you sad, Lucas. Tell me how this would work. Let's pretend we get married."

He lifted his head and smiled. "We could live anywhere you want. Have a normal life. No one would notice the age difference for years."

"And when twenty years have gone by, and you're twenty-five and I'm thirty-seven?"

"Still won't notice or I could grow a beard."

I had to laugh. "Don't think that would really help."

"Then plastic surgery."

"For me?"

"Never for you. I'd make myself older."

"Lucas, you're talking crazy now."

"Our kids wouldn't have to know. We could lead a normal life. I thought it all through, watched other Niners do it."

"Until their wife gets too old and finally—"

"You're getting ahead of yourself. You don't know what the future will bring." Lucas looked at me with such conviction; I almost believed it could work.

"What if I chose to live here?"

"We could do that, too. Whatever makes you happy."

"If you're safe, I'm happy." I leaned across the tiny table and kissed him. The little girls on the swings pointed and laughed. I waved to them.

I pulled Lucas up from his chair, and we continued to stroll, looking in the shop windows and stopping for lunch at a little café. People knew us and were friendly. As the afternoon began to wane, we started back for the house following the same route we took that morning. When we crossed the street to Lucas' house I noticed the brick didn't feel as hard as it should be. I bent down and poked it.

"Lucas, what's with the brick? It feels spongy."

"It's not brick. It's recycled tires."

"Oh, wow." Questions flew through my mind. "The first time I saw the village it was covered with snow but not the streets or sidewalks." I pointed at to the road. "Does that melt the snow?"

"There's a heating system running underground to keep the streets and sidewalks free of ice and snow. We heat the water at our solar power plant and run it through the pipes as needed. It also keeps us at a constant thirty-two degrees in winter. We never have a harsh one here."

We climbed the steps to the porch and sat on a swing in the front corner. "Lucas, do Niners share their discoveries with the rest of the world? I'm not saying they're selfish or anything. I don't blame them for wanting to be one step ahead of the world. Just wondering."

"Actually, we do share. Levi and Julian told stories of tracking R&D men, you know, research and development, to pass along ideas. They've found them at lunch, the theatre, baseball games and strike up a conversation, dropping the golden nugget along the way. Sometimes they go straight to the top and find a president of a company ready to listen."

"That's good to hear." I didn't want him to know I still needed information before I committed to living here. "Sharing the knowledge has to be hard."

"Now you see why we don't want the Task Force finding us or the compounds. They'd discover too many secrets. Call it 'too much information at one time' syndrome. It wouldn't be good, especially if it got in the wrong hands."

I shivered. I pictured Doug in control of those secrets. He wouldn't share. He'd just keep the power. In my mind, the Niners still had the edge. I saw them as the good guys.

"Cold? It's only seventy-eight degrees outside." Lucas teased as my thoughts returned to the present.

"You know I don't like the Task Force or Doug's part in it. I hate them and him."

"Don't hate the force. I don't. Now your brother?" He smiled.

"Really? After the STF drove you from your home? You don't blame them? You had to leave this." I swept my arm across my body.

"It was a low level breach. We probably could've stayed. Julian always errs on the side of caution. He consulted Levi. They thought it best to clear out for awhile."

"So all those people I saw today left for three years?"

"Yes. If families had young children, Levi sent them to the California compound. The rest of us were put in safe houses or given choices of other compounds. Remember, three years is not that long to us Niners."

"Refresh my memory. Julian's in charge here. Levi lives in California at another compound, but he's in charge of Julian?"

"Something like that. Levi lives and works from Spanish Village, located in the Napa Valley. He runs the California compound and also oversees the whole western half of the U.S. Julian reports to him."

A chain of command, like in the military. Lucas seemed afraid to say it. Both sides were an army. My resolve weakened again. Who exactly was the enemy?

He put his arm around me and pulled me closer. "Enough of the serious talk. How would you like to go shopping in Paris?" He helped me up, and we went inside.

The giant wall took us to places I only dreamed about. Paris became our backdrop for the evening. We ate dinner in front of the Eiffel Tower.

"I always dreamed of this." Lucas lips grazed me. "My girl and I below the Eiffel Tower." His mouth hungrily searched for mine, and I melted into his kiss.

"So I'm the first?" I took his arms and wrapped them around me, leaning against his chest. "I can't believe that."

"The first one I've ever been serious about." He kissed the top of my head. "I met a few girls over the years, but it never seemed right. Not until you. I eat, sleep and breathe you, Allie. You. Only you."

I untangled myself from his arms and pushed him down on the blanket we had spread on the floor. I nuzzled against him, kissing his ear and neck.

"Allie." Lucas breathed out my name. He ran his hands through my hair. His lips nipped my neck with soft, butterfly kisses. He kept whispering my name and kissing random spots. It was intoxicating. I ran my hands over his chest and around to his back.

"I love you." His mouth found mine again. He rolled me over onto my back. His eyes blazed with passion as he looked down on me.

"It's okay, Lucas. I'm ready." I closed my eyes waiting for his kiss.

CHAPTER TWENTY ONE

The warmth of Lucas' body disappeared. When I opened my eyes, I found him sitting next to me.

"You need to get to bed. You need your sleep." He ran his hand through his hair. "Go. Now."

It felt as if I was being sent to my room. "Lucas," I whispered.

"It's not going to happen, Allie." He wrapped his arm across my shoulders and kissed my cheek. "Goodnight."

I got up in a huff and pounded up the stairs to make a point. "I'm not a baby!" I yelled out when I reached the top.

"Then stop acting like one!" he called back.

I stormed to my room. Lucas didn't need much sleep, but insisted I get at least eight. We agreed on midnight as my bedtime. I glanced at my phone and saw I was right on schedule. Lucas must have a built-in alarm inside. He cut things off at just the right time. I'd show him. I set my alarm for three a.m. I'd sneak into his bed during the night.

When the alarm went off, it startled me awake. Lucas had excellent hearing so I tried my best to stay quiet. His door and mine had been left open. I tiptoed over to his bedroom and slid in next to him. I inched closer, and as I did, he rolled toward me. I breathed in a scent of citrus and spice, wanting to reach out and touch his face. If we weren't going to make love at least he could let me sleep next to him. I closed my eyes and dreamed of what would've happened if Lucas hadn't cut our evening short.

Eight a.m. I awoke, pretty unusual for me. I

blamed adrenaline. Last night's make-out session swirled in my head. I stretched my arms out to discover a body next to me. If waking up early seemed strange, Lucas sleeping late was definitely odd. I felt my hand grabbed and had to giggle. "You're not really sleeping, are you?"

"I've been up since five but didn't want to disappoint you." He kissed my hand. "When you snuck in here last night, I almost told you to go back to your own room."

"You heard me?"

"Of course. You tried so hard to make this happen. I didn't have the heart to ruin it."

I rolled on top of him and found him completely dressed. "I love you," I said.

We lay silent for a few minutes, our two hearts beating as one. Lucas rolled me back onto my side of the bed. "So I can sleep here with you?"

"Yeah, it's fine. You're asleep before I come to bed. I don't see the harm."

"The harm? Oh, you're so frustrating!" I playfully punched him in the arm.

Lucas jumped from the bed and started for the door before a pillow hit him. "We have a big day ahead so time to get ready."

I lounged in bed a few more minutes. I took his pillow, and hugged it to my body. His scent still lingered. I dozed off for a moment, and a voice startled me back to reality. "Allie, you coming?"

"Be there in a minute!" I dashed to my room, showered, dressed and raced to the kitchen. Lucas already had my lesson on the television screen.

"Try to pay better attention today."

"Got it!" I said after the travelogue ended. "I'll

watch it on the last day to refresh my memory. Where are we going today?"

"Headquarters. I want you to meet Julian and see how this operation is run."

"Does Julian know who I am?"

"Of course, he does. We all know you're not responsible for your brother's actions, if that's what you're thinking."

My nerves got the best of me. What if Julian didn't like me? What if he thought I was a spy? I played out all the scenarios in my head.

We jumped in Future Beetle, or Beetle as I had come to call the car. It would drive us anywhere we wanted all on its own. Lucas gave a command, and it moved along the road without a sound.

As we drove along, I looked beyond the homes of Victorian Village and saw the true natural beauty of the area. Ponderosa pines filled the landscape along with junipers, chokecherries and box elders. Wildflowers scattered among the various grasses took my breath away. Huge, craggy mountains surrounded the town. The village must be nestled in a valley between them.

We finally reached the large sand-colored facility. A door rose up, and we drove in. Beetle dropped us at the elevator and self-parked.

"Four." Lucas told the elevator. It whisked us to the top floor. The doors slid back, exposing command central. Conference rooms, a lounge area and rows and rows of work stations filled the area. Large white walls covered one side of the room. The other three walls were glass, giving a panoramic view of the area. Funny, I thought from the outside, the building didn't have windows.

A tall, muscular African-American man walked up,

extending his hand. He had that special look all Niners had, handsome and proud. "Allison, good to finally meet you. I'm Julian."

"Hello. It's nice to finally meet you in person. Please call me Allie." I shook his hand then he embraced Lucas.

"How's the family? Everyone settled in again?" Julian asked.

"Yes, we're all fine. Hannah and Joe like their schools. Stacy gave in and said we could stay in Virginia."

"Then it's good she came for a visit."

"Allie and I are here to see headquarters. I'd also like for you to tell her your story."

Julian gave a hearty laugh. "Not much to tell. Born a Niner, die a Niner."

That appeared to be an inside joke as they both chuckled. "Come on, let's sit."

Julian led us to a lounge area. A sleek white leather sectional with polished chrome legs filled up most of the space. It was arranged in the shape of a semi-circle with two round glass-topped ottomans in the center.

"Coffee?" Julian headed over to a large drink station behind the sofa and began to pour the liquid into a mug. "I hear you prefer lattes." Julian winked at me.

I nodded, overwhelmed by this futuristic place. Julian handed us coffee and settled in on the end of the sectional, crossing his legs, coffee cup in one hand and his other arm across the back of the couch.

"So, Lucas wants me to tell my story. Don't remember much of the first four years of my life. Like all Niners, complete memory function kicks in at the age of one, this might be a blessing. Wouldn't want to be reminded of how our parents fretted over our lack of growth."

"You're able to remember everything back to the age of one?" I felt my mouth open and snapped it shut.

"Pretty much. Not every detail, of course. Levi filled in the blanks for me." He shot Lucas a look. "She's heard of Levi, I hope?"

Lucas nodded, and Julian continued. "He came with Abe on the voyage to America to help set up the first compound in Pennsylvania. They kept their eyes and ears open for any rumblings about boys failing to thrive. That's what they called it in those days.

"Word about me made its way north. They plucked me from a little cabin right off a southern plantation in the middle of the night. They searched every home until they found the right one. They offered to take me, raise me, with my mother's blessing. She hid me for over a year and was afraid I would be found and killed. I don't know what my fate would've been if I stayed." Julian paused and took a sip of coffee.

It sounded like his mother was a slave before the Civil War. I had to wrap my mind around that. I tried to picture him alive back then. "You lived on a plantation? As a slave?"

"I was a well-hidden secret but yes, my mother and father were slaves."

"The Niners left your parents behind?"

"At the time, yes. My mother begged them to take me and not worry about them. Of course, Niners being Niners, they did worry."

I smiled. "I like that. Niners being Niners." More proof these men were stand-up guys, good-hearted men.

"They took me to the P.A. compound to live with

the rest of the Niners. Levi always treated me like his little brother. I think he was twelve at the time of the rescue. He insisted on going along and carried me the whole way back. Abe was like a father to me. Actually he was a father to us all. Levi never forgot my family. He made special trips south to check on them. When the time was right," Julian said as he gave me a huge grin, "they were brought north and lived outside the compound. I had three sisters. I was my parents' only son."

"I'm glad to hear your family was rescued." Tears pricked the corners of my eyes.

"I became a teenager in the early 1900s, married about twenty years later and brought my wife with me on the pilgrimage to Montana. By then my parents were gone and my sisters had lived long lives in Pennsylvania. I felt I could leave. We knew we needed more facilities. I would be in charge of this one."

"Are you the one who designed it?" I asked.

Julian expressed amusement. "I give some credit to my first wife, but yes, I did."

"I love it, it's so—"

"Nostalgic?"

"Yes, but it's more than that. It's so comforting and safe."

"She loved that time period, the architecture, the colors. Made sure everything was accurate, right down to the last detail. Once we were established here, Levi continued on to California to create another compound and set up the western regional base. Abe stayed here with me. He became the grandfather of the village."

"So you and your wife lived here the whole time."

"Yes, we did. I was in charge of the compound and needed to stay. My two children were born here. My wife passed away here. She's buried in the church cemetery on the outskirts of town as is my daughter. My son left the compound after college and now resides in Pennsylvania."

"Where you have your safe house."

"Yes, I like to be close by my son."

"May I ask his age?'

Julian chuckled. "He's pushing ninety."

"And now you have another wife?" I hated to bring it up but needed to know.

"Yes, I married again ten years ago. I went for many decades as a widower. Abe encouraged me to try again. He knew his time on earth was nearing its end and wanted to see me happy."

"Do you have children, a second family?"

"Yes, two girls, twins."

Still curious, I wanted to ask more questions, but a flashing light appeared on the wall. One by one, displays turned on. The dirt road we had taken just a few short days ago came on the screen.

"Someone's on the trail." Lucas and Julian used their phones to manipulate cameras. A dirt bike sped down the trail headed right for the dead end. We watched in silence until it turned around and away from the compound. "We need to add some diversions and more off-shoots to that road, Julian. Too many people have off-road vehicles these days." Lucas jumped up and pointed to different spots on the screen.

"Let's work on details while you're here. Draw up some designs."

While the two of them talked business, I wandered around the room, gazing out at the view from every angle. After seeing the dirt bike, it reminded me of Nate and home. It made me question if I could really leave it all behind. I felt so far removed from that world, like it didn't even exist. Oddly, I had no homesickness or regret. I realized I could do this.

The dirt bike on the security camera reminded me of Gene's passion for motorcycles. The streets of the village were not bike friendly. Where did he keep his bikes when he lived here? And where did he ride?

"A penny for your thoughts," Lucas whispered in my ear.

"Just wondering where Gene rode his bikes."

"And where we could ride? I'll show you when we leave. Julian and I are almost done."

Lunch miraculously showed up when we returned to the lounge area. Julian ate a sandwich and pointed for us to help ourselves.

"We're heading out after this." Lucas informed him. "I'll be back tomorrow for a few hours. How does four sound?"

"In the morning?" I asked, nearly choking on my sandwich.

"Yes. You'll be sleeping and won't even know I'm gone," Lucas said. "Ready to go?"

Rising from my seat, Julian came over and hugged me. "Good to finally meet you, Allie."

"You, too, Julian." We started to walk away, but I still had something on my mind. I turned and locked eyes with him. "Julian?"

"Yes?"

"I'm sorry about my brother."

"He's nothing more than a mosquito in our ear, Allie."

"Okay, if you say so. I'd never forgive him if he did something to any one of you."

"You take care and enjoy your time here." Julian

was so sincere; I had no choice but to believe him.

As we rode the elevator down to the second floor, I took Lucas' hand. "I like Julian, and I love it here."

"Good, then you're really going to love this!" He swept me off my feet and placed me in Beetle, waiting by the elevator door. I began to think of Beetle as another person, a friend we could rely on.

"Cycle barn." Lucas gave the command, and we flew off.

Beetle headed toward the village but at the last minute veered onto a service road running along the edge of town. Passing a cul-de-sac of futuristic office buildings and a few non-descript ones, I wondered what could be inside. We neared a curve in the road, but Beetle continued straight onto a dirt path taking us farther away from the village. Finally I saw a huge barn, similar to the one on the Montgomery property in Virginia. Beetle parked in front, and Lucas ordered the doors of the barn to open. The place held two bikes.

"We left a few if anyone wanted to ride." Lucas handed me a helmet from the counter, I slipped behind him, and we went roaring out of the barn. We swerved around the side of the building and into the woods. Lucas chose the closest trail among the trees and bushes. We came out into a field of wild flowers and traveled along in the warm sunshine. The trail took us past headquarters, then into to the forest again and finally back to the barn.

"That was great!" I removed my helmet and placed it on the workbench in the barn.

"We can go out of the compound and ride into town or anywhere you want to go."

"For now, this is enough." I wrapped my arms around Lucas and snuggled against him. He was my knight, my prince who would always protect me. He may be a bit conservative, but I'd honor his wishes. I'd leave the idea and the opportunity for making love alone. "Let's go home and spend the rest of the day just the two of us."

"Anything you want."

"As long as you don't make me go to school!" I laughed.

"I promise."

We kissed as if to seal the deal and climbed into Beetle for the ride back to the house. I leaned my head back against the cushioned seat and soaked everything in. I didn't want to forget one thing about this perfect trip. But in my heart I knew it couldn't last, perfect never does.

CHAPTER TWENTY TWO

Back to reality. On the plane ride home, Stacy showed me pictures of her sisters, telling me about their personalities, husbands, boyfriends, and children. We put pictures on my phone so I had something to show my parents. Lucas cropped me in so it looked believable.

The trip went too fast. I struggled with the thought of going home. Lucas and I had settled into a routine during our stay. We never left the village. I didn't want to see any sights or go into town. If we did go somewhere, we used the giant wall. I walked the Great Wall of China, hiked through the Amazon and went on a safari.

Toward the end of the week, I felt a little homesick and went back to my mall. As I headed for my favorite store, I saw Ashley and Nate right in front of me. I called out to Lucas, asking if I really saw them. He confirmed and joined me at the wall, telling me to give Nate a call. I watched my friend reach for his phone and explained I could see him. I begged him to find a way to turn Ashley around.

I watched Nate put his arm around Ash and spin her around. As he did, he gave a little wave, making my day. She gave him a little punch in the arm. I heard her ask who called, and he gave her the phone. We chatted for awhile without Ashley knowing I could see her every move. I watched them walk through the mall and sit at a table in the food court. I wished I could share with her, but knew better than to put Lucas in jeopardy.

Every night I slept in Lucas' bed. He made sure to be there in the morning when I woke. We strolled through the village, had lunch or coffee in the square, visited headquarters, and rode the bike through the woods. On the last day he took me up into the mountains. I cried as we packed, feeling like I'd never return again.

As the plane taxied to the gate, I sent a quick text to Ashley, making plans to meet her and Nate later. They went to prom, and she made a scrapbook while we were away. Nate had a memorable prom instead of going with me. The two of them radiated happiness that day, I pictured Ash in her sapphire blue dress and Nate in a black tux with a matching blue vest and tie. I think I missed them more than my parents if I ran away with Lucas and felt horrible.

Gene picked us up from the airport. We couldn't stop talking about the trip and asked what the Montgomery family did while we were away. Too soon, Gene pulled into my driveway. Vacation ended. Real life began. Lucas hopped out, removed my luggage from the back and walked me to the door. I couldn't stand to watch him walk away so I went in the house.

"Mom? Dad? I'm home," I called out in the entryway.

Mom scurried out of the family room. "My goodness, we didn't hear you come in. Did we, Jim?" She hugged me then held me at arm's length. "You look tan and healthy. You remembered to eat I take it."

"Of course. Did you think Stacy's family would let me starve? There was food everywhere." I teased Mom as she shook her head and smiled. I named the dishes and desserts Stacy said her family served.

"Well, it sounds like they fed you well." Mom linked arms and guided me to the family room.

"There's my girl!" Dad smiled and stood. I got a

big bear hug.

"Come." I motioned to him. "Sit here. I'll show you pictures. Mom, sit on my other side." In the back of my mind I knew I could look at my real pictures later. At least I could share the true vacation with Nate. After we finished I said, "Lucas and I are going out with Ash and Nate tonight so I won't be here for dinner."

Dad leaned back, eyes wide. "You just got home, and you're going back out? "Kids these days." He shook his head.

I laughed. "Didn't Doug and Dean go out all the time? Hang out with their friends?"

"If I wanted them to stay home for family time, they didn't go out."

I found that hard to believe, but kept silent. I didn't have the heart to say I would be at the diner with Lucas' family. I spent the rest of the afternoon with Mom and Dad, talking, watching TV, sitting on the deck, whatever they wanted to do.

A few hours later, I made the journey to the diner. It felt good to be back behind the wheel again although I'd never forget Beetle. I had a picture of her on my phone. I decided early on she must be a girl, and we became the best of friends.

As I pulled into the parking lot, I saw Nate's car. I hurried up the few steps to the diner and spotted Sean behind the counter. I froze in place. "Not again!"

He held up his hands in surrender. "Just helping out, Allie. Don't shoot me."

Lucas appeared from the back and grabbed a tray. "Allie, meet Sean. He's a good friend."

I lifted my hand in acknowledgment, not saying a word. He still scared me.

Lucas filled four sodas at the fountain machine and came around the counter. "We're over here." He nodded at Ashley and Nate already seated toward the back of the diner.

Ashley bounced out of the booth and hugged me like she hadn't seen me in a year. "Allie, I'm so glad you're home. I missed you. I want to show you the prom pictures."

We both slid in on the same side so we could view the scrapbook together. Lucas shrugged and slipped in next to Nate.

Stacy brought our food to the table. I couldn't believe she came to work on the first day home. "Stacy, I didn't expect to see you tonight."

"Need to keep busy, Allie." She seemed fidgety, unlike herself, but it had been a long day. "Here are some appetizers to keep you kids from starving."

She placed a few baskets in front of us filled with crispy battered green beans and baked flat bread with spinach dip. "Burgers and chicken sandwiches in fifteen."

"Thanks, Mom!" Lucas called after her as she returned to the counter.

Ashley asked a lot of questions about our vacation. Nate stayed unusually quiet. No snarky comments or jokes as I rambled on about the trip. I began to wonder how much he knew. Had Lucas told him more than I was aware? Or had he been doing undercover research on his computer again? Lucas asked him to stop any questionable searches months ago, but did he?

In an instant, my heart sank. I couldn't take another bite. Doug had gotten to Nate while we were away. That had to be it. He sat there taking notes to report back to the STF. My heart pounded through the rest of the meal. I analyzed everything Nate said or did. My fear overwhelmed me. Idle gossip became the furthest thing from my mind. Nate could be the mole.

"Lucas, can we talk?" I asked as we walked to the Jeep. When we finished dinner, he insisted I leave with Ash and Nate saying I needed my rest.

"Sure, I'll call you later."

I got a quick kiss at the car then Lucas strolled over to Nate's car to talk. I backed out of the parking space mentally begging Lucas to notice how hesitant I was to leave. I finally had to pull out into the street. I'd have to wait until I got home to talk to him.

All my plans went out the window when I saw an ambulance parked in my driveway when I got home. My heart pounded on the way home, but now the sound drummed in my ears. I ran into the house, bumping into someone I never expected to see.

"Doug! Are Dad and Mom alright?"

He stepped aside, exposing my parents standing together in the family room. Mom looked like she'd been crying for some time. Her phone lay smashed on a table, out of commission. Gene hadn't heard any of their conversation or I would have been alerted.

"What's going on?" I rushed to my mother's side. She wrapped her arms around me, brushing my hair away from my face and stroked my cheek.

"She's my baby, Doug." Mom's words scared me.

"Mom," Doug said as he stepped toward us. "We've been over this before. She's my sister. I'd never do anything to harm her. I'll protect her with my life."

What does that mean? What's going on here? "Someone needs to tell me what's happening." I trembled, and Mom held me tighter.

My dad took me by the arm, separating me from

Mom. "Allie, Doug's been doing an investigation of a certain cult for some time now. They've grown in numbers and have infiltrated mainstream America looking for young people to join their ranks."

What? Such a lie! That isn't what he told me. I tried to make sense of what he just said. Dad sounded a lot like Doug. I wondered how many times he heard that speech from his son.

"Doug's unit has been watching for movement in this area, targeting and investigating people new to the area."

"So Doug thinks Lucas' family is part of a cult?" I screamed, hoping the listening device wasn't disabled on Mom's phone.

"No, they're just one of many on the list. He wants to rule them out."

I convinced myself to go along with the lie. "I can vouch for Lucas."

"True, but Doug needs to do it for himself. Do you think you can get Lucas to come over? Doug has yet to meet him."

Alarms went off in my head. I'd never let Doug meet Lucas or come near him. It became clear in that moment, which side I was on. "Sure, I left my phone in the car. I need to get it."

"Good try." Doug took a few steps toward me. "I think your phone's in your back pocket. Check again."

I slipped my hand in that pocket and pulled it out. I fumbled with the buttons to send a message with no success. "Oh, I *did* bring it in."

"Hand it over." Doug put out his hand.

I slammed the cell into his palm. He grabbed some device off the table and placed it on top of the phone. The machine whirled and spun, then went silent.

I heard plastic cracking and my phone broke in pieces next to my mother's.

"Doug!" I took a swing at him, but my dad caught my arm. He captured me around the waist, pulling me back. I could hear Dad breathing heavily as I struggled to get away. It took a lot out of him to hold me back.

"See what's happened, Jim!" Mom yelled. "I told you this could turn out badly. We should've included Allie from the beginning." She took my face in her hands and turned my head toward her.

"At the beginning of the school year your brother came to visit. He informed me of the cult and said if you made any new friends to let him know. He wanted to check them out. When you brought Lucas home and said he was new to the area, I called Doug. That's why he came on your birthday, but he showed up too late."

She came closer, almost whispering. "After you two broke up, I was so relieved. I didn't like talking to Doug behind your back. I prayed you wouldn't make any new friends this year so it could be over. Doug insisted I keep track of you and who you saw, no matter what I said.

"Then you started seeing Lucas again. I felt Doug already had enough information but he persisted. I felt so bad deceiving you. You've done nothing wrong. Remember that. No matter what, you've done nothing wrong." Tears streamed down her face. "Jim, let her go."

Dad released me with a sigh. "Please cooperate," he whispered.

I ran my hands through my hair to calm down. As I did, I touched the scar. Suddenly my resolve to fight became stronger.

"We have to go now." Doug grasped me by the

arm, but I shrugged him off. I threw myself at my mother and buried my head in her shoulder. "I'm not going anywhere with you." I couldn't look at him. His hands were on my shoulders now. I squirmed to get away. Doug ripped me from my mom's arms.

"Jim, please! Don't let him take my baby." Mom cried like I never heard before. My heart ached for her. She stretched out her arms to ask Doug to return me to them.

"Clair, he'll take care of her. It's for her safety. Doug will bring her home soon."

I processed what Dad just said. He *knew* Doug wanted to take me somewhere, and he was okay with it? Mom seemed against it.

"Mom! He won't take care of me." I yelled, hoping she'd bring everyone to their senses. "Where's he taking me? Why does he need me?"

Mom shuffled toward me, but Dad got in between us. "Let Doug do his job, Clair."

"Mom! Mom!" I felt myself lifted into the air and carried out the door. I heard her screaming and crying, saying it wasn't right over and over again.

"Mom!" I kept screaming her name until I went hoarse. The back of the ambulance opened as Doug carried me out of the house. He placed me inside with two armed guards. The doors slammed shut.

I heard the engine start and saw red flashing lights through the windows. No siren. An ambulance rushing through the streets would draw less attention than a military van.

Very smart, Doug. I slipped down in the corner, trying to make myself as small as possible. The inside of the ambulance stayed dark except for the flashes of light from the streetlights and signs as we drove along.

The guards sat across from each other on benches, holding rifles between their legs.

So much for keeping me safe, Doug. Looks like they've been ordered to shoot if I try to escape. I fought back tears, refusing to cry. I needed my wits about me if I wanted to escape. Lucas couldn't find me. My phone destroyed. Mom's had been crushed for hours.

Then Lucas' words came back to me. "I'll always know where you are. I'll find you". He'd find me, and he *would* rescue me.

A slight smile crept over my face. I could almost hear the brakes of the ambulance screech to a halt as the Montgomerys came to the rescue. The victory fantasy lasted only a moment. Darkness filled the space where my liberation played out seconds ago. Panic gripped my throat. I realized a trap had been set. Doug won again. He destroyed any means of communication between Lucas and me. Doug put me in an ambulance. Anyone would assume we were headed to the hospital. If Lucas came for me, Doug would quickly figure out he was a Niner.

Kudos, Doug, kudos to you.

CHAPTER TWENTY THREE

I woke up in a small, neat room, surprised that I had fallen asleep. I had a hazy memory of pulling into an out of the way run-down motel. The one-story building stretched out from the office in either direction. I put up quite a fight and recalled something jabbed in my arm. It then became clear why I slept.

As I gazed around the room, I looked for an escape route. The room appeared too clean for an old motel. It took a second to realize everything was brand new. The double bed had crisp new sheets. A comfy, overstuffed chair sat in the corner next to the only window overlooking the front parking lot. Brand new patterned curtains with sheers framed the window. The dresser had a flat screen TV on top. I opened its drawers to find some of my clothes. I wondered who helped pack those things.

My only hope of escape could be the bathroom. I rushed in, hoping to find a small window to crawl through. No window, but the room had a shower big enough for one person, a toilet with a sink directly in front of it. The fluffy towels smelled brand new. *Good old Doug, always thinking of others.*

I walked back out to my prison, and turned on the television. The channel button didn't work. The remote did no good. A movie list appeared on the screen, comedies, chick flicks and some action movies. I shut the TV down and flopped on the bed. Staring at the ceiling, I tried to brainstorm ideas on how to break out and prayed Lucas stayed away.

The whole day went by without seeing anyone except delivery men who brought food. I only saw those people from the window and tried to figure out my location from the logos on the delivery trucks. The guards met them at their vans or stopped them before they reached the door. They got paid and sent on their way. Then I'd hear a knock, the door opened and one of Doug's goons handed breakfast, lunch and finally dinner to me. Of course, I handed breakfast right back.

I figured Doug wanted to break me down by leaving me alone for hours on end, worrying about what would come next. I finally gave in out of boredom and watched some movies well into the night. I could only take so much of Doug TV and shut everything down. I sized up the room and devised a workout routine.

The only thing left to do was sit in the dark and stare out the window through the sheer curtains. I could hear my captors talking outside the window. They probably thought I went to bed. I slid the chair closer and eavesdropped.

"Cap said to give her twenty-four hours to cool down. Then he'll be here." One of the goons said to the other.

"I thought he'd bring some men from the Special Team to help."

"They don't know we're here. Those self-righteous bastards wouldn't approve of our tactics. They want everything to be on a voluntary basis. Brains over muscle should be their motto." He laughed.

Special Team? Niners worked for Doug? Lucas never talked about the Task Force having a Special Team, maybe he didn't know.

"Yeah, those five guys don't realize they're being used as pawns. Too bad, I like them. If Cap doesn't increase their ranks, we'll never create the military machine he envisions. He needs answers from his sister. If he's wrong about the boyfriend being special, we'll move on to the next case."

"Didn't that contact say to watch Allison Sanders? She'll lead us to what we want?"

"That snitch has been inconsistent with their tips. We get a message here and there. So far they've led to nothing."

I almost forgot about Nate. Yesterday I figured out he was the leak, now this confirmed it. He sent messages to Doug. I heard it with my own ears. He passed along tips to Lucas' whereabouts. I hoped he was happy now that they locked me away in some prison motel with nothing to do except vegetate. Doug thought he could break me down? Just watch.

* * * *

A knock on my door came early the next day. I watched the door push back to reveal Doug on the other side. He stepped in, breakfast in hand. "I thought we could have breakfast together."

I sat in the chair, staring out the window, seeing nothing. He strolled over to the tiny table on the other side of the bed and set the bag down.

"Allison!"

I jumped. "I. *Don't*. Eat. Breakfast."

"Coffee?" He held up a foam cup.

Can't use that to slit his throat now, can I? I put up my hand in rejection. *Get a clue, Doug. You don't know anything about me.*

"Do I have to come over there and get you?" Doug's eyes burned through me. I didn't move.

He took a few threatening steps toward me. "Allison," he hissed. I froze. A few more paces, and he stood in front of me. "Get up!" he ordered as he grabbed my arm. "If you don't, I'll snap it in two." He squeezed my arm so hard I bit my lip to keep from crying out.

I rose from the chair, afraid of what he'd do next. His free hand flew to my other arm. I felt my feet leave the floor. My body slammed against the wall, the sound echoed through the room. My head bounced off the solid surface and back again. "When I tell you to do something, do it!" The rage in his voice made my heart bounce against my chest. I felt his hot breath on my face. His eyes became as large as saucers.

My brain scrambled. I didn't want him to see me come undone. I had to get over the shock of being thrown against the wall like a common criminal. Never in a million years did I think he'd go that far. I bit the insides of my cheeks, willing myself not to cry.

"Sit." He gestured to the chair across the room. I obeyed like a well-trained dog. "So, Allison, are you comfortable? Is the room up to your standards?" Doug asked as straightened his jacket and settled into the chair across from me.

"Really, Doug? That's all you have to say?" *Is he Jekyll or Hyde now?*

"Well, I do have some questions."

"I'm your captive audience."

"Sorry it has to be like this, but I can't get you to stay in one place long enough to talk."

"So you kidnap me? And throw me around?"

"I didn't throw you around. I needed to get your attention."

"Okay, if you didn't throw me around, what do you call it? And will it be alright to tell our parents?" I poked the bear.

"They won't believe you." He smirked. "That was

between you and me, right? Brother, sister stuff."

I gave in. "Right." I fought back tears. My stomach hurt, yet something inside me wanted to smash his face in. I fought down the fear and focused on the anger.

"Besides, Mom and Pop know where you are."

"Really? So I can call them?" I only had the bare essentials in the room, no phone to be found.

"Maybe later." He shifted in his seat. "So on your trip to Missouri, did you visit any place you'd consider unusual?"

"Yeah." I baited him as he leaned forward. "There was this huge building filled with people. I think it was called a wholesale warehouse."

"Very funny. Think! Did you meet anyone you thought was too friendly or happy to buy you anything you wanted?" Doug wouldn't give up on the cult angle.

"Nope."

"Any new friends move here recently? Beside your boyfriend that is."

"Doug, I'm sure the school system would be happy to oblige. I'm clueless."

"You like Lucas."

"Yes."

"How's his hearing?"

Doug changed topics, trying to bait me. I needed to focus. "Good, it's very good." His eyes lit up. "Like any teenager."

"I believe you said his birthday was in March. When did you celebrate it?"

"The weekend after."

"And he turned how old?"

"Seventeen." I wanted to say eighty but held back. My sarcastic remark could lead to the truth.

"Nothing strange about him or his family?"

"If you think they're part of this cult, they're not. They're just hard-working people trying to get by like the rest of us."

"Reclusive though."

"Yes, they only come out at night. I forgot to check for fangs. Is that what you're still looking for? Vampires?" I tilted my head and exposed my neck. "See any marks?"

"Allie, if you can't be serious—"

"Doug, they live in the country. Didn't you have a friend who lived out there? How often did you see him?"

"Not much until he learned to drive."

"I rest my case."

Doug stood to leave, taking all the garbage except for my coffee and a bottle of water.

"Leaving something behind for the inmates?"

"Come on, Allie, it's not that bad. I had this place painted, new carpet and all new furniture installed." He used my nickname as if that made it all better.

"Thanks, Doug, but I hate you. Dean's my favorite brother and you are—"

"I'm sorry to hear that."

"When I get out of here, don't ever talk to me again." I held my voice steady. "Don't buy me a single present or even send a Christmas card."

"I'm sure you don't mean that," he said so sincerely the hairs on my arms stood up.

He shut the motel door behind him. I threw the coffee cup across the room. Brown liquid ran down the shiny white door staining the fresh paint. Splatters of brown dripped on the blue carpet. Instantly I felt better. The room needed to get back to its roots.

* * * *

I flopped on the bed for what seemed like hours until I heard a car pull up in front of the room. *Please don't be Doug again!*

I ran to the window and spotted a delivery van with a strange logo on the side—Nuts Diner. *Great, my lunch is being delivered from a place with a logo of a crazy, crossed-eyed man wearing a bib.* He had a fork in one hand and a knife in the other as he waited for his food.

The van door opened. I blinked a few times. I couldn't believe who I saw. Sam. He talked with the men outside and placed their food on a small table between them. He made a move toward the door, but one man put out his arm to stop him. The other took the bag, nodded and sent Sam on his way. *He wanted to deliver the food himself.* I pounded the arm of the chair. He probably had important information to give me. I'd never find out now.

Keeper Number One, as I came to call him, entered the room and handed me the bag and a drink. "You got a half hour. Snooze, you lose."

I stuck out my tongue behind his back. They always came for the garbage, making sure I didn't keep a plastic fork or straw because I could do *so* much damage.

My favorite chicken sandwich from the diner sat in a clear plastic container. I unrolled the napkin when I got to the table and realized the writing on it must hold a clue. My heart began to pound. I wanted Keeper One out of the room so I could analyze the message. The door finally shut, and I breathed a sigh of relief.

I smoothed the napkin out and studied it. It read *Nuts Diner* at the top and the picture of the crazy man drawn below. Underneath him it said, *Use this to mop up the mess!*

I kept staring at the paper for the longest time. The words didn't make sense. Lucas knew the bag might be the only thing that would make it past the guards. The Montgomerys invented Nuts Diner so they could deliver the food. Still, I was stumped.

I stared and stared at the message while I ate the sandwich. I needed to figure it out before garbage time. I hated that they set a time limit. Not fair. I should tell Doug on them, but he'd probably be on their side.

Panic swept over me. For the first time since being locked in this hellhole, I couldn't shake the feeling. *I don't need a panic attack.* I lectured myself over and over until I calmed down. *Solve the riddle, and you'll get out of here.*

I finished the sandwich and started playing with the container. A clear plastic rectangle popped out of the bottom but didn't leave a hole. Another layer of clear plastic still filled the bottom. I slipped the plastic piece in my pocket, ran to the dresser and shoved the napkin in my underwear. I'd study the card later, the knock would come soon.

Keeper Number Two got garbage detail today. He checked the bag, started to leave then looked in the bag again. "The napkin?'

"Oh, I blew my nose in it and flushed it down the toilet. Is that okay?" I smiled sweetly.

"Sure." He stared at me like he had something more to say.

"Yes?" I blinked a few times and tilted my head to the side.

"Why don't you just tell Doug what he wants to know?" He sounded almost kind.

I couldn't hold back. Real tears fell from my eyes. "I don't know what he wants from me."

Keeper Two walked back and sat across the table. "Look. You know your brother can't give you any details. Everything's top secret."

I stared at him trying to look confused and innocent. "Oh."

His face relaxed. "I shouldn't tell you this. Your brother's working on something big. It's something that could affect the entire world, not just our country. These men, the ones he's looking for, can help. We already have five in our ranks. They're called the special team."

My eyes widened. Shocked he shared the information; I decided I'd given off a very clueless, sympathetic vibe. "Special team?"

"An international team of highly intelligent men. One's from the Netherlands, the others are from Brazil. Russia. UK. France. It goes beyond our country. It goes beyond us. Don't you see?"

"No, I guess I don't." From what I could tell, Keeper Two had no clue the real origin of these men. He thought they just had high IQ's, and Doug was searching the globe for more like them. *Very clever, Doug. Keep everyone in the dark.*

"These guys are working on a special project, one that could bring peace to the world. I want to be part of that. That's why we're all in. No questions asked."

"Wow!" I tried to sound impressed. I really wanted to say he sounded brainwashed. "Then why is Doug using force to achieve his goal?"

"Sometimes there has to be war before there is peace." Keeper Two rattled the saying off like a company slogan then looked as if he said too much. "I'll put a good word in for you. Just tell me where this Lucas kid lives, and you can walk right out that door."

He played the good cop to Doug's bad one. The false sympathy oozed off him. Little did he know he just gave me the information I needed. They wanted to find the safe house. Niner technology still won. I'd seen a map of the area. It looked like a dense forest. No signs of civilization. My moment of weakness dissolved. "I've never been to his house."

"Good to know." Number Two got up to leave. Being the go-getter of two, he looked disappointed. "If you think of anything?"

"I'll let you know." I pointed at him as if we made a connection.

When he opened the door, Doug stood on the other side. "Sir!" Keeper Two saluted and stepped back to let him in. They spoke in hushed tones and Keeper left the room after another salute.

I couldn't believe Doug had come back so soon. Another interrogation would begin. I had no time to study the items Sam smuggled in.

"Allison!" My body jumped at the sound. My mind flashed to his bout of violence that morning as I pictured my body hitting the wall again.

He stood next to my chair. "Let's end this today, and I'll take you home."

"I have no clue why I'm here, Doug. Why don't you tell me what you want from me?"

He slapped me hard across the face. "Just answer the questions."

Tears welled up in my eyes. I bit my bottom lip. "If you hit me again I will scratch your eyes out."

"Try it."

"Is that a challenge?"

He held up his hands. "I just get so frustrated with you."

"And I hate you!" I rose from my seat, made my hands into fists and beat on his chest.

Doug grabbed my arms and wrestled me back into the chair. "There. Feel better now?"

I reached up to massage the back of my head, still sore from the earlier beating and rubbed over the scar. *Am I dealing with a crazy man? Or one just filled with rage and jealousy?* "Keep away from me, Doug."

"You just have to tell me what you know about Lucas." Doug pulled back the seat across from me and sat down. "Where does he live? Where did he come from? Is that so hard?" He yelled as he pounded on the table.

"Why don't you tell me about this scar on the back of my head?" I screamed back. If he wanted crazy, I decided to match his every move.

Doug looked genuinely shocked. "Scar?"

"The one you gave me. Right here on the back of my head." I pointed to the spot. "What did you do to me? It had to be bad if your girlfriend broke up with you because of it."

"What?" Doug's face turned red. I thought steam would come out of his ears. "My girlfriend ended things after high school because she felt we were on two different paths in life."

"Yeah, she was nice, and you were a child abuser."

Doug pounded the table again. "You have no idea what happened."

I leaned forward and hissed, "What did you do? It's just you and me, Doug. Tell me. I'm not going anywhere." I taunted him.

"I loved you!" Doug leaned back and waved his hand in the air. "It's just that you were in the way. Kimmie loved babies. She always wanted to do things with you. Take you to the park. Take you for ice cream. She'd play with you when she came to the house. I never got to be alone with her. She was infatuated with you. Just once." He took a breath during the rant.

"Just once what?"

"I wanted to go somewhere without you," he whispered.

"Why didn't you just tell her that?"

"I did. You always clung to her and cried if she left the room. It was annoying."

"What did you do to me?" I asked again.

"We had plans to go to the beach. I had no idea Kimmie would want you to go along. Too much work dragging a toddler to the ocean. But she insisted. I made up a lie and said you'd been fussy all day, but she didn't seem to hear me."

I'd never agree with Doug, but I could see his point. "Go on."

"Kimmie went into the kitchen to talk to Mom while I watched you in the family room. Your favorite thing was to head to the dining room, climb on one of the chairs and look at the dishes in the china cabinet. You were a pain in the ass when it came to that. Pop finally put a baby gate across the dining room entryway to stop you from going in. Well, on that particular day, someone forgot to shut it. You got away from me—"

"Or you weren't watching me." I had to interrupt.

"Whatever. I followed after and found you climbing the chair. I decided it was the opportune time to prove you were fussy and pinched your leg."

"That's real nice." I crossed my arms and stared him down, trying to ignore the throbbing in my cheek. My one eye still watered from the hit.

"You didn't notice and kept climbing. I pinched

you harder. That time you let out a cry, but it didn't stop you. You just swatted my hand away and said 'no'. Finally you stood up on the seat of the chair. I went to pinch you one more time. You stepped back to get away from me. You fell backwards into the china cabinet and hit your head."

I covered my mouth to contain the gasp. "You let me fall?"

"Not really. It was too late before I realized what happened." Doug stared down at his hands. "Kimmie saw it all."

He appeared more upset that she witnessed the accident than about my fall. "And what happened to me?"

"There was blood everywhere, but you only needed some stitches. I think you had a mild concussion. You were fine." He looked up at me and smiled. "Look at you now. You're a beautiful teenage girl."

What is wrong with him? Does he think flattery will fix everything? I questioned if he was remorseful or just repeating a story from his past. He reminded me of a story Mom always read at Christmas, the Grinch with the heart two sizes too small. It made me wonder if Doug had a heart at all.

I bit my bottom lip to keep control. The harder I dug in my teeth, the more it helped to stay in the moment. I had to keep probing and deflecting until he wanted to leave. "What did Mom say?" Would this be the moment of truth or Doug's version?

"She realized it was an accident and blamed herself. She's the one who left the gate open."

Tears filled my eyes. I fought to keep my composure. Of course my beautiful, sweet mother took the blame so her son wouldn't feel guilty. Knowing her, she probably *did* blame herself. "Did Kimmie tell her you let me fall?"

"No." Doug's jaw tensed, and his eye twitched. "We talked at the hospital. She said she wouldn't tell."

"And that's when she broke up with you."

"How did you know?"

"I have my ways, Doug. Must run in the family." My emotions went all over the place. One second I felt like sobbing and the next I wanted to laugh hysterically. But the best thing that came out of the conversation? I distracted Doug from the reason he brought me here—Lucas—sat least for now.

"You know," Doug stood. "I'm going to give you some time to think about everything. You'll come to realize that I never meant to hurt you just like I don't mean you any harm now. You *are* my sister. You are family. Don't ever forget that."

"But you blame me for losing Kimmie. Don't you?" I stared at him hard, trying to get him to admit he hated me.

He didn't respond and turned his back. "I'll be back tonight, Allison. Try to get some rest. Hopefully we'll be going home tonight." The door opened. "Or not." I watched him leave without so much as a glance in my direction.

I threw myself onto the bed and muffled the sound of my screams in a pillow. I wanted to go home. I wanted to be rescued. I felt so helpless lying in the dingy motel room. The walls felt like they were closing in on me. I desperately needed to get out. I rolled on my back to calm myself, picking a spot on the ceiling to concentrate on. The remote lay next to me. I turned on the TV, raising the volume, just for appearance. Between Two's and Doug's conversations, I had so much to process.

As I went over both conversations, I focused on all the new information I learned. From what I could tell, Doug planned on taking over the world or at least the country. I laughed out loud. "That sounds ridiculous. He's just my stupid brother who has a giant ego, a dangerous one." A shiver went through me. I remembered back to a conversation I had with him after Lucas' birthday. He talked about the nuclear bomb.

Picture having an antidote, being able to diffuse it. Our country would be safe. No one could threaten us again. I wrapped my arms around my body and squeezed. I thought this was a game. Me against Doug. Brother vs. sister. Sibling rivalry. But it wasn't. Doug liked chess. He methodically planned each of his moves. I was the piece that wouldn't cooperate, wouldn't get out of his way.

Keeper Two said there had to be war before peace. Was that Doug's plan? War? I wished this was a badass novel, the kind of book Ash liked to read. I'd have super powers and would join forces with the good guys. We'd win the country back from the bad guys and lock them away. If only it was a story, I could write my own ending.

No one would believe me if I told them what happened over the past few months. "Look," I'd say. "There are these men called Niners. They're the good guys. Then there's the STF, short for special task force. They're the bad guys. I think they want to take over the country, maybe the world with Doug as their leader. Oh, and I forgot to add, Doug's my brother and the leader of the bad guys! What? You don't believe me? Why not? It makes perfect sense." I slapped my forehead. "Yeah, right. Makes perfect sense."

I turned the TV volume louder and stared at the screen. *You have to free yourself, Allison Sanders. Stop feeling sorry for yourself. Be your own independent woman. Get up and do something. Save yourself.*

I slipped off the edge of the bed and headed for the dresser. I took the napkin from its hiding place and pulled the plastic card from my pocket. Lucas had to make this simple enough for me to figure out. I carried the two items to the table, placing them side by side. As I studied them, I saw nothing. No clues. I had to give up out of pure frustration. I began to spin the napkin as a distraction. After a few spins I paid closer attention.

I squinted and twirled the napkin around as something jumped out at me. Nuts, upside down, made me see another word. Stun. Nuts spelled backwards. I read the message again, only this time with the new word. *Stun. Use this to mop up the mess.* The napkin was a weapon.

I placed the napkin on the bed and pressed the picture. Nothing happened. The crazy-eyed guy stared at me as if to say, "Try harder."

The word *nuts* could be the spot. After all, it really meant stun. My hand trembled as I touched the word, hoping it worked. I heard a snap and let out a sigh of relief. It would do more than that to my captors. Knowing Lucas, it would be lights out for awhile.

I moved on to the plastic card. That became a no-brainer. It unlocked the door. I had to find a time when I could catch the keepers off-guard, stun them and run. They had to think I escaped, not that Lucas rescued me. What a brilliant plan.

Keepers One and Two had to be getting tired of watching over a teenage girl. It couldn't be in their job description. After two days on the job, they might let their guard down.

I had to wait for the right moment to escape. The chance came as the evening sky glowed with sunset colors of orange and pink. I hear One tell Two he needed a quick break and would be in the office if needed. Translation: a bathroom break. My time to strike.

Two sat closest to the door, making it easy to zap him. I slipped the plastic card into the door slot. It silently opened.

Thank you, Lucas. The sun had begun to set behind the trees opposite the motel. It hurt the eyes to look at the sky, creating a great distraction. I placed the napkin on Two's neck and pushed hard. He looked up at me surprised, and crashed to the pavement. I stuffed the napkin and key in my back pocket, leaving no evidence behind. A decision had to be made. I looked in both directions then chose to run away from the office to the far end of the motel.

CHAPTER TWENTY FOUR

A closed, neglected bar sat next to the motel then miles of overgrown, neglected landscape. I could hide out in the building, but that would be the first place they'd look.

As I grew closer to the last room, I made my decision. *Run.*

My feet pounded the pavement until I reached the overgrown weed patch in front of the bar. I pushed through the tall grass and wild weeds, focusing on the next part of my escape. I couldn't run along the road. I'd be too easy to find.

The parking lot sat on the other side of the bar. I planned to stop and scope out the landscape. The street curved to the right with unkempt patches of wild grass and scruffy trees on either side. No sign of civilization. I headed for the overrun woods on my side of the street.

A black van slowed as it came to the curve in the road. My heart pounded against my chest, and a lump grew in my throat. *They found me.* I heard the side door roll back and thought I was doomed. I froze, unable to move.

Lucas jumped out, scaring me half to death. He ran into the woods, swept me up in his arms and started running. I clung to him with all my strength. The black van swung off the road to change directions. Lucas tossed me in the back, slid in next to me and we sped away. I wanted to cry I was so happy. Finally able to focus, I noticed Sean in the driver's seat. "What's he doing here?" I still thought of him as trouble.

"The most fun I've had in a long time." Sean

nodded his head as he looked back at us.

"Sean!" He drove so fast I couldn't believe he stared at us instead of the road.

"I got eyes in the back of my head, Allie, don't worry!" He laughed and turned back.

I snuggled against Lucas for the rest of the drive. He stroked my hair, my arm, kissed the top of my head. I breathed deeply, calming myself. "I'm good, Lucas. Thanks for rescuing me."

"I think you rescued yourself, Allie. I prayed you'd figure out the code on the napkin and not throw it away."

"You wanted them to think I planned the escape, didn't you?"

"Yes. I think it worked. I didn't have time to scan the guards before you came out of the room so I can't track them to see if they're following us."

"So that's how it's done."

"Tracking?"

"You never explained it. You scanned me with your phone?"

"Yeah, I did. The day I met you at the diner." Lucas smiled and kissed my forehead. "Thank goodness you're safe."

Safe. If only he knew. I'd never tell him what Doug had done to me in that room … ever. Lucas had threatened to kill him if he ever hurt me. Right now, I felt capable of doing the same.

Sean pulled the van into the Montgomery driveway and dropped us off in front of the house.

"Thanks, Sean." Lucas shook his hand as we got out.

Sam came to the front door. I hugged him. "Sam, you put your life on the line to bring me that lunch."

"That was nothing." He waved his hand in the air. Maybe I had misjudged him. What I assumed was disapproval might be an introverted personality. "Glad it turned out well." He stepped back, and we walked into the great room. "I'll leave you two alone."

Lucas and I sank to the sofa and kissed and kissed again. I felt liberated and happy to be out of the confines of my prison. I didn't realize how much until now.

I described how Doug carried me out of the house two nights ago to the waiting ambulance. He told me Gene heard a small bit of the conversation between Doug and my parents before Doug smashed and dismantled Mom's phone. Gene didn't want to alert us at the diner until he had more information.

By the time Lucas got home, it was already too late. He called, but my phone had been destroyed. They tracked me as I drove across town and out to the old Baker Motel. Lucas wanted to rescue me the first night, but cooler heads prevailed. They devised a plan and waited for the right time.

We got so caught up in telling our side of the story; I almost forgot the most important part. "Lucas, I don't think you're going to like this, but I have to tell you something. I overheard the guards talking about the Niners outside my room. I had no idea some of them worked for Doug."

"Yeah, I never thought to tell you. Many Niners join the Armed Forces. They want to do their patriotic duty. They want to help. Those five were discovered to have special talents while doing their tours of duty. The STF recruited them."

"Well, they're not being told everything. I had a conversation with one of my guards. You may want to get Julian on the phone."

Julian's face appeared on Lucas' phone. "I see you have her. Congratulations."

"Julian, I need to tell you something very important." I interrupted. "I think the Niners who work for the Special Task Force have been given little or no information about my kidnapping or that Doug's searching for others like them. The guards called them the Special Team, not Niners. So they don't know about the Niners' powers. Both sides are being kept in the dark."

"You're right, Allie. I hate to say it, but Doug's very smart. He's playing both sides. He's probably the only one who knows about the Niner skills. His men are led to believe the special team is just that—special. Men with high IQ's that can help the cause."

"The Niners don't know I was kidnapped or that Doug's looking for more of them. The guards said there are five special team members and more are needed. Doug's using his men to get what he wants."

Lucas leaned back and looked at me, eyes wide. "Not what we thought, is it, Julian? We felt it was their choice to do as they wished. How do we get word to them?"

"We don't, not yet, until we see the need. It's too risky. They won't believe us. They've been away too long and are loyal to the cause. We need something concrete, some proof. Allie, you're a brave girl. Thank you for sharing."

"Wait, there's more. At the time, I didn't think it was important. But now I do. I never told you this, Lucas. Doug wants to find an antidote to the nuclear bomb. I think he feels the Niners have the answer."

Lucas took me by the arm. "If we had the answer,

don't you think we'd share that with the world?"

"Yes," I whispered as I hung my head. "That's why I don't get it. Why is he so intent on finding *you*?"

"I was a solid lead and he followed it, Allie. I don't think he's specifically after me. You've heard the saying, 'two heads are better than one'. Well, it seems your brother wants lots of us Niners to solve his problem. Funny thing is we already know that doesn't work. We've been at it for years."

"The Niners have been working on an antidote to the bomb?" My jaw dropped.

Julian gave a small smile and a nod. "I'll get back to you later, Lucas, after I see what I can find out." His picture disappeared as we disconnected.

Lucas wrapped his arms around me." Thank you for being so brave. This changes a lot. Our intelligence work needs to be adjusted. You discovered something we didn't know. Those Niners are being kept in the dark. They think they're helping to save the world, not trying to find more of their kind."

"Do you think they're the ones who said they needed more brain power? They could be in on it."

"True. We just don't know. They've been away from us so long, they might think that. Or believe we found the answer."

"Oh!" I cried out as something came to mind. "One more thing." I sat straight up and faced Lucas. "I think Nate's the leak." I began to cry. "I don't want to believe it, but I overheard the guards talk about their informant. The person said to watch Allison Sanders. She'll lead you to what you want! That's why Doug's been stalking me." I sobbed harder.

"Nate would never do that." Lucas put his arm around me.

"How do you know?"

"Because he's been here the whole time."

Nate came out from the dining room, a distraught look on his face. "Hey, little one, you don't think I could ever betray you, do you?"

I flew into his arms. "No … maybe … no! I didn't want to believe it. I've been cooped up in that room for two days with a very active imagination. Please, forgive me!"

"Nothing to forgive."

"Nate designed our Nuts logo and slogan." Lucas joined us in the dining room and guided me to the table. "I'm going to make you a cup of tea. Then Nate's going to take you home."

"No! I don't want to go home. I don't ever want to go back there. You heard what I told Julian. I can't face Doug." I grabbed Nate's hand, hoping he'd agree.

"You have to, Allie." Nate sat with me and squeezed my hand. "Your parents have to believe Doug let you come home. There's no way he can take you again. Your mother won't allow it."

I smiled as he said that. "No, she was a mother lioness protecting her cub. She fought for me but my dad—"

"Was convinced it was the right thing to do. He trusts his son."

"Nate, I told Doug I hated him and never to talk to me again."

"Good for you." Nate rubbed my arm.

"Same goes for me." Lucas put a cup of tea in front of me and sat on the other side.

I stared into Nate's eyes. "Did you ever think it was this big? I thought it was Doug being Doug."

He shook his head, lowering his eyes to the table.

"Big doesn't describe it. Unbelievable? Maybe. Huge. Yep. The Niners have to be protected. I'll do whatever I can to help. And your brother? I don't know what to say. It sounds like this is his life's work. The only thing he cares about, sad to say."

"No, don't be sad. I learned a lot about him during these two days. I don't think he loves me or cares about our family at all. If he does, we are far down his priority list. It's up to me to protect the family." I slowly sipped the tea, trying to prolong the inevitable. "So I go home and act like Doug dropped me off, right?"

"That's the plan." Nate nodded.

"I can do that." I stood up, legs shaky. Lucas and Nate got on either side to steady me. I pulled the napkin and key from my back pocket and placed them on the table. "I loved the logo, by the way, Nate." I kissed his cheek in love and friendship, relieved I was wrong.

Walking to the car, I felt like the last two days had been a dream, but when I thought of my little prison, I assured myself it was real. Nate started his car. Lucas buckled me in the passenger side and shut the door. As we pulled away I breathed slowly, in and out, getting ready for the performance of my life.

* * * *

Before Nate dropped me at the end of the driveway, he reached in the backseat, catching me off guard. "You forgot this at the diner." He placed my handbag in my lap. "Good thing you did. You need it now."

"Why?"

"Do you have any makeup in there?" He pointed to the bag.

"You want to wear some of my makeup?" I half-laughed.

"No, but *you* need some." He pulled down the visor and lifted the flap to expose the lighted mirror. I gasped. One of my cheeks had a red handprint.

"Oh!" My hand flew to my face. I felt the heat coming from the spot. "I didn't want Lucas to know. Why didn't he say anything?" My eyes welled with tears.

"He sent me a text from the car on the way to the house. Said to act natural when I saw you. You'd been through enough. He was afraid you'd go into shock if we reacted."

"I wouldn't, and I won't." I sat straighter. I needed to explain the slap to Lucas and assure him it was a one-time occurrence.

"Allie, did Doug do anything else to you?" Nate's voice filled with anger as he glanced over at me.

"Please don't tell Lucas." I gave him pleading eyes.

"I won't."

"He grabbed me and threw me against a wall."

Nate pounded the steering wheel. "That bastard!"

I put my hand on his arm. "Please, don't. I'm okay."

"I'm sorry, Allie. Doug's worse than I thought. I'll keep my promise, for now. But don't hold me to it." He gestured to my bag. "Do what you need to do."

I had some concealer and powder in a zippered pouch. I hadn't looked in a mirror since this morning. Without a word, I applied the concealer then patted my face with powder. "How do I look?"

Nate examined my work after he pulled the car into my driveway. "Good. You just look tired." He grabbed my hand. "I'm next door if you need me."

I opened the truck door and slipped down to the pavement. The house looked warm and inviting, but I knew better. I had two clueless parents sitting inside. They loved their children and trusted them. I'd never convince them Doug was a monster.

I dragged my feet, fighting the urge to turn and run. I had no key to let myself in. No phone to call anyone. I rang the doorbell, and Mom answered.

"Allie, thank goodness! Doug said he wasn't sure when you'd be home, and here you are!" She motioned for me to come into the house, gathering me into her arms. "Jim, Allie's home!"

My dad walked out of the family room, looking sheepish. "Am I forgiven? I've been catching hell from your mother for the last two days."

"Of course you are!" I wasn't too happy with my dad, but it wasn't his fault. My Oscar winning performance had to start now.

"You must be starving. Let me get you something."

"Mom, I'm fine."

"How about a bottle of water?"

I nodded and waited for her to return from the kitchen. We settled in the family room. I couldn't wait to hear their side of the story. "So did you know where I was?"

Dad nodded. "The Baker Motel. Doug gave us his word you had an updated room and were well taken care of."

"Oh, yeah, the best."

"You helped him out to the best of your knowledge?"

"Yes, but Daddy, I don't really know anything and still don't understand why he took me there." I tried to act childish and innocent. I saw the pain in my father's eyes. Maybe he'd think twice if Doug ever tried that again. "I was scared, all alone there. It felt like I was in prison. The time dragged on and on. Where was Doug? I thought he'd stay with me. Didn't he promise to protect me?"

"Doug stayed here with us." Mom had tears in her eyes. "He gave us a full report each night. He said there were people with you. Why didn't he come in with you now?"

"He got called away, important business he said. I'm sure he won't be staying the night." I lied. *And if you do, Doug, you better sleep with one eye open.*

The house phone rang. Mom jumped up to get it. "She's right here, Doug. Yes, she got in alright. She said you were called away suddenly. Thanks for bringing her home safely. All of this nonsense is over, right? No more drama in this house. You'll give your poor mother a heart attack if there is."

I loved listening to her side of the conversation, wishing the Montgomerys could still hear, too. As she continued to talk I curled up next to my dad and shivered a little for extra effect. He rubbed my back and seemed to be talking under his breath, admonishing himself for letting it happen.

"Mom's right, isn't she? It's over?" I gazed up at him with puppy dog eyes, blinked a few times and saw him wipe tears from his eyes.

"Of course, it is. Doug gets a little carried away at times. He convinced me he was protecting you. I envisioned you being carried off by some cult, never to see you again. Forgive your old dad?"

"Yes, I do." *It's Doug I'll never forgive.*

"Clair, let me talk to him." Dad got up, and Mom handed him the handset. He left the room, but we could still hear him. "Allison's pretty traumatized,

Doug. This is not how you presented it originally."

No sound came from the other room as Doug tried to justify his actions on the other end of the phone. Then Dad talked again. His voice boomed through the room. "All well and good, Doug, but what did you find out? It seems like nothing. You held your sister captive for two days. You need to give her some time to recover. I suggest you stay away for the rest of the summer. I think it's best. I'm sorry, I don't mean to yell. You know I love each one of you kids and want what's best for you. I need you to apologize and mend fences with your sister, but now isn't the time." Silence again. "Son, call anytime. We love you."

Dad returned, placing the phone in its cradle. "All taken care of, Allie. Feel better?"

"Thanks, Daddy." I got off the couch and gave him a bear hug. I really wanted to do a happy dance. "I'm tired. I think I'll go up now. Good night."

I heard my parents' voices as I went up the stairs. I hoped they were discussing how much they hated Doug. In my heart, I knew they could never hate him. I wished they could see into mine. Was Doug that brainwashed after all those years in a secret military operation? Had those people become his family instead of us? Or was he just evil? He had so many secrets he couldn't share with his brother, his parents, his sister, it must be hard. Funny, he could talk to me since I know everything. A small part of me had sympathy for Doug. I chastised myself for defending him. A reminder of the abuse, the STF and my keepers was all I needed to wipe that thought from my mind.

My bedroom looked inviting. Fresh clothes sounded good. I opened my top drawer to grab some pajamas and spotted the envelope containing the money

Dean had given me months ago. I took it out and flipped through the cash, the contents still there. I hadn't spent a dime. Maybe I needed to go on a killer shopping spree and reward myself for being Prisoner of the Year.

At one time I planned to use the money to run away with Lucas. I learned I wouldn't need money if I went off with him. His needs were taken care of—food, shelter, safety. I didn't really know how or where they got their money. Next time I saw him, I'd have to ask.

I put the money back in the drawer, deciding not to spend it yet. As Dean said, "Save it for a rainy day." I would open a bank account instead and start saving. My plan to leave this small town was still a go. One more school year and I was out of here. The farther away from Doug, the better.

Collapsing on the bed, I reached for my phone and remembered I didn't have one anymore. *Strange*. I felt something in my back pocket. I pulled out a phone that looked exactly like Lucas'. I fumbled around until I found a contact list. I touched Lucas' name, and he came into view.

"Hey, I've been waiting."

"I didn't know I had a phone. When did you put it in my pocket?"

"I have my ways." Lucas smiled, the smile I remembered seeing for the first time in English class, the one that grabbed my heart and never let go.

"So in case Doug was here, you didn't want me to know I had it."

"You're catching on. Tell me what happened when you got home."

"I'm free of Doug for the summer. My dad told him to stay away from me and not come home for awhile. We can do whatever we want this summer without thinking someone's spying on us."

"Your parents are smart. They won't fall for any more of Doug's stories."

"I hope you're right. I'm so relieved to be home and so glad we avoided an explosive situation. We just have to get through one more school year. Then you can go off to college and be safe."

"With you by my side."

"Not if you're going to Harvard!" I laughed.

"Then anywhere you want to go."

"Somewhere far from here and Doug." I sighed. "Lucas?"

"What?"

"Do you think he'll ever stop looking for you?"

"He's got nothing concrete. We have to give this time. It could be over soon."

"Really? How can you be so sure?" I flopped back into my pillow.

"Because I'm Lucas Montgomery." He joked. He tried to make me feel better, but I still had a knot in my stomach. "Allie? Please believe me. Nothing will come between us again. I promised you. Remember?"

I took a deep breath. "So let's start making summer plans."

"I'll do whatever you want. After what you've been through, you deserve to call the shots."

"Mmm, let me think."

"Make a list. We'll sort it out tomorrow. You need a good night's rest. I bet you didn't sleep much at the motel."

"The first night I slept like a baby." I kidded then got serious. "If Doug doesn't behave, I might have to tell my parents about feeling something jab my arm.

The next thing I remembered was waking up the next morning."

"You don't want to scare them, Allie. But I see your point." He looked away for a moment then came back into view. "Are you ever going to mention how you got that mark on your face?"

"He slapped me. Please don't make me go there. It's over. Done." My brain played out the scene over and over again. The shock. The hatred in his eyes.

"You need to talk."

"I'm fine. Besides—"

"You're afraid of what I might do. When I said I'd kill Doug if he ever hurt you, I meant it."

"It was just a slap … to get me to talk. It's over and done with, I'm okay."

"I don't think you are, but I'll let it go. For now," Lucas said. "I know there's more to the story."

I needed to distract him so I kissed the screen. "You'll have to help me with this new phone. It's unlike anything I've used."

Lucas kissed his screen. "Just two teenagers in love?" he asked.

"Yes, for the summer. Let's enjoy summer love and forget the rest of the world. But since you turned twenty, you'll have to pretend you're a teen." I giggled.

"That's my girl. Hang in there. We'll act like any other high school couple all summer."

"All summer." I breathed in and out slowly, envisioning us as a normal couple. I hung up and got ready for bed. This morning I was in a tiny motel room and now crawled into my own bed. I shoved thoughts of Doug and my kidnapping to the innermost part of my brain, locked it away for now. Lucas could be right. I may need help dealing with all that happened. Some day. But now, I deserved a little happiness.

My phone rang early the next day flashing the name *Ashley*. I touched the screen and saw her face.

"Allie!" she wailed. This sounded serious. I bolted out of bed and hurried to find some clothes in case she needed me.

"Ash, what's wrong?"

"Nate's leaving me."

CHAPTER TWENTY FIVE

"I just saw Nate last night." I told Ashley. "He didn't say a word."

"You saw him? I haven't seen him for two days."

"So that's why you think he's breaking up with you?"

"No, not breaking up, leaving!"

I was totally confused. "You need to start from the beginning."

"You know how Nate wants to be a director or work in the film industry?"

"Yes, I'm aware."

"He got accepted to UCLA, one of the best film schools in the country!"

"That's wonderful news! That's why you think he's leaving you for good?"

"It's UCLA in California, Allie. It might as well be the moon. That's the other side of the country. Once he leaves, he'll never come back."

I hadn't thought of it like that. It would be hard to come home for the holidays, let alone weekend visits. "You'll have the holidays and summers. I'm sure the two of you will work it out."

"It's over. I just know it. How can I compete with California girls? How long can we do a long-distance relationship? How long before he doesn't have time for me? What about my senior prom?"

"All good questions, Ash, but you need to ask Nate." Nate had been in love with Ashley for so long I couldn't imagine him breaking things off. He'd try his best to make it work. But I could see her point, for how long? "Make the best of the summer. Don't worry about the future or what you have no control over."

Ash let out a sigh. "You might be right. It's just so hard."

I could relate. I almost lost my boyfriend when I thought he disappeared for good. "Let's try to have a great summer." I thought of the conversation I had with Lucas last night. "Summer love."

"Which ends when the school year begins. Haven't you seen the movie?" Ashley sniffed.

"Tell you what. I'll get a hold of Nate. We'll meet you anywhere you want." Lucas said he'd do whatever I wanted. Now I offered the same deal to Ashley.

"Bookstore? Coffee and lunch. And, by the way, where have you been?"

"Around. I'll see you soon."

I fumbled with the phone and finally connected to Lucas. I asked him to help me call Nate. He popped up on a split screen. I stared at the two most important men in my life. It dawned on me that Nate had a special phone, too. "Bookstore in an hour. Ashley needs us. And congrats, Nate."

"Is she upset?" Nate's concern was sweet.

"Yes, but she doesn't want you to know. California's pretty far away."

"I was just accepted. I don't have to go. I've applied to a lot of film schools."

"And which one do you have your heart set on? Which one were you dying to go to?"

"UCLA."

"Then you've made your choice. See you in a bit. You, too, Lucas."

Life could sometimes get complicated. We were cocooned for the first eighteen years in our hometown. Then friends began to spread their wings. Some stayed close to home. Others left and flew off to places they once dreamed about. Nate's dream was to head to California. He needed to make it come true. Me? I could build a new cocoon right in Victorian Village.

A knock on my door brought my attention back to the here and now. Mom stood on the other side with a huge package in her arms. "This was just delivered for you." She set it on the floor and turned to leave.

"Mom, wait. You need to be here when I open this." I had a hunch what was in the box. "I got a little bored at Stacy's and did some on-line shopping."

Mom hurried over to the bed and sat down. "Will there be a fashion show?" She clapped her hands lightly.

"If you insist." I giggled, and she joined in.

"I'm so happy to see you laughing again. You looked so traumatized last night."

"New clothes always help." I dug into the box and pulled out each piece, holding them up for inspection.

"You spent more than the gift card, Allie!"

"I had birthday money left over from Dean."

"Oh, that Dean, he's always spoiling you, isn't he?"

"Do you think he'll be upset if I don't come for a visit this summer?" I couldn't bear the thought of being away for a month.

"After what you've been through, I don't think he'd blame you."

"So he knows?"

"Oh, yes, I talked to him each night you were gone."

"And?"

"And he called your brother and gave him a piece of his mind, although it did no good. You know how stubborn Doug can be."

No, I didn't know how stubborn Doug could be. I didn't know much about him. I did know he was a tyrant, and that trumped stubborn. "I might be able to squeeze in a weekend visit."

"He would like that. You need to give Autumn a little push to start planning the wedding."

"Oh, Mom, ulterior motives!" We laughed again.

I decided to wear some of my new clothes after I finished the fashion show. "I'm going to meet Ashley at the bookstore, gotta run." I gave Mom a quick peck on the cheek, dashed downstairs and out the door.

A feeling of freedom swept through me as I jumped behind the wheel. I lowered the window to let in the fresh summer breeze and realized how much I missed it. Without warning, a flashback of my kidnapping ran through my mind. I saw the ambulance sitting in the drive. I heard my screams as I was carried away. I blinked and rubbed my eyes. Maybe it affected me more than I thought. My hands began to shake. I squeezed them into balls to stop the trembling. Resting my head back I stared at the house, zoning in and out, recalling the night I was taken away.

"Doug, you're a psychopath!" I screamed. Or was it sociopath? I desperately wanted an exact definition and reached for my phone. A quick connect to the internet, a dictionary search and I stared at the meaning. *Psychopath - A person with an antisocial personality disorder, manifested in aggressive, perverted, criminal, or amoral behavior without empathy or remorse.*

Strange, it made me feel better. "Psychopath!" I tucked the fear away, deep in my mind. After taking a few deep breaths, I started the engine and drove down the driveway.

I arrived at the bookstore and found Ashley and

Lucas already at a table. He must be working on cheering her up. I saw a tiny smile on her face. Lucas could keep her and Nate connected in ways she'd never imagine.

"Hey." I gave Lucas a quick kiss and sat down. "Ash, you okay?" Our eyes connected in solidarity.

"Yeah, just trying to wrap my head around the idea of Nate leaving and this guy," she patted Lucas' arm, "helped me. Did you know I can go there as easily as Nate can come here?" She laughed. "If only I had the money to do that. Babysitting gets in the way of a real job."

"I'm sure you and your mom can work something out or maybe she can pay you."

"You know she can't."

"Then let's find you a job on the weekend. I know the perfect place."

"Where?"

"Here! Your favorite place in the world. Go see if they're hiring."

Ashley's eyes lit up as she popped out of her chair. She headed to the checkout and talked to the clerk behind the counter. The employee pointed her in the direction of a work station at the back of the store.

While she was gone, I thought it safe to ask Lucas a few questions. "Is there a way you can help her?"

"I can get her booked on a flight for free, how about that?"

"All legal I presume."

"Of course. We have a standing business account with certain airlines."

"Where do Niners get their money?"

"All sorts of ways. We sell things. Don't forget some of us have been around for a long time. We have old coins, art collections then there's our inventions. The money's saved and invested wisely. We could own our own airline with state-of-the-art jets, but that would raise suspicion."

"So everyone shares. You don't have your own money?"

"Correct. We're issued credit cards, and our spending is tracked."

"So you don't go overboard?"

"No one would."

"Of course not. You Niners are perfect." I teased.

Lucas grasped my hand. "Enough about Ashley, money or Nate leaving for UCLA. How are you? How are you holding up?"

I had to fight back tears seeing the concern on his face. "I thought I was okay. Now I realize it will take awhile. I had a flashback in the car on the way here. I didn't sleep well last night, either."

"Of course it will take time. Stop trying to put up a brave front. I'll help you in anyway I can. If you need to talk, you know you can call me anytime. And if you want me in person, I'll be there."

"I just need time."

Ashley skipped back to the table. "I got it! I got a job. I can work Saturdays and Sundays. Thanks for the idea, Allie."

Nate joined us at the table. "What did I miss?"

Ashley jumped up and into his arms. "I got a job!"

I never saw anyone so happy to have a job, but I knew it meant more to her than just a job. She could save money and feel a little more in control of her life.

"Now onto Summer Love." I pointed to the chairs. "Have a seat. We're going to make a list of things to do, romantic things. Then we'll check them off as we do them."

"Well, I got an easy one. Fourth of July's next week so we go to the fireworks." Nate smiled.

Handing a sheet of paper to Ashley, I wrote it down on my own pad.

"Walks on the beach," Lucas added. "A lot of good beaches a few hours away."

"Picnics." I jotted down. "Simple but romantic."

"And that old drive-in, out by the Baker Motel, is going to be open on weekends this summer." Ashley said, completely unaware.

"Drive-in," I said a little too loud as I wrote.

"The local carnival." Nate seemed to be getting into it.

I set my pen down and looked at everyone. It was a start. Just the distraction I needed. We were going to have a great summer.

* * * *

Nothing like starting off the Summer of Love with a bang. The Fourth of July fireworks were extra-spectacular or maybe it seemed that way. The four of us lay back on our blankets, staring at the night sky. The sparkling colors showered down as if giving their blessing. After the show ended, we waited for the crowd to clear and talked of our next adventure. Ashley voted for the zoo.

"Romantic?" I wrinkled my nose.

"There's this old song about the birds do it, the bees do it, so let's fall in love." Nate tried to help Ash out.

"A Cole Porter classic." Lucas added. "Written in 1928 and introduced in the musical, *Paris*."

"When did you become a music major?" Ashley teased.

"An entertainment connoisseur, like myself." Nate saved the day. Lucas may not have been around in 1928, but knew many people who were and had been exposed to many decades of music.

"Well, it would be fun to stroll around." I changed the subject back. "Plus we all love animals. Don't we?"

"Fine, then let's add it to the list." Ashley nodded as she stood. She turned toward the parking lot and gestured across the street. "Ice cream!"

We strolled through the grass and over to the stand. Cars packed the lot. We stood in a long line waiting to order.

"Allie!" Chloe waved and skipped toward us, Josh in tow. "Hi, everyone!"

Her eyes sparkled like a girl in love. I could tell she had been working on her tan. It looked like she spent every waking moment at the beach. Josh could only nod, appearing a little uncomfortable. He acted like an animal in the zoo being paraded in front of the crowd. I understood why she came over to say hi, but felt a little sorry for him. I wanted to tell Josh that Chloe wanted to mark her territory. Wasn't that what the animal kingdom did?

"Awkward," Ashley sang as they walked away.

"I'm still happy for her."

"All Josh needs is a leash, and she'd be extra happy." Ashley said as we burst out laughing.

Lucas kissed the side of my head and whispered, "It's time for our own summer love. I've had enough of the crowds."

I smiled in agreement. I'd soon be whisked away to the Montgomery house where we'd spend the rest of the night on the deck. No mosquitoes or pesky insects to bother us. Niner technology took care of that. I hoped they'd get that secret out to the rest of the world soon.

We dashed for the car, hauling Ash and Nate with us. Lucas drove the family van so we had to drop them off. "Where to?" He closed one eye as he questioned Nate. "Name it."

"Drop us at Ashley's. I'll have Rob drive me home." Nate patted Lucas' shoulder. "Lead on."

After the drop-off, we rode in blissful silence to Lucas' home. He parked along side the barn, and we raced each other to the back deck. Soon I leaned against Lucas on the double chaise lounge, gazing out over the gorge. The moonlight illuminated the night. The air so still it added to the magic. I fell asleep in Lucas' arms and woke the next morning on the sofa in the great room. My parents stopped demanding to know my every move and didn't protest when I slept over at the Montgomery house. Lucas always called them after I fell asleep to let them know he wouldn't be waking me to bring me home.

The summer couldn't last long enough. Doug's absence added to the serenity of the season. In my heart I knew the peaceful feeling would soon come to an end, but planned to enjoy every minute while it lasted.

Throughout the rest of the season, we added new ideas and checked off old ones as we completed them. The dreaded first day of school drew near, marking the time we'd go our separate ways. Nate would leave for California in a few days. The rest of us would be seniors, counting the days until we, too, could leave and spread our wings.

For our last Summer of Love event, we had a surprise party for Nate at the diner. All his A/V buddies from school had been invited. He enjoyed seeing everyone. It was our last gift to the four of us, doing something for someone we loved. Nate's eyes shone as he held his plastic cup in the air, toasting his friends, Ashley, the summer and UCLA. I'd say he sounded a little drunk, but I made the punch and knew what I put in it.

It turned into a bittersweet night. We knew things would never be the same again. I wouldn't run over to Nate's every night or ride dirt bikes at a moment's notice. We wouldn't be chugging sports drinks or inventing more names for Doug. One of my best friends would soon leave the cocoon. Although he assured me he wouldn't change, I knew it would be a hard promise to keep.

Tonight I helped him pack so he could spend his last day with Ashley. She had to babysit Emma otherwise she would have been here, too. I placed some of his clothes in a box and taped it shut. His parents planned to ship some items to his dorm. Nate sorted what he'd take on the plane and what could be sent later.

"I can't believe you're leaving." I grabbed another box and began to fill it.

"It's surreal. I'll believe it when I'm there."

"Have you talked to your roommate yet?"

"Yeah, we compared notes."

"Do you think you and Ashley are going to survive this?"

"I hope so." Nate stopped and sat on the edge of his bed. "I wish I could pack her up and send her to California." We both laughed at the thought.

"She'd be kicking and screaming the whole way and asking way too many questions, especially, are we there yet?" We laughed again.

My phone buzzed and Lucas' face appeared wearing a look of concern. I switched to speaker so Nate could hear. "Lucas, is everything alright?"

"Can you come to the diner as soon as possible? We might have a problem. I promised I'd always let you know."

"I'm at Nate's. I've got to run home and get my car."

"I'll bring her." Nate took my phone. "It'll save time."

"Thanks, Nate. Try to get here as fast as you can, you know what I mean." Lucas disappeared from the screen. I didn't like the feel of this news and tried to remain calm. At least I was included this time.

We rushed to Nate's truck and sped toward the diner. Lucas gave Nate permission to speed, so he took full advantage.

"Nate, you're going a little fast."

"Don't worry. I won't be stopped."

"Did you just buy a police scanner or something?" I looked around inside the car.

"No, Lucas took care of it. Special circumstances."

"Is that what he meant by 'you know what I mean'? How much *do* you know?"

"Enough. I know he's a Niner. They have special skills, are extremely intelligent and live for a very long time. At first I thought Gene was really Lucas' dad, not his grandfather, but found out they're brothers. I feel privileged they trust me."

"I'm sorry I ever doubted you."

"Don't be. I can see how it could happen."

We made the turn off Gilbert, and Nate flew into the diner parking lot. The closed sign flashed on and off. Some of the family could be seen through the windows. I hopped out of the truck and slammed the door. "I have a feeling whatever's going on in there isn't good." I gave Nate a sideways glance. His jaw clenched as if he agreed.

CHAPTER TWENTY SIX

As we opened the door to the diner, I heard crying coming from the back storage area. Lucas sat in a booth with Hannah and Jonas. Hannah's sweet little face was tear-stained. Joe had a dark, brooding look. I called to Lucas, afraid to walk any further.

"What's going on?" I looked at his brother and sister then back at him as he came toward me.

"Sam and Stacy are fighting. Gene's back there trying to mediate. From what I've heard it's not good." Lucas turned to Nate. "Sorry to pull you into this."

"Not a problem." Nate slid onto a stool by the counter. "I'll let you two talk."

Lucas pulled me into another booth. We sat facing each other. "This could be nothing, but I wanted you here."

I grabbed both his hands and squeezed. "I'm glad you called."

Stacy burst out from the back, pulling her hands through her hair. "Let's just get it all out in the open. Let the kids decide, Sam." Sam and Gene followed behind her. Their expressions said it all, something was terribly wrong.

"Lucas, I'm sorry." Stacy stared his way. "I thought I could do this, but I can't. Going home this summer just reinforced my feelings. I want to be a good mother to you and my kids, a good wife to Sam and keep all of your secrets, but I can't do it anymore. I want to go home."

Sam put his arm around Stacy. "It's only one more year, honey. It's tough, I know, but we'll move back home soon."

"No, we won't, Sam, and you know it. There will always be a reason to protect Lucas. We'll have to be nearby or stand in as his parents or let him use our children. Sorry, Lucas, I don't mean to sound so cruel, but that's how I feel."

Lucas nodded, head down staring at his hands.

"Hannah, honey, come to mommy." Stacy put her arms out, and Hannah ran to her. "I know you don't understand what's going on. Someday you will. We're all going back to Montana to live. Won't that be nice?"

"I like it here, Mommy. My friends are here and Joe and Lucas and Grandpa."

"I know but you, me, Jonas and Daddy are a family. We'll be going home."

"Lucas is family." Hannah crossed her arms.

"Yes, yes, he is." Stacy tried again. "Sam, help me out here. You said you'd leave if I didn't think I could do this."

"That was three years ago." Sam answered. "We only have one more year to go. I don't understand."

"Well, I'll try to explain one more time. I'm at the end of my rope. I can't do this anymore, not one more minute. I want my family to move back to Montana."

"I won't do that to Lucas." Sam crossed his arms.

Lucas sat up and slid out of the booth. "No one has to worry about me, Sam. I can live here on my own. You don't have to take care of me."

Stacy shook her head back and forth. Tears streamed down her face. "Do you really believe that, Lucas? Your parents and Gene never allowed that. Do you really think they'd start now?" Stacy motioned to Joe. "Jonas, come here."

Joe got up, dragging his feet as he headed toward his mother. "I'm taking the kids and going, Sam."

"What?" Sam appeared shocked. Even the kids' faces showed surprise.

"I refuse to let my son be groomed to take over the care and protection of his great-uncle Lucas. If you're not coming, we're still leaving."

Joe backed away from his mother, raising both hands in front of his chest. "I'm not going, Mom. I won't go with you."

"Jonas!"

"I want to stay. I want to help. I'll be a part of Lucas' life for as long as he lets me. You can't make me go. I'm fourteen. I'll stay with Dad."

Hannah started crying again, looking scared and confused. She clung to Stacy. I knew she was afraid her mother would leave without her.

Stacy, now backed in a corner, said the unthinkable. "You won't have to worry about Lucas anymore, Jonas. He will be well taken care of. They're on their way to get him as we speak."

"Who, Stacy? Who's coming to get him?" Sam yanked her by the arm and spun her around to face him. His nostrils flared, and his eyes narrowed.

"The STF," she said so we could barely hear her. "They assured me it's the best place for him."

"So it was you all this time? You're the leak?" Sam's face grew red. "Every time we thought the family was in danger it was because of you?" Sam yelled so loudly that Gene pulled him aside.

"No one's in danger," she said too calmly, almost robotic. "They don't know any of our names. They don't know where we live. I only gave them locations where they might find him. Tonight it's the diner. I never had them come so close to home before." Stacy took Hannah by the hand. "I thought it would give us our life back. Lucas stood in the way of that. I had to do something. I tried to spare us when I staged the false alarm at the house, and we headed for Pennsylvania. We were so close. Julian said the compound was up and running again. I was positive we'd head back there, safe and sound. *All* of us. Then everyone voted to return here. I couldn't believe it."

Sam turned to Gene and said as if they were the only two in the room, "Makes sense, doesn't it, Dad? We never could trace the leak, didn't know how they were getting past the Niner technology. We had no idea *my wife* used that knowledge to her advantage. She gets rid of Lucas. We think he joined the STF with no idea how it happened, and we return to Montana." He spun back and faced Stacy, his eyes boring into her. "Well done, wife." He ran his hands through his hair over and over. "We need to get out of here. We probably don't have much time." He leaned over the counter and stared at us. "Lucas, go home and take the kids with you. I'll be there as soon as I can."

Hannah began to scream and wrapped her arms around her mother. "I won't leave Mommy!"

Stacy gathered Hannah up in her arms. "We're leaving, Sam. Don't try to stop us." She pushed past him and came around the front of the counter. Stacy hesitated in front of Joe, but he stood firm.

Before I could even process what happened, Stacy was in the car driving away. I still couldn't believe she was the one who caused all the problems. She was so nice to me. I thought she liked me. Maybe Stacy tried to keep me close as a confidante so I'd tell her our plans. She'd know where to send Doug so he could capture Lucas and get him out of their lives. She had used me. I covered my face to hold back the tears.

I thought back to the first time Doug came for Lucas. My birthday party. Stacy's information motivated him to come. She knew all of Lucas' movements and where he would be most of the time. After all, she acted as his mother and could insist on knowing. Guilt swept over me as I recalled blaming my mom.

During Thanksgiving and through winter break, Doug had to do his own intel. He hounded me for weeks trying to break me. Stacy didn't send any leads. I wonder why? Maybe she thought it'd be easier to convince everyone to leave if I wasn't around.

In June, she let Doug know I was on my way home from the diner so he could kidnap me and lure Lucas to the motel. Did Stacy realize all the pain and suffering she had caused? Anger erupted inside me, but I had no one to direct it at. Too late. She was gone. I needed to focus on the people in the diner and how I could help. "Lucas, what now?"

Lucas stood, took my hand and pulled me toward a booth farther from the noise. "We can't stay here anymore. I'm sure Gene and Sam will agree." He nodded toward them. Gene was on the phone. "We'll have to leave, go back to Montana or California or another safe house, whatever Julian thinks best. I'm sure Gene's talking to him now."

"I can't lose you again." I started to cry.

"You won't. Come with us. Nate can drive you home so you can pack some things. We'll come and get you once the plan is in place."

My head began to ache. I needed a moment to think. I could do this. I could go with them. "How will I finish high school?"

"The high school has courses you can complete on-line. You'll still be able to graduate from our high school, you and me both."

That sounded plausible. I wouldn't mind studying with Lucas at his home. "I'd like that."

"We could get married and have our own house in Victorian Village. I'd work with Julian, and you can do whatever you wish—teach at the primary school, work in the square, whatever your heart desires. I haven't shown you half of what the village has to offer. We have hydroponic gardening, recycling plants, creative think tanks, invention centers."

"Wow, you left out so much while we were there."

"You weren't into the school-thing so I backed off." Lucas kissed me. "Please say yes."

"Yes to going? Or yes to marrying you?"

"Both."

"Then yes, I'll go and yes, I'll marry you."

* * * *

I forgot Nate sat at the counter. He took everything in, not saying a word. He might try to stop me, but I hoped not. I rose to my feet, feeling a little wobbly, and made my way over to him. My throat constricted so I could hardly swallow. My chest tightened with each step I took. A chill washed over me. I was so cold I began to shiver. I sank onto the nearest stool, and clutched my head. *What have I just done?* I had to regroup and face the facts.

"Fifteen minutes!" Gene called out to Lucas. "Sean's closing down our house and is coming to pick us up. We'll go to Sean's and leave from there. We have a half-hour window before they reach the diner. Julian has them on camera and says they just reached the outskirts of town. Looks like a caravan of three trucks."

My heart beat faster when I heard those words. Doug could be in one of those trucks giving commands and staying in touch with his base. If only he knew I sat in the diner and would do anything to stop him from taking Lucas. He wanted Lucas to join his army and probably knew all along Lucas was a Niner. I made my final decision, one I could never look back on with regret. I needed to stand firm, hold my ground and be strong for everyone. The chill left my body. I got up, finishing the walk to Nate.

"Nate, can you wait outside for me? I need to talk to Lucas."

"Sure, little one, don't be too long. You heard what Gene said."

"Yeah, I heard. This won't take long." We hugged, and Nate went out to his truck.

I turned and gazed at Lucas, sitting in the booth, checking his phone like any other high school boy, only he wasn't. He was special and needed protection even though he didn't think so. Young adults thought they knew everything. Lucas thought he was smarter than his parents, but this time he got it wrong.

I needed to find the strength to tell him I couldn't go. I almost forgot over these months that I was the enemy. I thought back to the day on the beach when Lucas told me his story, I knew it then. I tucked the thought away in a box of forgotten memories. Now I needed to dust it off, open it and expose reality.

I. Am. The. Enemy. I was Doug's sister. He would never stop looking for me if I disappeared. That would confirm his suspicions. Tears filled my eyes as I slid back in the booth across from Lucas.

"Hard to say goodbye?" Lucas smiled his wonderful smile, unaware he'd be the one I was saying goodbye to. "After we get to Sean's, I'll call you."

I slipped my phone out of my back pocket and

pushed the device across the table. "I won't need this."

"Well, technically, you will." He started to slide it back, but I covered his hand with mine.

"I'm not going."

"You want to finish your school year here, I understand. You'll still need the phone so we can stay connected."

"No, you don't understand." Tears streamed down my face. He reached across the table to wipe them away. "Doug will never stop looking as long as I'm with you. If I disappear his suspicions will be confirmed. It will make him all the more determined. He suspects you're a Niner, and if I go with you, he'll know for sure. You keep forgetting I'm his sister. He'll do whatever it takes to find me and bring me home. He'll use me as bait. Then he'll take you away, never to be seen again. We have to break things off completely."

"No, never." His eyes pleaded with me.

"You know I'm right."

"I can't go on without you or least knowing I can talk to you, see your face on our phones—"

"I'm the enemy, Lucas. You have to face the truth." I finally said my fear aloud.

"Don't ever say that."

"Use your brain, not your heart. You have all the Niners to think about, Julian, Sean and the rest."

Lucas sat in silence then got up. He stood in front of the booth, tears in his eyes. His strong arms reached out. I let him pull me toward him. "My head's telling me you're right." He kissed me for a long time then drew back. "In my heart, I'm linked to you forever."

"And I, you." Lucas gave me one last lingering kiss, holding me for what would be the final time in our lives. I clung to him, fighting the urge to change my mind, say it was all a mistake.

Sean rushed back into the diner. I knew what it meant. Gene and Sam shut off the lights, closed and locked the place as Lucas and I headed for Nate's truck.

"Take care of her." Lucas pounded on the side of the truck.

Nate rolled down the window, looking confused. His face changed to one of understanding as they shook hands. "Good luck, and don't worry about Allie. I always have her back, no matter what."

I ran to Gene and Sam, giving them hugs. "Please take care of him." I whispered in Gene's ear. Even Jonas came over and gave me a one-arm hug. I couldn't help being touched by his action. They climbed into a large black van and slammed the door shut.

"Lucas!" Sean called from the van.

Lucas turned from Nate's truck and waved to Sean before he came over to me.

"I love you, Allison Sanders, forever." One, last, sweet kiss was shared.

"No contact, ever again. I beg of you. Do this for me." Tears rolled down my cheeks, and I didn't care. "I love you."

Lucas could only nod.

"In another life I would be your—"

He placed a finger over my lips. "I know." Under the moonlight, I saw tears glistening in his eyes.

I didn't want to prolong the pain any longer so I ran to the truck as Lucas climbed into the van.

"I'm not going with him! Start it up. Get me home!" I screamed at Nate through the open window, wanting to get out of here as fast as possible. The black van already skidded through the gravel parking lot speeding for the street.

Something came over me. I couldn't help myself. I didn't get in the truck. Instead I turned and ran after the van, through the parking lot, right out into the street. I wanted to chase it down and take all my words back. I heard myself screaming and crying as I watched it disappear into the darkness. I wondered if Lucas could hear my cries. I said I loved him over and over and would never forget him. I felt as if I was on fire, going up in flames. I envisioned flames bursting from my hands igniting the rest of my body. I burned to a pile of ash as I crumbled right in the middle of the street, sobbing.

Hands were on my shoulders. Nate pulled me to my feet. He guided me back to the truck, opened the door and put me inside. All this felt vaguely familiar. I mumbled Lucas' name over and over, not able to stop. Nate tolerated my behavior. I knew he felt sorry for me otherwise he'd tell me to knock it off or pick another name.

He pulled into his drive and up to the garage. "Parents are out tonight. Come in. We'll get you calmed down before you go home." He ran around to the passenger side and lifted me from the truck. I couldn't believe he tried to carry me and managed to get inside the garage. He placed me against the wall by the door.

"I can walk," I said in a monotone voice.

"I know. Just shut up and let me help you." He picked me up again, entered the house, dumping me in a chair in the family room. A cold drink was put in my hand and a cool cloth held to my face.

I grabbed the washcloth from his hand and threw it down. "Enough. I have to stop feeling sorry for myself."

"You did the right thing."

I sat up in the chair. "Did I?"

"Yeah, you did. Lucas knows it, too. Just not yet."

"I need your support, Nate."

"You've got it."

"You're leaving in two days."

"We have video chat and our phones—"

"I gave mine back to Lucas."

"What? That thing was awesome."

"Nate." I gave him a stern look.

"You had to cut all ties. I get it. And besides, what if Doug found it?"

"Don't speak his name ever again."

"Alright, then let's make one up when we need to speak of him. How about Captain Un-America? The Dork? Brother-Who-Shall-Not-Be-Named or also known as BWSNBN. Or is that too long?"

I gave him a small smile. I wouldn't be laughing or finding things funny for a long time. Nate would be different. "Psychopath," I mumbled under my breath.

"What did you call him?" Nate cocked his head to one side.

"Never mind. I should go. Promise you'll come see me before you leave?"

"Promise." We hugged, and I went out the back door to take the path home. As I walked along I swore I'd never look for Lucas or hope to see him again. I chose a star and sealed the promise. I hoped Lucas would do the same thing on that same evening star tonight.

CHAPTER TWENTY SEVEN

Senior year. I got ready for the first day of school in a daze. I said goodbye over and over to my old life and made methodical plans for the new. My strategy would be to save as much money as possible so I could get out of town after graduation. I got a job at the bookstore café working as many hours as possible. I mindlessly made lattes, mochas and cappuccinos for customers.

My paycheck went into the birthday money account. Maybe Dean would sense I needed a few more dollars and be as generous this birthday. I applied for a recent opening at the bookstore, hoping they'd let me work both sides of the store for more hours.

The high school offered community college classes that counted for both college and high school credit. I signed up for as many as I could take so I wouldn't have to be in college for four years. I could be out in two if I started summer semester. The new life I designed for myself needed to begin as soon as possible. My parents had no idea I wanted to leave and never come back. I didn't want to hurt them, especially Mom, but Doug made the need to escape that much stronger.

I had to pretend everything was okay. I told anyone who asked I was fine with Lucas moving away. I could focus on my senior year without distraction.

The dreaded family barbecue took place the weekend before school started. My parents invited Doug so he could make his apology. He acted all humble and said he was sorry for his behavior. I didn't buy it for a second. As I listened to his lies, I kept thinking, *Yeah, how many brothers kidnap their sisters and keep them in a small room? Oh, right, just psychos like you, Doug.*

I had to hold back from slapping his face when he got too close, but I had to make amends for Lucas' sake. He still was my number one priority. To keep him safe and off Doug's radar was worth the pain.

At one time, Lucas told me he'd always keep me safe, and now the tables had turned. I kept him safe. I had to hug Doug and tell him I forgave him which made me nauseous. Mom and Dad thought we were one big happy family again. If only they knew he resented them for not being born a Niner.

Dean and Autumn discussed their wedding plans at the barbecue. They'd get married next summer, and I was relieved they'd chosen a date when I'd still be home. I never wanted to disappoint Dean. Since being the maid of honor came with multiple duties, I'd have plenty to keep my mind occupied. Autumn said she needed lots of help even though it would be long distance. They felt sorry for me and making me a big part of the wedding was their way of helping me cope.

Our class voted Chloe senior class president at the end of junior year. She asked me to be on some of her committees. Funny how things had a way of turning around. We might eventually become friends. I took her up on the offer. Besides, it would look good on my college applications. I planned to stay so busy I'd pass out every night from exhaustion.

Sleep didn't come easy these days for so many reasons. When I slept, I sometimes dreamed of Lucas and me happy and in love, but most were nightmares of him being stripped from my arms. Then I searched for him, never finding him. Many dreams had me confined in small places with walls closing in on me. Often, I was beaten and left for dead. I woke up in cold sweats, breathing so heavy I thought I'd never catch my breath. Love and hate filled my dreams. I didn't like to sleep.

I hoped Lucas had stopped tracking me because it upset me to think about it. I hoped he'd grow tired of knowing my whereabouts. If he thought I could be in danger there would be no way he could save me, and that would be painful for him. He couldn't call Nate for help as he now lived in LA. Lucas could be in California, too, for all I knew.

Doug confirmed I made the right decision when he left the family barbecue. He looked straight in my eyes, took my hands firmly in his and said, "You know, Allison, sometimes there has to be war before there is peace."

My skin crawled every time I thought of that conversation. Keeper Two had been the first to say the words, but it made me ill hearing the phrase come from Doug's mouth. His sly grin and cold eyes verified what I already believed. He said that to his unit every day.

I snapped back to reality. It was the first day of school. I looked around my bedroom and grabbed my book bag. I needed to stop dwelling on the past and get myself out the door. After gathering my things, I went down the stairs, forcing one foot to work then the other. Mom stood at the door with my breakfast bar and a bottle of water. She didn't notice my hesitation. I kissed her cheek and walked out into an already hot, muggy day. I tossed my bag on the backseat and climbed into the driver's seat.

Ashley and I planned to meet in the parking lot. She drove to school now, inheriting the Rob-mobile. The year would be so different we made a pact to be there for each other. I saw her heading toward the car as I parked. She appeared to be reading something on her phone.

"Aww, Nate sent me a message. He set his alarm to wake up early so he could text me as we walked into the building." She looked up and into my eyes. "Ooh, sorry."

"No it's fine. Tell him I said hi."

"He also sent a message for you. It doesn't quite make sense. 'Wish you still had that phone, or any phone for that matter, but I understand. Hope you have a good year.' What does that mean?"

"I downgraded my phone to save money. You know that."

"So having no phone is considered a downgrade? I hope you get one soon so we can text and stay in contact. Why exactly did you get rid of it?"

I needed to change the subject before she came up with more questions. "It's just for a while, Ash, to save money. Let's go in and get this over."

I smiled at my innocent best friend and wished she could stay that way as long as possible. She had no idea what really transpired over the last year.

The good, the bad and the ugly came to mind as we strolled toward the building. I naively labeled my life with those very words last year. The good had changed from having a boy I liked show up in my English class to having that boy turn out to be one of the most unique, special people in the world. One I would always love.

The bad? Running into my ex, Josh, and finding out he was in one of my classes ruined the beginning of my junior year. I'd have to see him everyday. How trivial that sounded now! The bad was having your heart ripped out over and over again and never knowing if it would heal. The bad was losing the love of your life, knowing you'd never see him again. The bad was finding out your brother was a monster.

And the ugly? Well, Doug still won that category. He was capable of more evil than I could ever imagine. I wondered what the future held for us. Would he back off? Or would I always be on his STF radar? Time would tell. I wondered if he had a heart, ever truly been in love, or really loved his family.

Ashley opened the door to the school, and the scent hit me right away. I'd always been sensitive to smells. Maybe that was how I identified with things. I couldn't find words to describe the school scent, just like the bookstore.

"Are you going to be alright?" Ashley took me by the arm, turning me toward her. "No Loner lurking in the corners?"

"I'll be fine, Ash, really. I'll see you later." I walked down the hall. The district had done away with homeroom this year. No extra time to think or brood over what could have been. Grateful for the change, I didn't glance around, just headed straight to my first class. My foot ached as I limped along. I glanced down and smiled at my new tattoo in the arch of my right foot. X-X-I-X. It calmed me whenever I looked at it. It gave me peace and reassurance that I had done the right thing.

This was my new life. A fresh start. No Loner. No Heathcliff. No Lucas. I accepted that. Like the Phoenix rising from the ashes to start a new life ... so shall I.

ACKNOWLEDGMENTS

If not for Leap Year, this book would never been written! It's been a work of love—written, rewritten, torn apart and started over again. When I finally felt it was ready, I entered the story in a competition. 29 came in fifth place in the Critique My Novel (now known as Ink and Insight) contest for unpublished manuscripts giving me the confidence to continue.

I have to give major props to my editor, Elizabeth Housing, for all her hard work. You have made the book better, and for that, I thank you.

Big thanks to my son, Matt, for just liking the book and being a fan. He pushed me to get it published. His excitement throughout the project kept me going. Besides that, he designed the awesome cover. His creative skills never seize to amaze me.

Another giant thanks to my sister, Sue, who is my beta reader. She's always the first to read my manuscripts, plowing through them in less than a week. My question to her always is, do I keep going? And for 29, she answered yes.

Many characters in this book have special meaning to me. One is named after a student I had, another for a good friend's son. As always, somewhere in my book I find a special place for the name Gilbert. Dad, your name manages to find its way into my stories and always will. That's a promise. This time you're a road, but I know you wouldn't mind.

Finally, I have to thank my husband. He is my rock, my support, and I couldn't do this without him. He's also very good at catching grammar and punctuation mistakes. Thanks, Ron, you know every book is dedicated to you.

OTHER BOOKS BY NANCY PENNICK

Waiting for Dusk Series

Waiting for Dusk (Book 1)

Call of The Canyon (Book 2)

Stealing Time (Book 3)

Taking Chances (Short Story)

Broken Dreams (Prequel)

ABOUT THE AUTHOR

Nancy Pennick, author of the Waiting for Dusk series, has been writing nonstop since retiring from teaching. She credits her new series, *29*, to the originator of Leap Day, basing her story on that distinctive day. Born and raised in Northeast Ohio, she resides in Mentor, OH. Nancy is married and has one son.